# Sherlock...
## The S...
## Que...

### Mike Hogan

**KALEIDOSCOPE**

Copyright © 2019 by Mike Hogan

All rights reserved. No part of this publication may be reproduced, distributed or transmitted in any form or by any means, without prior written permission.

Kaleidoscope Productions
www.kaeidoscopeproductions.co.uk

Publisher's Note: This is a work of fiction. Names, characters, places, and incidents are a product of the author's imagination. Locales and public names are sometimes used for atmospheric purposes. Any resemblance to actual people, living or dead, or to businesses, companies, events, institutions, or locales is completely coincidental.
ISBN 9781096802181

Sherlock Holmes: The Scottish Question/ Mike Hogan. – 2nd illustrated ed.

It was a' for our rightfu' King
We left fair Scotland's strand;
It was a' for our rightfu' King
We e'er saw Irish land, my dear,
We e'er saw Irish land.

Now a' is done that men can do,
And a' is done in vain;
My Love and Native Land fareweel,
For I maun cross the main, my dear,
For I maun cross the main.

Robert Burns

SONS OF THE THISTLE

# ICONS OF SCOTLAND

I came down from my bedroom to the sitting room of our lodgings at 221b Baker Street and found my friend Sherlock Holmes already at the breakfast table clad in his threadbare, mouse-coloured dressing gown. Our pageboy stood on a stool by the fireplace in his Sunday best clothes under a white apron, changing the old gas mantles for new ones.

"Well, Watson, I fear we are entering the season of equinoctial gales," said Holmes.

"Good morning, Holmes, and to you, Billy."

I went to the window, opened it wide and peered out. "Why so? We are barely past the *ides* of July, and the weather is beautiful, with not a cloud in the sky. I imagine that we are in for another stifling day."

"Local portends suggest stormy weather," Holmes replied, tapping his nose with his finger. "Note the new lace curtains."

I joined him at the breakfast table, helped myself to toast and leafed without enthusiasm through the morning newspapers. Billy's *Police Gazette* lay on the arm of the sofa with his box of Sugg's gas mantles, and I snatched it, chuckling at the lurid headlines. "More airship sightings in America, ha, ha."

"Pass the coffee, old man." Holmes snapped his *Times* and turned the page.

I slid the coffee pot across the table. "Did you see the droll story last year from California in which seven-foot beings emerged from an airship and attempted to abduct a colonel in the United States military together with his female companion and horse and buggy. He fought them off."

Holmes sniffed from behind his newspaper.

"Now, repeated from the *St Louis Post-Dispatch* is a story that a certain W H Hopkins of Springfield, Missouri encountered a grounded airship twenty feet in length and eight feet in diameter. The vehicle was propelled by three large propellers and crewed by a woman and a bearded man, both, ahem, unclothed. Mr Hopkins tried to communicate with the crew to ascertain their origins, and eventually understanding what Hopkins was asking of them, they pointed to the sky and said 'Mars'.

I turned the page. "And here is a more sinister account from three months ago. A story published in the *Table Rock Argus* claims a group of 'anonymous but reliable' witnesses saw an airship sailing overhead. The craft had many passengers. The witnesses report that among these passengers was a woman tied to a chair, a servant attending her and a man with a pistol guarding the prisoner. Before the witnesses thought to contact the authorities, the airship was gone."

I laughed aloud, threw Billy's paper back onto the sofa and wiped my eyes with my handkerchief. "Oh, dear, what drivel people may be hoodwinked into believing."

Holmes flipped down a corner of his newspaper. "Hmmm?"

"Anything in the post?" I asked.

Holmes smiled. "An intriguing summons by messenger."

Mrs Hudson bustled in with a tray. "Here's your breakfast, Doctor." She laid a bowl of steaming grey gruel in front of me. "Mrs Campbell at number ninety-seven had a sack of fine oats sent from Clackmannan just yesterday. She gave me a pound, and I made a braw porridge."

She wagged her finger at me. "Simple Scots oats boiled with a pinch of salt and served hot as you'd like with cold milk on the side and none of your honey or syrup nonsense." She turned to Holmes. "Have you finished yours, Mr Holmes?"

"I have," Holmes said, passing her his empty bowl. "And I am in an excellent mood for eggs and bacon, if that could be managed?"

Mrs Hudson beamed at him. "The porridge will set you up for the day."

She left us, and I stared doubtfully at my bowl. "You say you finished yours, Holmes?"

"Not quite". He sniffed. "I don't feel any need to be set up on such a bright day." He coughed softly and signalled to Billy. The boy stepped down from his stool, brought a retort from Holmes' laboratory bench to the breakfast table and opened the lid to disclose a heaving grey mass. Billy raised his eyebrows, I nodded, and he scraped the contents of my bowl into the retort and returned it to the bench.

I buttered my toast as I glanced at my *Telegraph*. "Not much of interest this morning. I see the Queen is going to Balmoral earlier this year than is her usual practice. I expect she is looking forward to a change of scene after the exertions of the Diamond Jubilee celebrations."

"Mmmm?"

"I could wish for a trip to Scotland, Holmes: the scented heather, lofty bens, trickling becks and noble lochs. Do you not yearn for the fresh, clean air and romantic vistas of the Highlands?"

"I do not," he answered.

"Balmoral is a fine building, by all accounts," I said. "It's on the River Dee."

Holmes flicked down a corner of his newspaper again. "A baronial Scots mansion adorned with the necessary turrets, battlements and crow-stepped gables, but with touches of *Saxe-Coburg und Gotha* from the drawing board of Prince Albert. A curious hybrid of Celt and Teuton, much like the sovereigns of these British islands."

"Who rule a significant portion of the earth," I reminded him.

Holmes smiled. "Hybrids are often hardier than their progenitors."

Billy whistled an annoying music-hall tune as he moved his stool to the gas jets on the far wall. I gave him a sharp look, and he desisted.

"You mentioned a summons, Holmes?" I asked.

"The dean of Westminster Abbey requires my presence at the West Door of the Abbey at noon precisely. He wishes to consult me on a matter of some delicacy."

I chuckled. "Have you been up to anything indelicate, Holmes? You've not denied the Trinity or disallowed the forty-nine articles, I trust."

Holmes ignored my gibe. "If you are as intrigued as I am, you might like to accompany me. It will be good for our souls, slightly spotted as they are this morning, to confess our sins."

"I do not indulge in the practice of confession," I said stiffly.

"Weel, all may," said Holmes in a faux Scots accent, "none must, and some should, as the saying goes."

We finished our breakfast and smoked our morning pipes in companionable silence until the mantel clock struck ten, when we dressed, went downstairs and collected our hats and canes from the stand in the lobby. Billy followed us with the retort.

I sniffed as I caught a whiff of carbolic soap in the air. It came from Billy. "Where's your uniform?" I asked him.

"On the line in the back yard, Doctor," he said, looking down at his toes. "Which, Mrs H took my suit of buttons apart and scrubbed it. She sewed it back up again, and it's being aired."

"That retort needs cleaning, Billy," Holmes said loudly enough to be heard in the kitchen. "At the drain in the backyard, I suggest, as the contents are toxic."

Holmes snapped his fingers. "Lend me thruppence, will you?"

I handed Holmes the coin, and he flicked it to Billy and tapped his finger to his lips. "Hush."

The day had already grown hot, and bright sunlight glinted off the metalwork and glass of the carts and carriages pressing around our cab as we threaded through heavy traffic towards central London. I shielded my eyes from the glare with the rim of my bowler.

Billows of dust rose from the rumbling carriage wheels, and the city smells – smoke, horse dung and rotting rubbish – were augmented by the sharp tang of hot leather and horse sweat.

After a weary journey, our cab dropped us at the West Door of Westminster Abbey where a young man in clerical garb met us and introduced himself as Canon Isaac Blood. He ushered us through the Nave and Choir of the church, and I appreciated the cool and tranquil atmosphere that prevailed in the Abbey after the dust, oppressive heat and jangling noise outside.

I gazed in awe at the vaulted ceiling high overhead. It seemed astonishing that such a magnificent structure had been built by manual labour without the aid of steam engines and cranes. I wondered whether, with all our inventiveness and skill, modern man could create a monument that would stand as a testimony to faith and the human spirit for as many hundreds of years. I feared that as we neared the end of the nineteenth century, the focus of our scientists and inventors was more on destruction than on construction, on more efficient means of defeating our enemies rather than on soaring towers of faith to exalt our spirit.

"Are you related to General Binden Blood of the Malakand Field Force?" I asked the canon. "I read of his exploits in the *Telegraph*."

"Distantly," Canon Blood replied in a soft voice tinged with a Scots burr. "Binden Blood's is the cadet branch of the family, mine the Irish-Scots."

He stopped at the chapel of Edward the Confessor, screened by a black curtain. "We have closed this section of the Abbey to visitors, gentlemen. If you step behind the cloth, you will see why."

I raised my eyebrows.

"A matter of sacrilege, Doctor," Canon Blood said, lifting the curtain. "And burglary."

I followed Holmes through the curtain and found myself in the chapel of Edward the Confessor, who I recalled from childhood history lessons was a 'good' king and the last of our native Anglo-Saxon monarchs.

I looked about me. Standing on a dais was a tall, high-backed, ornate wooden throne constructed in the Gothic style with carved and gilded lion feet. The sides and front of the chair were painted with what looked like images of animals, but the designs were so faded that it was difficult to make them out.

An elderly cleric stood beside the chair wringing his hands in agitation. He introduced himself as George Bradley, Dean of Westminster Abbey. With his white side-whiskers and benevolent expression, he was the very image of the aged clergyman whom Holmes had imitated on many occasions with varying degrees of success.

"In your note you mention a matter of delicacy," Holmes said.

The dean sighed. "The Coronation Chair before you, gentlemen, otherwise known as King Edward's Chair, dates from exactly six hundred years ago. All anointed sovereigns of England have been crowned on it since 1308 (save for Mary the Second who used a replica while her husband William occupied the original). And all sovereigns of Great Britain since the Union have sat on it. Queen Victoria was crowned on this chair."

"It looks rather battered," I suggested.

"And the Stone of Scone is missing from its place under the seat," said Holmes.

The dean saw my puzzled look, and he turned to Canon Blood and gestured for him to explain.

"Known also as the Stone of Destiny, Doctor," the canon said in his soft Scots accent. "It was the coronation seat of the *Dál Riata* Gaels, brought with them from Ireland when they settled in Scotland. Scots kings were crowned on the Stone from at least the ninth century until it was seized by King Edward the First of England as a spoil of war in 1296. It was then placed on a shelf below this chair."

Holmes whipped out his magnifying glass and pounced on the Chair. I watched complacently and the dean and canon gaped wide-eyed at Holmes as he crawled around the chair, peering at the battered wood and the flagstone floor.

He stood. "Pray describe the missing item."

"It is a block of sandstone," said Canon Blood. He gestured with his hands. "It measures about twenty-six inches by seventeen by ten or so, and its weight is three hundred pounds, or twenty-odd stone. The top bears chisel-marks. At each end of the stone is an iron ring."

"You say it was taken by Edward the Confessor?" I asked.

"No, Doctor, by King Edward the First, two hundred years after the Confessor," said Canon Blood. "He was otherwise known as *Malleus Scotorum*, or the Hammer of the Scots. The English and Scots were at war on and off for centuries. When the English took Dunbar Castle in April 1296, King John

Balliol of Scotland was forced to abdicate, and Edward seized the Honours of Scotland: the kings' crown, sword and sceptre, and (so it is said) the Stone of Destiny."

"Well," I said mildly, "spoils of war as you say, Dean Bradley. It was the custom at the time. I understand that the Scots were not averse to cattle raiding across the border, ha ha."

My attempt at humour fell on stony ground, and I endured two cold stares.

"Coming back to the present," said Holmes. "When was the stone last seen?"

"Yesterday evening after Evensong," the dean answered, "by a choirboy, James Elwood. I caught him carving his initials into the back of the throne, and I thrashed him. I was too scandalised by his behaviour (though it is common enough, I'm afraid, with tourists and with servitors) to notice whether the Stone was in its usual place. The boy swears it was. He was bent over at the time, you see, so he had a good view."

"Could the Stone have been removed and carried out of the Abbey in daylight?" Holmes asked.

"Impossible," said Canon Blood. "Abbey officials are everywhere during the day, and the exits have lay attendants posted nearby to assist visitors. The Stone is large and heavy. Someone would have noticed."

Holmes nodded. "Are any repairs being carried out in the building? Are there workmen in the Abbey?"

"Thankfully no," said the dean. "There usually are, of course; we are constantly repairing and restoring."

"When did you realise the Stone was missing?" I asked.

"Early this morning," Canon Blood replied.

"It was taken last night, then," I suggested.

Canon Blood nodded and turned to Holmes. "And there is something else."

"Come, come, Isaac," Dean Bradley said testily. "That is unrelated; a triviality. Mr Holmes should concentrate his efforts on the Stone."

Holmes smiled. "I thrive on trivialities, Dean Bradley; they are catnip to consulting detectives."

We said our goodbyes to the dean, and Holmes accompanied Canon Blood through the curtain. I was about to follow them when Dean Bradley put his hand on my arm.

"Is that really Sherlock Holmes, Doctor? I had thought him a character in your admirable detective fictions. I had no idea he was an actual person until the Home Office official this morning directed we consult him. It is rather like the French detective from Mr Edgar Poe's *Murder on the Rue Morgue* coming suddenly to life."

"You refer to *le Chevalier* Auguste Dupin? I had coffee with him on the Champs-Élysées in, let me see, June or July of last year." I bowed, slipped through the curtains and chuckled to myself as I hurried after the canon and Holmes.

They stopped at the tomb of Mary, Queen of Scots. A fresh-faced boy wearing a black cassock stood by the marble effigy of the queen with a wreath of thistle flowers tied with a blue and white silk bow at his feet.

"James Elwood, I presume?" Holmes asked the boy.

"Aye, sir," the boy answered in a soft Scots accent. He smiled a warm smile as he looked from Canon Blood to me and back to Holmes.

"I am a Sherlock Holmes, the consulting detective," Holmes said sternly. "I know everything, Master Elwood, about you and the other fellows. You meant it as a jape, and if you tell me where you put the Stone, I shall plead for you with the dean."

The boy gasped and blinked at Holmes. "I don't know what you mean, sir."

"Come, come, Elwood, you were beaten by Dean Bradley yesterday evening and in revenge, but just as a prank, you and the others removed the Stone of Scone and hid it, intending to return it in a few hours. But now the matter has become serious, and I am here and you are afraid, and rightly so."

Holmes loomed over the boy. "Take me to the stone this instant." He waved his hand over the Elwood's head. "And *ego te absolve*: you are absolved."

"I say, Holmes!" I exclaimed.

The boy turned to Canon Blood. "I did not steal the Stone of Destiny."

I took Elwood's chin in my hand, turned his face to mine and looked into his eyes. "He is telling the truth, Holmes." I took a packet of peppermints from my pocket and handed it to the boy.

Holmes sniffed dismissively and knelt to examine the wreath through his glass. Elwood offered peppermints to Canon Blood and to me.

"The thistle wreath was noticed early this morning, Mr Holmes," said Canon Blood.

Holmes stood. "By whom?"

"I found the wreath as I did my morning rounds at dawn," the canon answered. "I saw the Gaelic inscriptions on the silk ribbon and I decided to check the Coronation Chair. I was not thinking of theft or damage, but of some further expression of nationalist sentiment."

"You can read the texts?" Holmes asked.

Canon Blood nodded. "There are three, two in Scots Gaelic and the last in English. The first is from Ossian, the third-century Scottish Homer." He picked up the wreath of thistle and unwound the silk bow to reveal a line of writing. "I loosely translate,

> *I have seen the household of Finn.*
> *No men were they of coward race.*

And the third in English,

> *Unless the Fates be faithless found,*
> *And prophet's voice be vain,*
> *Where'er this monument be found,*
> *The Scottish race shall reign.*

The source of the verse is an ancient Latin epigram; the translation is by Sir Walter Scott."

"Finn? Was he not an Irish hero of legend?" I asked.

"He was and is, Doctor, but the lays of Ossian were brought to Scotland by the Tara kings with the original Stone of Destiny, and so his exploits are part of Scotland's heroic past as well as Ireland's."

"The second inscription?" asked Holmes.

"That is also in Gaelic, but I do not know its origin. It says,

> *The Crown of Gold shall be returned,*

*And Hibernia's Glory
Restored.*

"A modern stanza," the canon said. "Or so I suspect by the metre, but I am no expert."

I frowned. "Hibernia, the Roman name for Scotland. What is the connection between the poems and Mary, Queen of Scots?"

Canon Blood glanced at the marble grave effigy adorning the tomb of the queen. "There are Scots who bear a grudge against the English for the execution of Mary by Queen Elizabeth. For many of us, the nobility of the death of the Queen of Scots atoned for her many faults."

"Yes, yes," Holmes said. "I assume the police have been summoned."

Canon Blood turned to the boy. "Run along now, Hamish, and have your luncheon. And not a word to the other boys, mind."

Elwood bowed to us and left.

"I notified the dean when I saw the stone was missing," Canon Blood continued. "He and I formed the same conclusion as you, Mr Holmes. We woke Elwood and asked him where he'd hidden it. Like you, we expected he was in a conspiracy with his friends (the stone is heavy) and it was a prank.

"He convinced us of his innocence, under oath, as he did Doctor Watson. We therefore swore him to secrecy and put him here to guard the wreath while Dean Bradley communicated with the Archbishop of Canterbury at Lambeth

Palace. As a royal peculiar, the Abbey is not under the archbishop's control, but the dean thought it wise to solicit the advice of His Grace. It was decided at the highest level that the matter was too delicate for the police to be involved. A gentleman from the Home Office expressed the view that Scotland Yard was hand-in-glove with the gutter press and the story would inevitably be leaked, with unpredictable consequences. I understand there is a violent precedent: after their defeat by the Scots in 1327, the English promised to return the Stone to Scotland, but rioting Londoners prevented its removal from the Abbey."

I raised a sceptical eyebrow.

"You decided to consult me," Holmes said.

"The dean, archbishop and the representative of the Home Office met here this morning," the canon said. "I was not party to their discussions, but I understand your name was mentioned."

Holmes bowed. "Very well."

"The Home Office, not the Scottish Office?" I asked.

"The view was taken that the Stone is the property of the Crown and in the custody of the English Government," Canon Blood replied. "Its theft is therefore a domestic matter."

I frowned. That attitude seemed high-handed. Morally the Stone was the property of the people of Scotland, and it was mean-spirited and short-sighted not to inform their representative in London of the theft. I glanced at Holmes, but he was deep in thought.

The canon bowed. "If there is nothing more?"

"You have been most helpful, Canon Blood," Holmes said, looking up. "I wonder if you would be good enough to copy the Gaelic inscriptions and your translations into Doctor Watson's notebook, and then, if you will lead me, I will examine all the entrance doors at this end of the Abbey."

I handed the canon my notebook and pencil and waited as he transcribed the poems and translations.

"Young Elwood strikes me as a bright boy," I said.

"Indeed, but he has a delicate constitution," Canon Blood replied. "I advised the family that he should not follow his brothers to Eton."

"Are there any anniversaries or important days coming up that might appeal to the Scots and fire their nationalist sentiments?" Holmes asked.

Canon Blood returned my notebook and considered. "The hundred and first anniversary of the death of the Scots poet Robert Burns on the twenty-first of this month will be commemorated by some Scots, but it is his birth date in January that is celebrated most commonly."

Canon Blood led us to the entrances on the south, or river side of the Abbey. Holmes stopped at each door we passed and examined the locks and the stone floor. At the door leading to the cloisters, he scrutinised the floor inside and the ground outside and scraped some material from the flagstones.

"Can you conceive of any connection between the wreath and the missing Stone?" I asked as Canon Blood saw us out of the Abbey and into the bright sunshine and oppressive heat of the Broad Sanctuary.

"None," the canon answered, "other than the obvious fact that the Stone and the bard Ossian are icons of Scotland. The placing of the wreath at the tomb of Mary, Queen of Scots may have significance, but it is deeper than I can fathom."

I thanked him, and Holmes and I shook his hand. I hailed a passing cab and climbed aboard, and Holmes was about to follow me when Canon Blood stayed him with a hand on his arm.

"I should make it clear Mr Holmes that the stone until recently in our possession may not be the true Stone of Destiny. A body of opinion suggests the true Stone was hidden by the canny Scots, and King Edward was fobbed off with a drain cover."

The canon smiled. "Nor stone nor iron makes us who we are; it is blood we must stand true to, is it not, gentlemen?"

THE STONE OF SCONE AND CORONATION CHAIR

## 2. CAUSE FOR GRIEVANCE

"So, Watson, the Stone of Destiny has been stolen for a second time," Holmes said as our cab trundled along Victoria Street towards our lodgings.

"A second time?"

"Edward the First filched it from the Augustinian canons at Scone Abbey in 1296. A clear case of robbery and sacrilege."

"I'm surprised the Scots have not required its return, rioting Londoners notwithstanding."

Holmes sighed. "I know little of Scotland, and it's vexing to be burdened with this missing rock when I have an intriguing little matter of espionage on hand towards which I had hoped to direct my attention."

I cleared my throat. "Holmes, old man, there is a subject on which I am charged to speak to you. Mrs Hudson has asked me to make representations concerning several of your recent clients and most of all the ragamuffins you call your Baker Street Irregulars. She says she is the object of ridicule from other landladies in regard to the class of persons who visit our rooms. That fellow last week, for example, was in rags."

Holmes frowned. "On Thursday? That was Barker, the enquiry agent. He wished to consult me on the murder of Cardinal Tosca in '95. Barker is dogged by thugs employed by the Vatican, so he came in disguise. Any peppermints left?"

"I gave them to Master Elwood."

Holmes sniffed. "I doubt he deserves them. Ah, here we are." We stepped down outside our lodgings in Baker Street, and Holmes indicated a closed carriage at the kerb. "We have company."

Billy opened the door of 221b looking resplendent in a bright, newly laundered suit of buttons.

"You look very fine Billy," Holmes said. "But your uniform has evidently shrunk in the wash. I must urge Doctor Watson to require you to undo the top button of your jacket on medical grounds. Oxygen is as essential to pageboys as it is to other low orders of Creation."

I hung my bowler on the hat stand. Billy plucked at my sleeve. "Doctor, sir, I must tell you—"

I turned to Holmes. "I say, where is our stair carpet?" The stairs to the sitting room were bare wood.

"More cleaning, Mrs Hudson?" Holmes called along the corridor towards the kitchen. "Did we not endure enough dislocation during the season appointed for spring-cleaning? Are we to be discommoded all year through?"

He thundered up the stairs, and I hurried after him, anxious not to be associated with his remarks.

"Brother Mycroft," Holmes exclaimed as he opened our sitting-room door. "The mountain is come to Muhammad."

Mycroft Holmes, my friend's older brother, heaved his considerable bulk from our sofa. "A most offensive remark, Sherlock, particularly as on the instructions of my physician I am maintaining a strict diet."

He shook my hand. "My dear Doctor, always a pleasure to see you hale and hearty – as much as anyone might be with Sherlock as his fellow lodger."

He slumped back into his seat. "Where is your stair carpet and the Axminster that graced this room? Have you sold them? Are you auctioning off your things? Hard times, Sherlock?"

Our sitting-room carpet had also disappeared.

"Moths," Holmes answered as he settled himself in his usual seat in front of the empty fireplace.

"I helped myself to a cigar and a whisky," Mycroft said. "Your Scotch is a most inferior blend. I'll send you a case of the true malt when you have found the Stone of Scone."

I glanced at the whisky and brandy Tantalus on the sideboard and frowned. As far as I could see, it was still locked, and I wondered how Mycroft had opened it without a key. I turned to see the Holmes brothers smiling at me. I reddened and took my accustomed seat by the fireplace opposite Holmes.

"The Stone," Holmes said, raising his eyebrows.

Mycroft leaned back and sipped his whisky. "A potent symbol of Scottish sovereignty. It is a serious matter we do not have it in our hands. Or, to be precise, beneath Her Majesty. Figuratively, it signifies the Queen keeps her Scottish subjects in a special place not only in her heart, but under her, ah, thumb." He pulled a large white handkerchief from his sleeve and mopped his brow. "Where we all are, in our various ways, of course."

I stood. "I'll open the windows wider and let in what air there is."

"Would you, my dear Doctor?" said Mycroft. "You are too kind."

"And call down for coffee," said Holmes. "I would do so myself, but I fear Mrs Hudson may have taken my earlier remarks amiss."

I opened the windows, then went to the landing and looked over the rail. Billy was in the hall plucking at his collar. He started at my call, blinked up at me with a pale countenance and stage-whispered something. His discretion swallowed his meaning, and I ordered coffee and returned to my place in the sitting room.

"It is difficult to know how seriously to take the matter," Mycroft said. "A rock is, when all's said and done, a rock." He shrugged. "And it will be replaced with a replica quarried by convicts on Dartmoor. But the prime minister was especially troubled by certain lines from one of the poems attached to the wreath found by Mary's tomb."

I read from my notebook.

*"Where'er this monument be found,*
*The Scottish race shall reign."*

"Exactly," Mycroft said with a weary sigh. "Whoever took the Stone of Destiny now possesses a powerful emblem of national pride. Of course, the most puissant symbols of Scottish sovereignty are hardly to be found these days as there are so few chaste maiden's laps on which they may rest their weary heads."

I frowned, and Holmes glossed his brother's remark. "Unicorns. The beast sinister supporting the crown in the British coat of arms represents the Scots."

"There may be a demand for ransom," I suggested.

Holmes shrugged. "That is possible. I suppose we might offer the thieves Berwick-on-Tweed in exchange. The town has been hostaged and ransomed on several occasions."

He turned to Mycroft. "There was a good deal of sandstone dust on the floor under the chair; the rock may have cracked as it was extracted."

"In which case one person could handle the pieces," I said. "We do not need a conspiracy. Perhaps it was deliberately destroyed by someone who has a grudge against Scotland."

"You spoke to the constable on duty in Parliament Square?" Mycroft asked his brother. "And the one stationed in Old Palace Yard?"

Holmes smiled. "I did not, for I knew you had."

Mycroft nodded. "I was called to a meeting with the Dean and the Archbishop of Canterbury at an absurd hour this morning. I represented the government, the Home Office in this case. We interrogated the police constables on duty in Parliament Square and on the river side of the Abbey. They noticed nothing unusual last night."

"You examined the chair?" I asked.

"I did," Mycroft said, yawning. "I saw the sand and stone crumblings on the floor, and the clean swathe where they dragged the stone away using a sack or cloth under it."

Holmes nodded. "The trail led south, towards the river."

"The great lock on the door to the cloisters would have been easy enough to pick," said Mycroft, "but there were no marks or scratches on it or on the locks of the other doors. Yet Canon Blood is certain all the doors were locked. He checked them in company with another cleric when the Abbey was closed after the final service."

Holmes stood and scrabbled along the mantel. "You saw the sandstone particles scattered inside the cloister door, of course. There were none outside." He shook out a cigar from my packet and lit it.

"The dust might have been blown away," Mycroft said. "It is often windy by the river."

"Ha!" Holmes puffed a stream of smoke across the room. "Not a hint of a breeze has stirred the air these last three days."

"The gang could have been spirited the Stone out of a side door and taken it away by boat," I said. "The Thames is busy, even late at night. No one would have thought anything was amiss, particularly if the Stone was in a sack."

"A gang?" Holmes said as the door of the sitting room opened and Mrs Hudson marched in with a tray of coffee cups and a coffee jug. "I certainly believe it was the work of more than one man, but doubtfully of a whole number of men."

Mrs Hudson glared at Holmes and then at me as she slammed the tray on the table. "That sitting-room carpet was a disgrace to a Christian household, what with your pipe tobacco and cigar ash and all the nasty chemical stains. The man from Whiteleys said he'd do what he could, but he feared it was a lost cause."

She narrowed her eyes and gave Holmes and me further dark looks. "I had to boil Billy's uniform and scour him from-head-to-heel with carbolic soap to kill the mites brought in by your ragamuffins, Mr Holmes. And I'll tell you straight, Doctor, the tar on the stair carpet won't come out even if Bessie scrubs it ever so."

Mrs Hudson turned to the door but stopped on the threshold and glowered back at Holmes. "And the drains are blocked solid!" She stamped out, closing the door firmly behind her.

"The tar from the road repair last week," Holmes said, blinking at me. "The Baker Street Irregulars could not leave their shoes at the door as we did, for they wear none."

"And the drains?" asked Mycroft.

Holmes shrugged. "Porridge."

Mycroft laughed. "I haven't seen Sherlock so chastened since Nanny caught him at the nursery window burning a hole in his fingernail with a magnifying glass held to the sun."

"Mrs Hudson has a Caledonian temper," Holmes said with a rueful smile.

I handed cups of coffee to Mycroft and Holmes. "Is there a movement advocating independence for Scotland?" I asked. "If so, they are remarkably reticent; we have spent the last three decades wringing our hands over Irish Home Rule, but hardly a word has been spoken of Scotland."

I passed Mycroft the sugar bowl and he spooned in several measures. "They do not seethe under our administration as their cousins in Erin do," he said, "but the Scots have cause for grievance; their country is not well managed. As you might expect, the discontented Scots grumble about money. While most tax revenue from Ireland is disbursed on projects in that country, almost all Scottish revenue comes to London: a state of affairs with which the Imperial Treasury is well content."

He sipped his coffee. "The Scots have their cabinet minister now, but he is absurdly understaffed and not at one with their MPs in Parliament. The Scots MPs complain the Imperial Parliament does not allocate enough time for Scottish affairs, a Scottish Secretary sitting here in London is divorced from the people of Scotland and the country is run (as far as it is not governed by the Kirk and the Boards) by a dictatorship untrammelled by parliamentary checks and balances, albeit more or less benevolent."

"What are the chances of a separate parliament for Scotland?" I asked.

Mycroft shook his head. "Slim to none: the Tories will brook no erosion of the Union, and the Liberals are afraid that without Scottish Liberal support in Westminster they will be condemned to perpetual opposition."

Holmes helped himself to coffee. "If I were a Scot, I would consider that lamentable."

"If you were a Scot, Sherlock, you would be governing New Zealand, Jamaica or Basutoland. The Scots have done well out of the Empire. It would not be in their best interests to leave us."

Mycroft took out his pocket handkerchief and mopped his brow. "Besides, the Queen would be livid. I should not like to be the prime minister who informed her the Scots wish to run their own affairs."

"The Queen loves Scotland," I said. "She spends months of every year at Balmoral. And even in England, she is surrounded by Highlanders."

Mycroft chuckled. "In their kilts and sporrans and tartans amid the stag heads and the skirl of the pipes. She loves the theatre of it all, as do the Scots themselves. That romance writer fellow Walter Scott stage managed the Highland revival. He gave them their symbols, all as mythical as Alfred and his burnt cakes, Canute's watery ambitions or King Arthur and the round table. And just as wearingly trite."

Mycroft pulled a gold watch from his waistcoat pocket. "As is this blessed missing rock." He checked the time and sniffed. "The royal train trundles at its stately pace from Windsor to Scotland at least twice a year, but the Queen sees little of how her subjects on either side of the border live: the curtains of her salon are drawn tight until the tenements are passed and bosky woods and tumbling streams grace the Imperial eye."

He noticed my furrowed brows. "We must face facts, Doctor, and concentrate on more important problems than stones of destiny and frothy nationalist maunderings. In contrast with the civilisation you, I, Her Majesty and even Sherlock in his less Bohemian moments enjoy, many of the Queen's subjects in our industrial cities live in circumstances as desperate as at any time in our island's history. And in the north of Scotland and Ireland, existence for peasants in their crofts is as stark as in a kraal in our African territories."

He sighed. "They are admonished that, like all Britons, they are masters of their own fate and must pull themselves up by their bootstraps, even when they do not possess boots."

"Samuel Smiles, the celebrated author of *Self-Help*, is a Scot," I said.

"I am no radical, gentlemen," Mycroft continued, "but the reports that pass my desk on conditions in the slums of our great cities are damning of all recent governments. Only our native phlegmatic character has prevented the bloody uprising the nihilists predict will end our high civilization and usher in a reign of dog-eat-dog socialist demagoguery."

He mopped his brow again. "I grow heated, in every sense. I know we should all strive to rise above the corporeal and into airy spirituality, but when a fellow has to forgo his regular breakfast mutton chop and sustain himself on a single peeled apple, he may be excused if he is easily vexed."

"Would oatmeal porridge by permitted in your diet?" I asked. "It is boiled Scots oats, water and salt, and reputedly very nourishing."

Mycroft's eyes lit up for a second and then he sighed. "No, Doctor. Only fruit may be taken during the hours of daylight. For dinner, I am allowed a boiled fowl with vegetables and, as a treat, a dish of semolina."

Holmes stood. "Another whisky, Mycroft, or would you prefer a carrot?"

"What of the thistle wreath and the poems?" I asked, quickly changing the subject.

"Ossian!" Mycroft exclaimed. "I thought we were well rid of that nonsense. The so-called Scots Homer is quite exploded. He is a sham: a deliberate fakery. It is a disgrace that Macpherson, the author of these nuisances, is interred in the Abbey, and in Poet's Corner forsooth! Do not worry your head over such melancholic nonsense, Sherlock. Let's find the Stone of Destiny, or replace it, and have done with the matter."

"Is there no ancient crown of Scotland?" I asked. "The last poem mentioned a golden crown."

Mycroft pursed his lips. "There is not. The Scots have their 'Honours' (a crown, sceptre and sword) found in a dusty trunk in Edinburgh Castle by that bothersome fellow Scott. And we have our Crown Jewels in the Tower. I know of no other crowns, ancient or modern, Scotland might lay claim to."

He checked his watch again. "I leave the matter in your hands, Sherlock. I can't go fagging about London chasing lumps of stone; I have an empire to manage. I am here to introduce you to a certain personage who has an interest in the case, no more. And he is late."

"A personage; how very portentous," Holmes murmured.

The doorbell rang downstairs. "At last," said Mycroft, heaving himself from the sofa. "We are to address him as the Duke of – let me see, I wrote it somewhere." He held his shirt cuff to the light from the window. "The Earl of – I cannot read it. Never mind, HRH is incognito, 'sir' will do."

I heard a thunder on the stairs, and Billy came in with a telegram. "For Mr Mycroft Holmes."

Mycroft slit the envelope open with our paperknife and glared at the slip. "We are summoned to Clarence House. It seems there has been a development." He shrugged. "I know no more. Come, I have a carriage outside."

Holmes stood. "We might stop at the telegraph office on the way. I have one or little things to attend to.

MYCROFT HOLMES

## 3. OUTRAGE IN PALL MALL

We clambered down from Mycroft's carriage outside the doors of Clarence House, just off the Mall, the London residence of the Duke and Duchess of Edinburgh. A platoon of soldiers under a young officer guarded the gates.

Mycroft spoke to the officer, and we were ushered into the building and upstairs to a second-floor reception room luxuriously furnished with gold-inlaid chairs and over-stuffed sofas set on a vast Oriental carpet. A white grand piano stood in the far corner, its lid covered with religious pictures and icons.

Exotic blooms displayed in a dozen or more vases crowded occasional tables and credenzas, and my nose twitched as their powerful scent wafted across the room.

A bearded, heavily built gentleman in a frock coat paced up and down before the silk-curtained windows muttering to himself in what might have been German. A line of fidgeting maids and liveried footmen was ranged against the opposite wall with a pale-faced chamberlain before them fingering his chain of office. At the far end of the row, a long-haired, bearded man in a flowing black gown and strange veiled hat glowered at us.

The gentleman by the windows turned and nodded to Mycroft and I recognised Edward, Prince of Wales, son of Queen Victoria and heir to the throne. He held out his hand to

Holmes and then to me. "Doctor Watson, I have read your stories."

I mumbled an appropriate reply as His Royal Highness turned back to Mycroft. "Earlier this afternoon, my brother, the Duke of Edinburgh, was—" The prince frowned. "Kidnapped seems an awkward word to use of a prince and royal duke."

"Abducted, Your Royal Highness?" Mycroft suggested.

"Very well; my brother, the Duke of Edinburgh, was abducted, Mr Holmes, and I wish—"

"What of Grand Duchess Maria Alexandrovna," one of the maids cried in a thick Russian accent, pointing to a portrait of an imperious-looking lady that hung over the fireplace. It showed the grand duchess in court dress with a cascade of diamonds and pearls across her ample bosom and a scintillating coronet of precious stones set in her elaborate hairdo.

The Prince of Wales glared the maid to silence, and the chamberlain pushed her back into line.

The prince turned to us. "The duke was travelling to his club for luncheon when armed men stopped his carriage and threatened his wife with violence if he did not go with them."

The prince opened his frock coat and disclosed a shoulder holster and pistol. "We go armed these days against the Irish devils, and Alfred would have engaged the brutes, but the duchess would not permit him to do so; in fact she insisted on accompanying him into captivity. Thus the fiends not only have a prince and royal duke, they possess an Imperial Russian grand duchess. The Tsar will be upset; Grand Duchess Maria is his aunt."

The bearded man at the end of the line of servants pushed past the chamberlain, shook his fist at the prince and let loose a storm of what I presumed was Russian. The maid we had heard from earlier translated the tirade as well as she could into her halting English.

From what I understood, Her Imperial Highness Maria Alexandrovna had been warned at her home in Germany earlier in the year that a calamity would befall her if she came to England with her husband the Duke of Edinburgh.

The bearded man, a Russian Orthodox priest, had seen the evil portends in a dream. The duchess had therefore been unwilling to visit London for the Jubilee, but she had done so as a matter of duty to her husband. The priest reminded us that the last tsar had been assassinated by raving democrats, and he declared his emphatic belief that the grand duchess would be sacrificed in a vile satanic ritual by members of the nihilist wing of the Church of England.

The maid broke down, and we understood no more of the priest's outburst. Fellow servants took her arm and led her and the priest from the room. I would have offered my medical services, but Holmes laid his hand on my arm and shook his head.

The Prince of Wales murmured to the chamberlain, and the other servants were ordered to leave, taking vases of flowers with them.

"You see what my brother has to put up with?" he asked, gesturing to the furniture and the icons on the piano. "The poor fellow is half-choked with scent from his wife's flowers and incense smoke from the woman's private chapel, and her every motion is subject to the whims of her *verdammt* chaplain."

The prince led the way to a pair of over-stuffed sofas in front of the grand fireplace. He lowered himself into one and waved for Holmes, Mycroft and me to occupy the other. It looked a tight fit for the three of us as Mycroft was almost as extensive in proportions as the prince, so I stood and leaned against the mantel.

The chamberlain returned and offered refreshments, which we refused. The prince ordered cigars, the chamberlain brought a humidor, and we helped ourselves.

"Your brother assures me you are not one of these prating fellows, Mr Holmes," His Royal Highness remarked as we lit our cigars. "As I know myself from your association with the Tranby Croft affair and the Balmoral attempt." The prince accepted a light from the chamberlain, nodded dismissal and waited as the man bowed and left the room, closing the door behind him. "If you were a tattletale," he continued, "I would not have agreed to meet you on the subject of this ridiculous stone."

He bent forward and spoke in a confidential murmur. "The stone be damned, gentlemen. Events have overtaken us, and our first task now is to find my brother – and his wife of course. We must determine who would benefit from the removal of the duke, and who might be involved in a potential coup."

Holmes frowned. "Against the Crown? I understand the Duke of Edinburgh is well down in the order of accession to the throne after you and your children."

"Against Saxe-Coburg and Gotha," the prince said sharply. "My brother is the sovereign duke of that nation. I was next in line to the Saxe-Coburg throne, but for obvious reasons I renounced my claim in my brother's favour and Alfred took the ducal throne in '93."

Holmes blinked at him. "Is there a republican movement in Saxe-Coburg and Gotha?"

The prince laughed. "Of course not, *Saxe-Coburg und Gotha* is a German dukedom, not a mutinous Ottoman province." He shrugged. "There was a difficult period at first when my brother was thought too English by some of his subjects, but he is a fine fellow, and he brought them around. He is now universally loved, and his manly son is being groomed to succeed him."

The prince lowered his voice. "But there are those who would like to see the duchy dissolved and amalgamated into a larger union. Already the army of Saxe-Coburg is controlled by Prussia."

He took a fierce pull at his cigar. "I am sure you will agree with me, gentlemen, that we can place no trust in the word or the intentions of my nephew the Emperor of Prussia. Wilhelm is peeved: it is his natural state. This time he is upset he was not guest of honour at the Queen's Diamond Jubilee celebrations last month, even though it was explained to him the festivities were to be focused entirely on the Empire."

Prince Edward looked around, evidently for an ashtray as, not finding one, he tapped his cigar ash onto the carpet. "Wilhelm thinks his exclusion from the Jubilee was my doing, when in fact I urged the Queen to invite him, but she declined on the grounds it would open the floodgates to hundreds of European royals who would demand to be invited and put up somewhere. Our palaces were and still are packed tight with colonials; we had to draw the line."

He chuckled. "The Kaiser is also vexed I beat him in the yacht races at Cowes, ha ha."

The prince's expression darkened. "Wilhelm is a dangerous schemer who accepts no bounds to his whims and ambitions; he would love to pull *Saxe-Coburg und Gotha* from under my brother."

"Is there any evidence to suggest a German plot," Holmes asked, ending the long silence that had occurred while we digested the prince's remarks. "To kidnap a British prince (and a Russian grand duchess) on the streets of London is a wilful act."

"The abductors did not wear spiked helmets, if that's what you mean, Mr Holmes," the Prince said in a cold tone. "They did not click their heels or address my brother in German. The coach driver's testimony suggests they spoke English with the accents of Dublin rather than Berlin, but accents can be assumed." The prince banged his fist on the arm of the sofa. "All is not as it seems, and for once I believe the damned Irish are innocent. No, no, the strings are pulled by the Kaiser."

I glanced at Holmes, but his face was an inscrutable mask.

"I see you doubt me, gentlemen," the prince said stiffly. "But I know my nephew, and you do not. His mother is my sister, and although she and her son are estranged, she knows him best of all. She agrees with me that Willy is the most capricious and irresponsible monarch in Europe (which has its share of rum sovereigns, I may say)."

"We should bear in mind the possibility the German emperor is behind the abduction, Your Royal Highness," Mycroft said carefully. "But we might want to explore other, more domestic motives for the outrage."

It was clear from the Prince's expression and his silence that Mycroft's suggestion did not engage the royal mind.

"If this is not a plot against the Duke of Edinburgh in his German capacity," I said, "could it be an attack by Irish or Scottish Nationalists on the ruling dynasty here in Britain?" I frowned. "Although I confess I do not see a clear Scottish connection, apart from His Royal Highness's title."

"There is none," the prince said shortly. "I am the Prince of Wales, but that does not make me Welsh. I am the Duke of Rothsay and Lord of the Isles, but that does not make me Scottish. My brother is as English as I am. He is, or was, a senior admiral in the Royal Navy. He is now the Duke of Saxe-Coburg and Gotha, still Duke of Edinburgh and a British prince. He has no personal connection with the city of Edinburgh or with Scotland generally."

The prince sniffed. "Alfred is a Knight Grand Cross of the Order of the Wendish Crown, with gems, but that does not make him Mecklenburgian. Touch the bell would you, Doctor?"

I pulled on the rope that hung by the fireplace.

"The Queen has a particular affinity for Scotland," the prince continued. "My brothers and I do not. We visit Her Majesty at Balmoral, and we fish and shoot there, but, to be frank, we find the Highlanders loud and coarse even when sober (seldom the case) and we consider their dancing wild, their music deafening and their cuisine disgusting."

Again a long silence ensued, and I attempted to re-establish an atmosphere of amity.

"Who is the rightful heir of Scotland?" I asked.

"I am," the Prince said in a frigid tone.

I reddened. "Yes, of course, Your Royal Highness. I meant the claimant to the Stuart succession."

The prince heaved himself off the sofa, and I stood and stiffened to attention.

"Again, that would be me," he said. "I have Stuart blood in my veins: my ancestor George the First was great-grandson to James the First."

The chamberlain entered with the prince's hat and cane, and Mycroft and Holmes shook the royal hand. I received a brief nod of dismissal.

"I wish you good hunting, gentlemen," the prince called back as he left the room.

"HRH has taken against the Scots," Mycroft said as the door closed and he settled once more on the sofa. "That fellow John Brown was irritating, and the other Highlanders can be a trial (they are not deferential men), but they are fiercely loyal to the Queen and far too whisky-sodden to plan anything more sophisticated than their next debauchery. I don't think we need worry about a Scottish coup from that quarter."

Mycroft turned to Holmes. "I didn't know you were involved in the baccarat scandal, Sherlock."

I too could not recall Holmes mentioning he had a role in the Tranby Croft affair, when the Prince of Wales had been called as a witness in a case involving cheating at cards at a house party.

Holmes shrugged. "I was consulted, no more. That Lieutenant Colonel Gordon-Cummings cheated was amply proven; he was perfectly brazen. After an interview with the prince, other principals and witnesses, Gordon-Cummings was forced to sign a confession and swear off card play for life. All involved were pledged to secrecy."

He smiled. "It got out, of course, and the Prince of Wales was the subject of adverse comment in the Press for illegal gambling. He wanted to know the source of the leak."

Mycroft considered the end of his cigar for a moment. "Wilhelm sent an ill-advised letter to his uncle criticising him for embroiling himself in a gambling squabble and playing cards with men young enough to be his sons. It did not endear the German Emperor to our future king."

Mycroft shook his head. "The unpleasantness is not all one sided; the Prince of Wales can be mightily rude when he has a mind to be. In '95 he demanded his nephew postpone the carefully planned grand opening of the Kiel Canal because it conflicted with the Ascot races!"

Mycroft's tone darkened. "With such bad blood between the princes, we may be heading for a conflagration of European dimensions. Relations between the British and German empires are governed by a family in a continuous state of spat. If we go to war, as I fervently hope we will not, Britain must have her Scottish regiments."

"The duke is married to the daughter of an assassinated tsar and aunt of the current tsar," I said. "Perhaps as the priest said, nihilists perpetrated the abduction. Not Church of England nihilists, naturally."

"Whoever the perpetrators," said Mycroft, "the Tsar will be mightily annoyed."

"You did not discuss the Stone of Scone with His Royal Highness," I said after another silence.

Mycroft gave me an odd look as he heaved himself from his sofa. "I thought it politic to concentrate on the missing duke. I doubt the Prince of Wales will continue to involve himself in the theft of the Stone under the present circumstances. The Prime Minister informed the prince of its loss this morning, and HRH contacted me by telephone to ask for details. He asked whether I was the source for the character portrayed in your detective stories, Doctor, and I was obliged to admit Sherlock is, for better or worse, a real person. The prince expressed a desire to meet him to discuss the robbery."

Mycroft took out his handkerchief and mopped his brow. "And now this."

Holmes stood. "High politics aside, we have a crime to solve; let's interview the driver of the duke's carriage and his footmen."

I rang for the chamberlain, and he conducted us through the house.

"The duke and duchess were on their way to luncheon," he said. "The duchess intended to take hers at the home of her friend the Countess of Minsk in Cadogan Square. The duke was to be dropped off at his club in Pall Mall."

"The couple's habit was to take luncheon separately, he at his club and she with her friend?" Holmes asked.

"Invariably, when in London, sir."

"And they would drive together, taking the same route?"

"They would."

The chamberlain led us out of a side door and across a stable yard to the mews. Two of the young footmen we had seen earlier in the salon, one tall and fair and the other a little shorter and dark-haired, leaned against a set of empty stalls. An older man dressed as a driver sat on a barrel, his head bandaged. They stood to attention as we approached.

Holmes addressed the driver. "Pray describe to me exactly what occurred today. My friend will take notes."

The driver frowned, looked down at his toes and began to answer in a mumble.

"Speak up, man," Holmes snapped.

"Which, his wits have been knocked about sir," the taller footman said in a Welsh accent. "I can tell you the way of it."

Holmes nodded curtly, and I opened my notebook.

"Your names?" I asked.

"I'm Evans, he's Raines and the driver's Poole."

"Go on," said Holmes.

"Well, sir, we'd just turned in to Pall Mall when a wildly driven carriage pulled ahead of ours. It stopped, and three men jumped down. One grabbed our horses' bridles, another waved a revolver at me and Raines and the last dragged Poole from the box."

"Describe the men."

"Thin men of low to middling height, sir, all with heavy beards and wearing bowlers; fierce, energetic men with glinting eyes, savage snarls and dangerous miens."

Holmes blinked at Evans, and I stifled a chuckle.

"I'm sorry, gentlemen," said the chamberlain, "Evans is taking classes at the Institute. He means no disrespect." He turned to Evans. "Answer plain and respectful if you know what's good for you."

Evans was unabashed. He smiled. "What struck me, sirs, what amazed me, was the girl up on the box of their carriage holding the reins."

"A girl drove the kidnappers' carriage?" I asked incredulously.

"She did, and she kept the horses quiet till they took off again. Can't say who drove then, as I was flat on the ground. Two of the scoundrels pulled me and Raines off the back of our coach, pushed us down and jumped in with the duke and duchess. They held them at gunpoint and tried to force the duke out and leave the duchess. She scorned them and their threats and would not let go of her husband no matter how much they threatened or he entreated her."

The footman lowered his voice. "The duchess is not easily persuaded, if you take my meaning, gentlemen. If she will, she will, and if she won't, well there's no moving her in the matter."

"Watch it," the chamberlain said, wagging his finger at the footman. "We'll have no talk of that sort."

"Always has a kind word for us footmen," Evans continued. "In foreign, like, as she does not care to speak English any more than she can help."

"Go on," said Holmes.

"The beggars escorted the duke and duchess to their carriage and forced them inside. The third man cut the reins of our carriage, jumped back up beside the girl, and they drove away. As soon as they turned the corner, I left Raines to care for Poole, grabbed a passing cab and followed the villain's carriage. I stopped to report the matter to a bobby and lost sight of them in the traffic in Waterloo Place."

"Naturally, they did not take the gaudy ducal equipage," Holmes said. "They used something nondescript; probably a hired carriage."

"How was Poole injured?" I asked.

"He stumbled and cracked his head on the pavement, sir," Evans answered.

I unwound the bandages on the driver's head and peered at the wound. It bled, as cuts to the head always do. I strongly advised Poole to consult a doctor as his slurred speech and vacant manner suggested a serious concussion.

"Continue," Holmes said impatiently.

Evans shrugged. "Not much more to say, sir. I came back, picked up the others, and we returned here to raise the alarm."

"Accents?" asked Holmes.

"Irish, sir, without a shadow of a doubt."

"Did they sound like this, begorrah?" Holmes said in a dreadful faux Irish tone.

"They did, sir."

"*Eh, voilà*," Holmes said with a sniff. "False beards and false accents. All is, as the prince suggested, not as it seems." He turned back to Evans. "Were there other witnesses who might have seen more than you?"

Evans considered. "No, I'd say not, sir. The street was quiet at the time, and it was all over in seconds."

Holmes nodded. "Thank you."

"Now, Poole," I said. "I strongly advise—"

"Evans," Holmes said over me. "Why did the duchess refuse to leave her husband?"

The footman smiled. "I heard the duke urging his wife to do what the kidnappers wanted and stay put while they dragged him away, but she wouldn't take orders from them would she now, commoners like as not? I mean, being Russian and a grand imperial duchess and all?"

"Talking of accents," I said with a slight chuckle as we were led through the house to our carriage, "I was expecting His Royal Highness to have a more German streak in his, but I noticed few Teutonic notes in his English."

"The prince's expletives are entirely Germanic," said Mycroft. "But he saves them for the billiard room. The Kaiser is proud of his perfect English accent, and he teases HRH on the imperfections he perceives in his uncle's pronunciation. Wilhelm has made a study of English humour and he strives to outdo his uncle in what he calls *badinage*. His quips are not well received by the Prince of Wales."

We passed through the cordon of guardsmen and crossed the street to where Mycroft's carriage waited.

"Stable doors," Holmes murmured.

"I drop at the Diogenes Club, Sherlock," Mycroft said. "You may borrow this government carriage for the duration of the investigation. It is signed out to me, so you must promise to return carriage, horse and driver to the mews in Whitehall every night, preferably before ten, in good condition with no scratches or injuries. The coachman, Rankin, expects a daily meal allowance and a half-crown tip, more if you keep him out after dark. Do not underestimate the fellow."

I climbed in after Holmes and Mycroft, and our carriage set off. Even with the windows down, the atmosphere was stifling, and my face and hands were soon damp with perspiration.

"The question of the duchess's motivation is an interesting one," Mycroft said as we trundled along Pall Mall through heavy traffic. "The Duke of Edinburgh and his wife are not close. They do not agree in temperament or on any matter on which they are obliged to converse, and Her Imperial Highness is rarely well disposed towards any activity in which her husband engages. Her insistence on following him into captivity is odd, even perverse."

"Evans puts it down to her native haughty contrariness," I said.

Mycroft nodded. "It's a persuasive notion."

"So, Prussian machinations, Russian (or Church of England) nihilists and the Scots," said Holmes. "What are my instructions, Brother?"

Mycroft bent forward and spoke in a voice scarcely audible above the creak of harness, the clatter of the horse's hooves and the street noises. "Above all, absolute secrecy. Her Majesty would be deeply affronted by any suggestion of disloyalty among her Scottish subjects, and she would not accept any notion of foul intentions on the part of the Kaiser (other than his characteristic bad temper). She considers nihilists to be a Continental plague despite the seven attempts against her life."

"Mostly by madmen and Irish Nationalists," I said.

Mycroft shrugged. "Her Majesty understands that certain disaffected elements in Ireland do not have her well-being at heart, but she puts that down to the pernicious influence of the Pope."

"Coming back to the matter at hand, Mycroft," Holmes said. "Does not Scotland Yard have information on nationalist groups?"

"Only on Irish secessionists." Mycroft delved into a valise at his side. "The Special Branch is directed against Irish outrages. I have compiled this slim file on two possible Scottish Nationalist organisations, but neither is a likely nest of sedition, and one has been defunct these many years."

"They advocate disunion?" I asked.

"No, I cannot in truth say they do. The first is the National Association for the Vindication of Scottish Rights, wound up in the '50s after the Crimean War, and the other the Highland Land League from the '80s. Neither was rebellious in character. They did not wish the overthrow of the Hanoverian dynasty and the return of the usurped Stuarts, or to secede from the Union and form an independent Scotland. Their members wished to preserve the Union but create a more effective means of managing the affairs of Scotland."

"Is there no seditious newspaper or broadsheet," Holmes asked. "How do these people communicate? Are there meetings, gatherings?"

Mycroft considered. "Large public meetings were held in the fifties, when the National Association for the Vindication of Scottish Rights flourished. As for publications, the Gaelic paper the *Highlander* was purportedly radical (it is long gone). The *Peoples Journal* has a huge circulation around Perth and Dundee, but I believe it focuses on local events and on all things Scottish: Burns, Wallace, haggises and so on. I have not seen a copy."

Mycroft took a sheet of paper from his bag. "I have examined the Duke of Edinburgh's schedule and that of Grand Duchess Maria for this week. We may cancel several unofficial engagements, but the couple are invited to a gala dinner by

Lord Rosebery on Wednesday, and that cannot be missed without exciting comment.

"The gossip-mongers will poke their noses in, as will newspaper reporters and friends of the couple. Then there is the Queen: while she would be happy to see the back of Maria, she will not be pleased if her son Alfred fails to visit his mother before her train journey north arranged for Wednesday morning. You thus have two days to rescue the Duke and Duchess of Edinburgh and restore them to married bliss at Clarence House."

I heard a low rumbling noise, and I frowned at Holmes. "Thunder? Is there hope of rain?"

Holmes' lips quivered, and he would not meet my eye, but he said nothing. Mycroft stared out of the window, his hands joined across his ample belly.

"*Quid est Veritas?*" Mycroft said at last. "You recall the reference? 'What is truth, said jesting Pilate, and would not stay for an answer'. You have no idea, Brother, how much the departments of government groan with mendacity."

"I can quite believe it, Brother," Holmes answered.

The carriage stopped outside Mycroft's club near the end of Pall Mall.

"I bid you good day, gentlemen," Mycroft said as he clambered out. "It is time for my afternoon apple."

Holmes ordered Rankin to continue east towards St Paul's.

"Let me see whether I can recall my schoolboy history, Watson," Holmes said, numbering the monarchs on his fingers. "The Scottish king, James the Sixth took the English over as James the First of England after Queen Elizabeth died. As a thank you, we beheaded his son Charles the First, brought back Charles the Second, deposed his son James the Second and invited Dutch William and Mary to take over. After a brief period with Anne, the Stuart dynasty in Britain effectively ended when we imported George the First from Hanover; he spoke so little English he instructed his British ministers in French. A sorry spectacle."

I chuckled. "Are you a Jacobite, Holmes? Would you favour the return of the Stuart dynasty to the throne?"

"I am not, and I would not. I don't see what advantage would accrue from exchanging our current Hanoverians for another dynasty. However, I understand several members of the Government are and would. Mycroft tells me they pass their wineglasses over the water carafes when they drink the loyal toast."

"Who is the pretender, the 'king across the water'?" I asked.

"Here will do," Holmes said, rapping on the roof with his stick.

The carriage stopped before an imposing building in Queen Victoria Street screened from the busy road by a set of tall ornamental gates. Holmes opened the carriage door and stepped down onto the pavement. "We must follow your line, Watson."

"Ah, yes, good idea," I said as I dropped down to the pavement next to Holmes. "What line is that?"

GRAND DUCHESS MARIA ALEXANDROVNA

## 4. THE NEW PRETENDER

Holmes and I passed through the tall gates into a small courtyard, and my friend took me by the arm. "The line of enquiry you started with the Prince of Wales, to his understandable annoyance, we must now vigorously pursue."

We crossed the courtyard, ascended a short flight of steps, and Holmes led the way into the lobby of the building. After identifying ourselves to a surly porter, we were shown upstairs to a pleasant sitting room furnished in the style of a gentleman's club, with leather chairs, buttoned sofas and potted plants. Open double doors on our right led to a large library.

The walls of the room were adorned with paintings of medieval heralds and framed representations of elaborate coats of arms.

I cleared my throat, but nobody appeared. Holmes made himself comfortable in one of the club chairs in his relaxed fashion, and I stood by the empty fireplace and glanced about me.

Stacks of leather-bound books lay on every table and even on the carpet, and the two desks in the room were piled with bulging folders of manuscript papers and drawings. I leaned over the nearer desk and peered at a coloured illustration of a unicorn.

As I angled it towards me, I heard a sharp intake of breath. I looked up and started at two figures who stood in the doorway of the library arm-in-arm. One was tall and thin and the other shorter and so rotund as to be almost spherical. They wore scarlet smoking jackets and fez hats in the same hue with gold tassels. They looked from Holmes to me, and then to the mantel clock.

"I do apologise," said Holmes waving an airy hand in his Bohemian way. "We are a little early."

"Gentlemen," the short man said, frowning, "you catch us in our shifts—"

"Garter exaggerates," the tall man said, pursing his lips. "It is our smoking hour, when in fine weather we take our post-luncheon cigars on the Library balcony." He pulled a gold watch from his waistcoat and checked it against the clock.

I held out my hand. "I am Doctor John Watson. May I introduce my friend and colleague Mr Sherlock Holmes?"

The men blinked at me, shuffled arm-in-arm back through the door, slipped through it and left me standing with my hand out.

Holmes chuckled and put his feet up on a pile of books.

I dropped my arm. "They must be deranged, Holmes. Is this a madhouse? The porter downstairs was a gruff fellow; perhaps he is the warder."

"Not quite a madhouse, but a strange world. This is the College of Arms of England, and the stout fellow, if I am not mistaken, is the Garter Principal King at Arms. He oversees all matters of precedence, emblems and coats of arms. We briefly met him and his companion at the time of the Queen's Golden

Jubilee. I telegraphed him earlier today regarding the Stone, but now we have a graver matter on which to consult."

I hardly knew whether to be annoyed or amused at the antic behaviour I had observed, and I waited with what equanimity I could muster for the Garter King and his companion to return.

The mantel clock chimed three and the sitting-room door opened again to reveal the gentlemen we had seen earlier, now hatless and clad in sober black frock coats. They bowed, and the shorter man welcomed us to the College of Arms, introducing himself as the Garter King as Holmes had surmised. His companion was Bluemantle, a herald of arms.

Holmes leapt from his chair, introduced himself and me and reminding them of our earlier meeting. He shook the gentlemen's hands. I hesitantly offered my hand again, and we were ushered to seats before a desk at one end of the room. The Garter King took his place opposite us under a portrait of the Queen, and Bluemantle pulled up a chair next to me.

The Garter King took a notebook from a drawer in the desk. "You are a doctor, sir?"

"I am."

He smiled. "In which particular academic field, if I might enquire?"

"Medicine. I am a general practitioner."

A frown flitted across Garter's face. "Your practice is in London?"

"I had a practice in Kensington. At the moment I do not regularly see patients."

Garter's frown steadied and deepened. "Watson, general practitioner, late of Kensington."

"Before that, my practice was in Paddington," I added.

The Garter King exchanged an amused look with his companion. "And you, sir?" he asked Holmes. "I recall you are connected with the police."

"My profession is consulting detective; my practice is in Baker Street."

"Holmes," Garter said in a musing tone. "Consulting detective." He reached behind him for a thick book, flicked through its pages, stopped and peered at one page. He ran his finger down a column of text. "Clairvoyants, consorts, consulates (see appendix), consulting physicians—"

He looked up and smiled first at me and then at Holmes. "No consulting detectives, I am afraid." He closed the book with a snap.

"I fear there has been a misunderstanding," said Holmes. "We are not here to lay claim to coats of arms. We investigate a matter of some moment, gentlemen, on orders from, ah, a person of eminence: *Wir dienen auch*, as it were."

Garter and Bluemantle exchanged knowing looks. "We quite understand," said Garter.

"More than I do," I muttered, earning reproachful looks from the heralds.

"What is the present status of Scots nationality?" Holmes asked.

"Scotland," Garter said, blinking at Holmes. "We have no knowledge of affairs of arms in Scotland. It would hardly do for us to meddle as they have their college, the Court of Lord Lyon. No, no, we would not presume to interfere. *Nemo me impune lacessit* is the motto of the Order of the Thistle, and therefore of the Scottish nation, insofar as that entity still exists within the Union."

"No one attacks me with impunity," I translated, not without a certain satisfaction.

"No one cuts me might be closer to the original," said Holmes, "presumably referring to the thorns of the thistle. But let us agree that the Scots, like their cousins in the south and west of these islands do not care to be provoked."

I recalled the image of the unicorn I had seen earlier. "Why is the Scottish unicorn in the royal coat of arms chained?" I asked.

Bluemantle leaned close to me. "Unicorns are dangerous beasts, Doctor." He stood. "A glass of Madeira, gentlemen?"

We accepted, and Bluemantle went to a sideboard laden with decanters.

"We wish to know the name of the current Jacobite pretender to the throne," said Holmes.

Garter frowned. "The Stuart heir-general? Again, I do not know. I fear the British red books will be of no use to us in that particular inquiry, and we must therefore consult our European rivals." He swung his chair around and ran his hand along a shelf of books behind the desk.

Bluemantle handed Holmes and me small glasses of Madeira and laid a plate of biscuits on the desk. He sat, leaned forward and put a hand on my knee. "There is a question of remuneration, gentlemen. We are a private institution. Our meagre salaries are supplemented by fees our clients are kind enough to disburse for genealogical research on their behalf."

I stood and moved to the fireplace. "The authorities, the Home Office for example, will defray your expenses. Or a simple application to the Palace would deal with considerations of payment."

Bluemantle chuckled. "I may venture to suggest you have not had extensive dealings with either institution."

"*Pro bono publico*," Garter said as he searched another shelf of books. "Or *Edwardus princeps Wallie*, if I may be allowed some linguistic latitude. Where did you put the *Almanach de Gotha*, Bluemantle? It is not in its accustomed place. Kindly fetch it."

Bluemantle pouted, stood and went to another desk in the far corner of the room. He picked up a thick, red-bound book and came back flicking through its pages.

"I asked you to get me the book, not to start the investigation yourself," Garter snapped. "Give it here."

Bluemantle sniffed. "My German is better than yours."

Garter stood and put his hands on his hips. "As you well know, the *Almanach* is in French." He turned to me. "The *Almanach de Gotha* is the Continental equivalent of our *Debrett's* or *Burke's Peerage*."

Bluemantle passed the book across the desk, gave Garter a cold look, turned and went into the Library. Garter called after him. "Peace, Brother Bluemantle. Come, let's have a little fun."

His colleague returned with another hefty red-leather-bound tome. He sat, balanced it on his knees and flicked through it.

I watched as the two heralds thumbed through their books, running their fingers down the pages and making occasional observations.

"Savoy is a *cul-de-sac*."

"The Cardinal Duke of York: a dry well."

I yawned and turned to Holmes. He was staring into space in one of his reveries.

I coughed to stifle another yawn. "What of the Duke and Duchess of Edinburgh, gentlemen? What connection have they with Scotland?"

Garter looked up. "None. One is Anglo-Hanoverian and the other Russian. Pass the biscuits, Bluemantle."

Garter took one from the plate and held it up. "Did you know *Marie* biscuits were created by the Peek Frean company to commemorate the marriage of Grand Duchess Maria to Prince Alfred, Duke of Edinburgh?"

"I did," said Holmes, coming out of his reverie, taking a biscuit and complacently nibbling it.

I sighed. "Can you tell us anything of the duke's wife?"

Garter shuddered. "Grand Duchess Maria Alexandrovna of Russia? Dreadful woman; she has caused us a great deal of inconvenience. She arrived on our shores with a vast treasury of jewellery, several wardrobes of extravagant gowns, her own Russian Orthodox Priest and a stupendous yearly allowance from St Petersburg. She estranged herself from London Society with her haughty manner and distaste for all things English. Marie deeply distrusts the British Parliament, convinced the institution is dangerous and radical." He shrugged. "She has a point."

"Tsar Alexander II insisted that, as the daughter of an *emperor*, Maria be styled 'Her Imperial Highness'," Bluemantle said with a sneer. "She would then have precedence over the Princess of Wales, the daughter of a mere *king* of Denmark." He smiled. "The Queen was unamused."

Garter nodded. "The Queen requires Maria be addressed as 'Her Royal Highness'."

"In retaliation," said Bluemantle, "Marie makes undignified attempts to upstage her mother-in-law by wearing jewels that surpass those of the Queen."

"What of the Duke of Edinburgh?" I asked.

"He was a successful naval officer," Bluemantle answered. "Often away from home, which must have been a comfort to both parties." He smiled at me. "The Navy knows the value of emblems and standards. Where would we be, Doctor, without our jolly tars?"

I blinked at him.

"But you'll have heard of the outrage in Sydney?" Garter asked. "No? The duke, in command of his armoured cruiser, visited Australia for several months in 1868. In Sydney he was invited to a picnic to raise funds for a sailors' home where he was shot by an Irish Nationalist. The Prince miraculously survived."

"He is now Duke of Saxe-Coburg and Gotha," I said.

"Indeed," said Garter. "And on her husband's ascension to the ducal throne, the Grand Duchess Marie Alexandrovna became Duchess of Saxe-Coburg and Gotha, in addition to being Duchess of Edinburgh. Unfortunately, as the consort of a sovereign German duke, she outranks her English sisters-in-law. We managed to keep them apart at the Diamond Jubilee celebrations by stuffing the dining table with maharajahs and other Empire and foreign worthies who muddled the precedence sufficiently for Maria to feel snubbed, but not know quite why."

"Does Saxe-Coburg and Gotha have any diplomatic representation here in Britain?" I asked.

"None," Garter answered. "They have no independent representation at all. It is all subsumed now under the German Empire."

I yawned and found my eyelids drooping. I stretched my arms and shook my head to clear it. "I might take a breath of air, with your permission."

I strolled into the Library. The French windows were open, but not a breeze stirred. The afternoon was stifling, the balcony was bathed in harsh sunshine and I did not choose to venture outside. I slumped onto a sofa and considered our progress on the two cases thus far.

We must be doing well, I thought, as very soon I found myself discussing designs for my own coat of arms with the Garter King. He showed me Shakespeare's blazon, a quill pen or spear on a yellow background, and we discussed how to combine the twin threads of my life, medicine and literature. We had almost reached an agreement and Garter was explaining the significance of the Scots lion that surmounted my emblem when I felt a hand on my arm.

"Wake up, old man."

"Eh? Oh, it's you, Holmes. I was resting my eyes."

He smiled. "We have a contender."

"Another Maria, without the biscuit," Garter said as I sat opposite him and Holmes took my place at the fireplace. "Maria Theresa of Bavaria is the niece and heir of the childless Francis the Fifth, Duke of Modena; she became the Jacobite heir-general to the thrones of England and Scotland after his death in 1875."

"Oh," I said. I yawned and blinked at him. "Who is she, again?"

"A Bavarian hausfrau," Holmes answered. "She and her husband stand to inherit the Kingdom of Bavaria, but for now they live a humble life on their farm south of Munich, where Maria Theresa tends her rose gardens."

"They live quietly and frugally," said Garter.

"Frugality is a Scottish virtue," said Holmes. He held out his hand. "Gentlemen, you have my thanks. I wish you a pleasant afternoon."

I stood, rendered my thanks and shook hands. When I had extricated my hand from Bluemantle's, I followed Holmes to the door, where he stopped.

"One more thing, gentlemen," he asked. "Do we in England possess any symbols of Scottish nationhood other than the Stone of Destiny at Westminster Abbey? A golden crown perhaps?"

"The Scots have their set of Crown Jewels, their 'Honours'," Garter replied.

"I thought Edward the First took them," I said.

"Indeed, Doctor, but they were returned with certain other items, (Berwick-on-Tweed, possibly) as a provision of the treaty that followed an English defeat."

"We also agreed to return the Stone of Destiny to Scotland," Bluemantle added. "But the London mob prevented its removal from the Abbey. Or *so they say*."

The two heralds exchanged arch looks.

"You know of no ancient crown of gold that pre-dates the Honours?" Holmes asked.

Garter glanced at his colleague, who shook his head. Neither met our eyes. "Not to our knowledge."

We passed through the ornate gates of the College of Arms into the glare, dust and noise of the busy road beyond and boarded our carriage.

"Jonathan Swift contends that all sublunary happiness consists in being well-deceived," said Holmes. "We should therefore be delighted."

I took out my handkerchief and mopped my brow. "How so?"

"Those fellows were lying, and my dear brother Mycroft also prevaricated; I know his deceitful look."

"What about, and to what end?"

Holmes laughed. "I am not quite sure."

"The Westminster theft, the thistle wreath and a royal kidnapping," I said as our carriage trundled towards Baker Street through heavy traffic. "Connections?"

Holmes shrugged. "Suspicions, but little data."

I puzzled in my mind over the various strands of the abduction of the duke and duchess, but the more I thought about the facts before us, the less I could imagine a connecting link.

The Prince of Wales was adamant the abduction was a plot of his nephew, the German Kaiser, but it would be a madcap thing for Wilhelm to kidnap his uncle, an English prince, so he could get his hands on the tiny duchy of Saxe-Coburg and Gotha. Would he do away with Prince Alfred and with Grand Duchess Maria? If discovered, that would inevitably lead to war with England and Russia, with other Powers joining in on either side in what Mycroft described as a pan-European conflagration. No, I dismissed the notion out-of-hand as an action that would cause the Kaiser's advisers to push him off the throne and into the madhouse.

"The Kaiser is surrounded by sycophants since Bismarck was dismissed," Holmes said, playing his mind-reading game.

"But what a terrible risk for such a trifling gain."

"Wilhelm is impulsive." Holmes shook two cigarettes from his packet and passed me one. "If the Kaiser's mind is fixed against his Uncle Edward, what better way to humiliate the prince and this country than by engineering the abduction of the prince's brother Alfred by supposed Irish fanatics? Perhaps the Kaiser thinks he could manipulate the Duke's young son into agreeing to merge his dukedom with Prussia."

I was struck with the gravest sense of dread that the incident in Pall Mall might be a catalyst leading to the ruin of Europe. Against that possibility, the question of the missing Stone of Destiny and the aspirations of the Scots for independence seemed ludicrously trivial.

"England is not well-loved after our attempts to bully the Boers," Holmes continued. "We might well be the laughing stock of Europe rather than the object of pity if something were to happen to the Duke and Duchess of Edinburgh."

We were held up by a jam of traffic in Holborn, and I took the opportunity to call a newspaper vendor to the carriage and get the late afternoon editions. I passed the *Evening News* to Holmes, and I leafed through the *Pall Mall Gazette*. I was relieved to see no mention of either the missing Stone or the royal couple. I judged from Holmes' silence as he looked through his paper that the cases were not featured.

We picked up speed as we left the City and made good time to Baker Street. We got down on a pavement thronged with people leaving their places of work and catching cabs or boarding omnibuses for home.

Mycroft's driver stepped down from the box and confronted me at the door of our lodgings. He was a tall, heavily built fellow with thick eyebrows and a mop of unruly black hair under a battered and crushed top hat. I gave him a half-crown, dismissed him for the day and ordered him to report for duty at eight the next morning. Rankin gave me a surly look and growled something unintelligible in a Scots accent. I added another shilling, firmly wished him good evening and turned away.

I opened the front door as quietly as I could, and Holmes and I left our hats and sticks in the hall and crept upstairs to our sitting room.

Holmes dropped into his chair by the fireplace and tucked his legs under him, adopting his usual position for thinking through a problem. I had considered buying him an Oriental hookah pipe for his birthday, but with Mrs Hudson on the warpath about smoking, I decided that another tartan scarf might be more politic.

"Any cigars left?" Holmes asked.

I stood, hunted along the mantel and found a packet with one cigar inside. I furrowed my brow as I tried to remember when I had opened it and how many cigars had been consumed. I was sure it had been new and unopened that morning, with three cigars inside. I had suspected for some time that our page was filching not only a pinch or two of our tobacco for his cigarettes, but the occasional cigar. I decided to confront him when I saw him next.

"You forget Mycroft," said Holmes, playing his irritating game. "He not only helped himself to our whisky, he made free with your cigars."

I passed Holmes the remaining cigar, and I filled my pipe.

"Where is Billy?" I asked. "I hope Mrs Hudson hasn't locked him up somewhere for the porridge outrage."

"He is on an errand for me."

I struck a match and lit my pipe. "You are right about Billy's suit of buttons, Holmes," I said between puffs. "We should get him a uniform more suitable for his age. I saw an advertisement for servants' uniforms this morning, in the *Telegraph*, I think. Whiteleys is having a sale this month at their temporary premises after the fire."

Holmes made no answer, and I turned my mind away from our domestic concerns and back to European politics. "Does it not seem strange we should be at odds with Germany? We fought beside Prussia against Napoleon through the Great Wars, and I don't think many Britons were unpleased when the Prussians defeated the French in 1870."

I blew a stream of smoke across the room. "The German Army is a counter to French aggression on the Continent, as our navy keeps watch on the French Navy in the Atlantic and Mediterranean. Germany is our natural ally."

Holmes nodded, but he did not pick up the conversation. His mind was evidently elsewhere, so I reached for the *Telegraph*, settled in my chair and hunted for the Whiteleys advertisement. I could not find it, and I may have dozed off, for I was startled when Holmes leapt out of his chair.

"Ha!" he cried. "Smoke and mirrors, Watson, we are being played." He bounded across the room to his desk and began throwing papers backwards and forwards. "Pass me down the 'F' Index, would you, old chap?"

I heaved myself out of my chair, yawned, and took a volume of Holmes' meticulous Index down from its shelf.

"Do try not to get cigar ash on the floor, old man," I said. "You know Mrs Hudson—"

"Three men in Europe might attempt such a crime," said Holmes.

"The theft of the Stone of Destiny?" I asked.

Holmes turned from his desk and raised his eyebrows. "I think we might concentrate our efforts on the abduction of the Duke of Edinburgh and his illustrious wife," he said in a tone of mild rebuke. "We might attempt to avert pan-European destruction and the end of civilisation, rather than pursuing the theft of a drain cover."

I looked down at my toes. "Of course, Holmes."

He held up a telephone directory. "Only one of the three men I have in mind enjoys the confidence of the German Emperor. That man is Baron Otto von Feldberg."

"I've heard the name. Wasn't he the fellow behind the attempt at the Windsor castle jewels in '91?"

Holmes nodded. "He was, although we could not prove it. He is in Society. He has offices and rooms in Regent Street and a villa near Windsor where he holds receptions during the Season and intimate dinner parties throughout the year. He plays the Anglophile and *bon vivant*, but Feldberg is the eyes and ears of the Kaiser in the capital; he collects information, intelligence if he can get it, but often mere gossip, that can be used by Wilhelm against this country and especially against his uncle, the Prince of Wales."

I laid the 'F' volume of the Index on the table and Holmes pounced on it and flicked through the pages. "We talked of the Tranby Croft affair earlier," he said. "The source of the information on the Prince of Wales' gambling was obvious; one of the ladies present at Tranby Croft was the most notorious gossip in the kingdom. But who leaked the details to the Continental newspapers and provided the Kaiser with intimate portraits of the participants?"

"His agent, von Feldberg?"

"Indeed. Pass me the large-scale map of London."

I handed the map to Holmes, and he spread it across the table. "From Pall Mall to Regent Street – no great distance."

Holmes pored over the map, flicked through directories, scribbled notes on scraps of paper and wrote sheaves of telegrams. He was too focused for conversation, so I settled at my desk and wrote up my notes of the two current cases – slim pickings, of course and I soon put down my pen and slumped into my comfortable chair in front of the empty fireplace with the latest issue of the *Lancet*. The evening was stifling, and I had no desire to venture forth despite the uninviting prospect of Mrs Hudson's infamous liver and bacon for supper.

I was woken some time later by a knock at the sitting-room door, and our maid Bessie brought in a sealed package. "By messenger, Doctor, with thruppence-ha'penny to pay."

I gave her the coins, and Holmes ripped open the package to reveal a wreath of thistles identical to the one we had seen earlier at the Abbey. A note was attached.

"From Mycroft," said Holmes. "This wreath was fixed to the door knocker at the Scottish Office. Oh dear, if I am not mistaken this is more Ossian. I had hoped for Burns, Macdonald or even McGonagall." He threw the wreath onto the table, strode to the window, drew one of our new curtains aside and peered out. "I have a notion we are being watched."

"By whom?"

Holmes shrugged and went back to his papers.

I picked up the wreath. The verses were similar to those on the first wreath and just as incomprehensible. If the person or persons who stole the Stone of Destiny were those who left the wreaths, then they were using a most allusive and allegorical medium to make their political statements.

Bessie brought up supper at nine, and Holmes and I washed down our contrite liver and bacon with a fine Beaune from a case given Holmes by a satisfied client. That, and the excellent rice pudding we had for dessert lightened my apocalyptic mood, but after our busy day I found I was suddenly exhausted. I wished my friend goodnight, went to the door, stopped and turned. "I say, Holmes, I've just remembered. What was that—"

"The motto of the Prince of Wales is, for some reason, in German, '*Ich Dein*', meaning 'I serve'. I hinted at the august 'personage' behind our enquiries by informing the heralds we also serve, or in German, *Wir dienen auch*. As you saw, it encouraged their cooperation."

I nodded and yawned. "Good night."

THE CHAINED UNICORN OF SCOTLAND

## 5. WE ARE DOGGED

I came downstairs at about eight the next morning and saw Holmes had breakfasted before me as his place was not yet cleared.

Breakfast was a frugal affair. I had to be content with a couple of over-boiled eggs and a chop that had seen better days. As I ate, I considered how Holmes and I might assuage the wrath of Mrs Hudson without looking even more foolish than we already did.

I had noticed a fine Chinese pot in the window of the glass and ceramic emporium down the road, and I thought, if the price was reasonable, I could purchase it, get Billy to plant an aspidistra and give it to Mrs Hudson as a peace offering.

As I thought of Billy, he appeared in the doorway.

"Ah, Billy," I said. "You're back. Can you—"

"Gentleman for Mr Holmes, Doctor." He ushered a stout gentleman wearing a grey frock coat over a gaudy purple waistcoat into the room.

The man laid his stick, gloves and a white homburg-style hat on the side table and held out his hand. "Pennington, George Arthur, sir. I have an appointment with Mr Holmes at nine." He spoke in a soft voice with a faint accent I took to be American or Canadian.

I introduced myself, showed Mr Pennington to our sofa and offered refreshments, which he declined. I explained Holmes was out, and I expressed my conviction he would return shortly to keep his appointment.

Mr Pennington folded his hands in his lap and said he was perfectly happy to wait, and I should not go to any trouble on his behalf.

"Do I detect a North American accent, sir," I asked to make conversation.

Mr Pennington smiled. "You are very kind, Doctor."

I blinked at him, and, feeling I had not made myself clear, I continued. "From what part of America do you hail, Mr Pennington? Or are you Canadian, perchance?"

He considered for a moment. "I am not quite sure. I decided on the East Coast, as more likely from the commercial point of view, but I have no indication a particular city is required."

I frowned as I tried to understand Mr Pennington's cryptic answer to what I had thought a simple enough question. I decided to abandon that line of enquiry in favour of the topic of the Diamond Jubilee celebrations of the previous month, the searing heat of the summer and the remote possibility of rain.

Mr Pennington and I made idle conversation for ten minutes or so. He was polite, but he did not make any effort to let a conversational hare have a run. He replied to my observations on the inauguration of the new American president, Mr McKinley, in monosyllables and then, smiling his soft smile, he fell silent once again.

Having again offered refreshments, I racked my brain for other subjects on which we might converse. In my awkward circumstance, with a stranger in the room to whom I owed a duty of hospitality but who would accept none, who sat before me with the blank, benign image of an Oriental potentate, I found that my mind focused once again on the abduction case and the terrible consequences that would ensue if the Duke of Edinburgh and his wife were not rescued.

My brow furrowed, my hospitable smile grew rigid and my fingers twitched. I mopped at my face with my handkerchief in a gesture as much a response to the dark affair Holmes was investigating and to my awkward situation as it was to the stifling heat of the room.

The mantel clock chimed nine, then a quarter past and there was no sign of Holmes. I was about to make a remark on the bimetallic question and the plight of the Indian Rupee when I heard Holmes' footsteps echo on the still bare stairs.

He strode in, waved a greeting and studied his guest in silence for a long moment, then, to my chagrin, he disappeared into his room.

I smiled weakly at Mr Pennington. "Mr Holmes will be with you very soon, I am sure."

Mr Pennington nodded.

After ten more minutes of what was for me a most uncomfortable tension, I stood, went to the door of Holmes' dressing room and knocked. "A gentleman is here to see you, Holmes. A Mr Pennington; his appointment was at nine."

There was no answer save for a soft rustling noise and the clink of something – metal, glass, china?

I returned to my seat and spread my hands in a gesture designed to show Mr Pennington I had done all I could.

"Might the window be closed, sir?" he requested in his soft voice. "And the curtains drawn. I think Mr Holmes would want them so."

I complied with our visitor's odd request, and when I turned back to the room, I was astonished to see that Mr Pennington had taken off his frock coat, removed his colourful waistcoat and put his coat back on over his shirt.

"It is warm," I said, as he laid the waistcoat on the sideboard with his hat, stick and gloves. "Do feel free to make yourself comfortable, Mr Pennington. Are you sure I cannot offer you any refreshment?"

"Indeed, it is warm, Doctor," Mr Pennington replied, sitting down again. "But I am perfectly comfortable."

The door of Holmes' bedroom opened a crack. "Are the curtains drawn?" he called.

"They are," I answered.

The door opened fully, and I was amazed when the same stout gentleman who sat contentedly on the sofa strode into the sitting room in his shirt with a grey frock coat over his arm. He put on Mr Pennington's purple waistcoat and his own coat. He nodded to his twin, picked up the gentleman's hat, gloves and stick, wished me a pleasant afternoon in an American accent and left.

I frowned at Mr Pennington. "You *are* Mr Pennington?" I asked.

"I am, Doctor. And that gentleman was Mr Holmes, I presume."

I frowned and felt the circumstances were such that I might question Holmes' guest without impropriety. "May I ask how you come to be here, Mr Pennington, if that is not a private matter?"

Mr Pennington considered. "I am charged not to discuss anything I see or hear in this room with anyone outside, but as I am *in* the room with you, Doctor, I conceive I am not bound by that injunction."

He smiled his pleasant smile. "I am an actor, currently resting between parts. My agency contacted me yesterday afternoon with a proposition for a private performance. The part required me to wear a bright-coloured waistcoat and a white hat, preferably in the American style. I had both in my actor's wardrobe as I had a supporting role in *The Colonel* at the Comedy Theatre a few years back. I therefore accepted the part, which is very well remunerated, with great pleasure. A note that came by messenger this morning gave me more details of my character and instructed me to come to 221b Baker Street attired as I am (or was), and there I was to wait for a Mr Holmes. When he arrived, after ensuring the windows were closed and curtains were drawn, I should take off my waistcoat and sit quietly until Mr Holmes dismissed me."

I frowned. "That is all? You have no idea when or where you are to play your role?"

"None whatsoever," Mr Pennington said. "In my profession, at least at the meagre level of professional advancement I have achieved, one has learned to be patient and to grasp avidly at any straws whisking by. And one does not look a gift horse in the mouth, if I may mix my metaphors."

He smiled again. "You mentioned refreshments earlier, Doctor. Would it be an imposition for me request a whisky and soda? It is early, but as you observed the weather is close today."

I gave Mr Pennington his drink and, as he seemed content to sit on the sofa and sip his whisky soda, I picked up my *Times* and sat at the breakfast table leafing through it. I still found it most awkward having a stranger planted Buddha-like on the sofa in our sitting-room, but I found that if I half-turned away from him, I could almost forget he was there. After ten minutes or so, Mr Pennington cleared his throat, and I offered him another whisky, which he politely accepted.

It was with relief that I heard the front door open, then footsteps thumping on the staircase and the second Mr Pennington appeared at the sitting-room door. He slipped off his frock coat, removed his purple waistcoat and handed it, his gloves, stick and hat to Mr Pennington.

"We agreed three guineas," he said in Holmes' voice. "Watson?"

I gave Holmes the required coins, and Holmes counted them into Mr Pennington's hand. "Do not worry about the agency percentage, my dear sir," he said. "I saw to that yesterday."

Mr Pennington bowed. "That is most generous, Mr Holmes. If there is ever any other little—"

"Yes, yes, our page will show you out." Holmes strode into his bedroom and closed the door behind him.

Mr Pennington dressed, shook my hand and made to go, but he turned back. "That gentleman is the famous Sherlock Holmes?" he asked in his soft voice, this time with an English accent. "I had expected someone more (how shall I say?), more imposing. Good day to you, Doctor."

"Now, what was that about?" I asked Holmes as he came out from his bedroom in his usual clothes and without wig and make-up.

"We are watched," Holmes said as he picked a pipe from the rack and scrabbled along the mantel for the Persian slipper in which he kept our tobacco. "I am now certain we are dogged. I employed Mr Pennington as my shadow. He came here as a client, and, as you saw, I left as him. I was able to get close. Let me show our watcher to you."

He strode to the window and gently pulled aside one of the curtains to allow us a view of the street below. "You see him? The young man on the corner, lounging in that languid manner."

"A common loafer, Holmes."

"No, no. This fellow lounges with an aristocratic languor. He is used to leaning against the mantel in the billiard room rather than against the counter in a public house. His hair under that disreputable cap is neatly trimmed and anointed with an expensive Macassar Oil. His patched and threadbare jacket is at least two sizes too big for him, yet his trousers are of excellent quality, well-tailored and ironed in the Prince of Wales style with the creases at the side. The trousers legs have been let down at least twice as the wearer grew. They are frayed and threadbare and the cloth is shiny on the seat. The assiduous ironer must know the trousers are in need of repair or replacement. No wife who loved her husband, or servant who cared for his master would let him out in public in such attire."

Holmes took his usual seat, filled his pipe and lit it. I continued to peer at the lounger in as careful a manner as I could manage. As far as I could see, the young man's attention was on the street and not at all on our windows.

"His shoes are also of the best quality and they shine brilliantly," Holmes continued between puffs on his pipe. "Not only the front of the shoes have been diligently polished, but the back of the heels the brigades of shoeblacks who infest our London streets do not trouble themselves with is buffed to a mirror finish."

Holmes blew a stream of smoke across the room. "Yet our lounger is a lazy, careless fellow. You see how he smokes his cigarette with no concern for the ash which spots his shirt front and jacket? His shoes were therefore polished by another – a servant, or some person acting in that capacity."

"Not an officer's servant," I said. "He has not the bearing of a military man."

"Ha!" said Holmes, turning to me. "You are coming along, Watson. Your association with the world's foremost consulting detective has sharpened your deductive faculties."

I accepted the compliment with a smile. "Whisky?"

"Thank you." Holmes leaned back in his chair. "I managed to get close in to the young man. He bites his nails, and he has done a good deal of writing recently."

"Ink stains on his fingers?"

"Exactly. The shiny patch on the seat of his trousers suggests a sedentary life, but he is spare and muscular, and his gait is that of a young fellow who plays regular sport."

I offered Holmes a tumbler of whisky and soda. "No ice, I'm afraid."

Holmes took the glass "He is an enigma."

"Did you speak to him?" I asked. "Do you think he means us harm?"

Holmes considered. "It depends which faction he represents. If the Prussian, then we must be wary. I had thought of precipitating a confrontation, but I need more data before I act. The surveillance may be unrelated to the present cases. He could be a minion of Brooks, or Woodhouse, or any of a dozen men who think my term of life on earth should be violently curtailed."

"Prussian? You agree with the Prince of Wales that Prussia is involved in these affairs: the Stone and the royal abduction?"

"I have formulated a plan of action I hope will answer that question. May I rely on you to second me?"

"Of course, Holmes."

I poured myself a drink and returned to my seat at our breakfast table. "By the way," I said. "At the Abbey you mentioned a case of espionage in which you were involved. Could the watcher be connected with that?"

"Hmmm? Did you know our prime minister, Lord Salisbury, was so badly bullied at Eton he had to be withdrawn from the school?"

I frowned and blinked at my friend. "What has that to do with—"

Holmes leapt up. "Let me have your copy of *Dickens' Guide to London*, would you?" He scrabbled among the papers on his desk. "Where did I put the telegram forms?"

I passed Holmes a sheaf, took the *Guide* from the shelf above my desk and handed it to him. He flicked through the pages. "Nothing on term dates. I would telegraph, but I don't want to draw attention to the subjects of my enquiry."

He smiled and put his finger to his lip. "I might use the telephone. You know, the telephone apparatus has an extraordinary potential for fraud. One can adopt an accent and pretend to be whomever one wants to be. No record can be kept of the conversation."

Billy came in with an envelope. Holmes opened it, read the message and handed it to me. "A report from my crow in Regent Street." He frowned. "I should have liked to have spent another day or two establishing our target's routine, but we have no time. It must be today."

The message was written in a scrawl, but I managed to read a line that suggested no change had occurred. "You are even more inscrutable than is your irritating wont, Holmes. What must be today?"

He bounded to the door. "Come, my friend, and see."

Rankin, just as surly in the morning as he had the previous evening, drove us across London to the neighbourhood of Fleet Street. I computed with some satisfaction what we had saved in cab fares by using the official carriage, despite the three-and-six I had been obliged to tip the fellow the previous day.

"I telegraphed the offices of the *People's Journal* in Perth yesterday regarding subscriptions," said Holmes. "I was referred to their London agency at an office in Poppins Court, off Fleet Street." He checked his watch. "They open at ten."

We passed slowly along Fleet Street along a constricted lane between the newspaper vans parked on either side. The pavements were thronged with pedestrians, grateful no doubt for the awnings extended over almost all the ground floor premises that shaded them from the sun's glare.

Rankin stopped at the entrance to a small alley too narrow for the carriage to negotiate. Holmes and I stepped down and Rankin called to me that he and the horse were dying of thirst – at least I presumed that was the gist of his remarks as his voice was even gruffer than it had been the previous evening, and his accent thicker.

I tossed him a shilling, and he flicked the reins and moved up the street towards the horse trough, and, I didn't doubt, a gin shop.

Holmes led the way into the alley. Small businesses lined the left side. A leather repair shop had harness, shoes and bags in its crowded window, and a second-hand bookshop displayed its volumes not only inside, but on shelves and in boxes on the already crowded pavement, leaving precious little room for pedestrians. We picked our way among the books and then passed a spectacle shop and a wigmaker. Between that and a servants' apparel emporium, of whose location I made a note, was a narrow shop front with a bow window in which pages from newspapers were stuck on boards. In peeling gilt lettering across the glass was the legend 'The News Agency of the North'.

A ragged boy leaned against the wall of the alley a few doors farther along. He tapped his nose and gave me a most impertinent look and a wink, which I ignored.

Holmes pushed through the door and a bell tinkled, startling a pale young man who was rising from his desk.

"Good morning to you," said Holmes.

"We are just closing for luncheon," the man said in a faint Scots accent. He reached for his bowler hat hanging from a stand.

I looked at my watch as Holmes gave the man his business card; it was ten to eleven.

"Mr Sherlock Holmes the detective?" The man smiled and turned to me. "Then you must be his Boswell, Doctor Wilson."

"Watson, in fact."

Richard McNair, proprietor and sole employee of the News Agency of the North, introduced himself and shook Holmes' hand and mine. "Do I detect some Scots in your accent, Doctor?" he asked.

"I do not think so, although I believe I may have Scottish ancestors."

"We are interested in the current state of the movement, if there is one, for Scottish independence," said Holmes.

Mr McNair shrugged. "Not my line, although in my personal capacity I have views of the subject, as any Scotsman may. My job is to have articles from the *Peoples Journal* and other Scots and border newspapers accepted by the London agencies and reprinted here. It is an uphill climb; interest in Scotland and Scots affairs is not white hot."

"Is it not?" said Holmes in a sympathetic tone. "I wonder why?"

"Take a seat, gentlemen." Mr McNair took an almost empty bottle of Scotch from a cabinet and held it up "Will you take a dram?"

"Thank you, no," Holmes said, and I smiled and shook my head.

Mr McNair poured the dregs of the bottle into a tumbler, added water and took a sip. "You are pursuing a case, sir?"

"I am," said Holmes. "And I am on a generous expense allowance. Might I suggest a change of location, perhaps to the Coal Hole in the Strand?"

Mr McNair raised his eyebrows. "That was where I was about to go for luncheon."

"What a coincidence," Holmes said with a smile.

"Let me get my keys, and I am your man," Mr McNair said as he heaved himself from his chair, leaning on a walking stick, and went through the door into the back of the shop.

"Behave yourself, Holmes," I whispered. "Think of Walter Scott, Robert Stevenson, James Watt and Thomas Carlyle."

Holmes frowned. "Thomas who?"

I stood and examined a needlepoint tapestry framed on the office wall. "According to the label, it is a lay of Ossian,

*No, never Finn;*
*The sun ne'er saw King*
*Who him excelled.*
*The monsters in lakes,*
*The serpent by land,*
*In Erin of saints*
*The hero slew."*

I turned to Holmes. "I thought Saint Patrick expelled the serpents from Ireland."

Holmes shrugged. "He missed one."

Mr McNair appeared carrying his stick and gloves. "If I may correct you, Mr Holmes, Ossian pre-dates Patrick, or perhaps they were contemporaneous. For history, you'd best speak to my friend and colleague, Angus Macdonald. He's on at the Alhambra as an illusionist. He'll set you right on matters of history. I look forward; he looks back."

We returned along the alley to Fleet Street where our carriage waited. The ragged street Arab followed us and officiously held open the carriage door as Mr McNair heaved himself inside. Holmes insisted I tip the boy thruppence before we set off for the Strand, and the impudent child took the money with another impertinent wink.

"What of the National Association for the Vindication of Scottish Rights?" Holmes asked Mr McNair as we clattered along Fleet Street.

He shrugged. "A talking shop; no, a defunct talking shop."

"Very well. Could you give me a succinct account of nationalist feelings in Scotland?"

"And the significance of the Stone of Destiny to the Scots," I added, earning a bleak look from Holmes.

Mr McNair smiled. "The Stone of Scone? I understand it was stolen by your King Edward and now it forms what must be an uncomfortable perch for British monarchs. It can have no significance for the rational Scot, or Englishman for that matter – if such a creature exists."

I offered Mr McNair a cigarette, which he accepted as he continued.

"That rational Englishman might not find Scottish independence such a peculiar idea if he looked at it with the cold eye of logic."

I passed him my matches, and he lit his cigarette.

"Not being an acquisitive race, the Scots are respected by Europeans and Americans. Even the Irish tolerate us. And we have men in key positions in the Empire, particularly in Canada, Australia, New Zealand, the Cape Colony and India. And it cannot be said of the Scots, as it used to be said unfairly about the Irish, that they are undeserving of independence, or unable to govern themselves. Scots have been far too successful in governing other people (including the English) for that argument to make any sense."

He chuckled. "I am reminded of the old story that a fellow from Edinburgh goes to London to meet the leaders in politics and business here. When he gets back, his friend asks him what he thought of the English. He says he didna meet any: all the managers he dealt with were Scots."

Our carriage stopped outside the Coal Hole, and I frowned as I wondered whether I should take offence at Mr McNair's glib manner. I got down behind Holmes, and Mr McNair followed us, stepping down with some difficulty.

Rankin climbed down from his box and told me he was going for his dinner. He indicated a pie and mash shop on the opposite side of the street and held out his hand. I gave him a shilling and then another sixpence. He growled at me and fixed me with his fierce glare, but I turned away and followed Holmes and Mr McNair into the bar of the Coal Hole. I bought drinks at the counter as they settled at a table by the window. I joined them with a tray of whisky sodas.

"My feeling is that an independent Scotland would be looked upon very favourably by most of the world," said Mr McNair, evidently in answer to a question from Holmes. "We have steel and shipbuilding, productive farms, competitive merchants and our fine fishery: we would not starve."

I passed drinks to Holmes and Mr McNair.

"How would you propose to achieve independence?" Holmes asked.

Mr McNair considered. "Few Scots would want to sever their ties to the Union and Empire entirely; no, such a proposition would gather little support in Scotland. Scottish merchants thrive within the Empire. The success of Scottish arms in its defence has created our shared military history: the charge of the Scots Greys at Waterloo and the thin Red Line at Balaclava and many other exploits are justly celebrated." Mr McNair smiled. "And are the more Scottish when connected to heroic failure, a Jacobite motif." He took a sip of whisky.

"With the Empire," I said firmly, "Britain is far greater than the sum of its geographical parts. Scotsmen, whether as statesmen, financiers, scientists, educators, engineers or, as you say, merchants and soldiers have held their own in all our colonies, nay, risen to positions of eminence. Scottish missionaries are hugely influential; the name Livingstone cannot be said without a lump coming to one's throat."

"Livingston," said Holmes. He blinked at me, shrugged and turned back to Mr McNair. "Are all members of the movement for Scottish independence, of the same mind? Would none desire disunion? Is there no equivalent to the Irish Fenian organisation in Scotland?"

Mr McNair frowned. "Dynamitards and assassins? Well, I cannot say there are none in Scotland. Madmen exist on both sides of the border. But I know of no populist movement calling for disunion. My view is that Scotland can exist and even thrive on its own, but I would be content if my nation ran its own affairs from Edinburgh, without meddling from London. We'll stay in your Empire, continue to fight your wars and respect your alliances, but we must impose and spend our own taxes and govern ourselves domestically."

He shook his head. "The Fenians use violent means, and they have merely hardened opinion against them. They offer no example for the Scots to follow." Mr McNair took a puff of his cigarette.

"And what of loyalty," I asked stiffly. "What of the Queen?"

"Scots are loyal to our Queen as head of the United Kingdom and the Empire, but she is the head for them because she is descended from a long line of Scottish kings going back and back till lost in the Scots mists of antiquity. The fact that she is also descended from the kings of England is of no consequence."

Holmes nodded to me, and I held my notebook open to the light from the window.

"What do you make of this?"

"Quotes from Ossian, Doctor." He lifted his glass and began to declaim.

> *"When shall Ossian's youth return?*
> *When his ear delight in the sound of arms?*
> *When shall I, like Oscar, travel in the light of my steel?*
> *Come with your streams, ye hills of Cona!*
> *Listen to the voice of Ossian.*
> *The song rises, like the sun, in my soul.*
> *I feel the joys of other times."*

Mr McNair raised his glass to me. "Is that not sublime?"

Holmes stood. "Thank you. You have been most helpful."

Mr McNair rose, wincing, and he and I shook hands. "Boswell was a Scot, Doctor," he murmured.

"And Johnson was not," said Holmes. "He called Ossian a mountebank, a liar, and a fraud, and held the author Macpherson guilty of as gross an imposition as ever the world was troubled with. A very good morning to you, Mr McNair."

We emerged from the dim coolness of the public house into the harsh sunlight, and I sent a boy to the pie and mash shop to call our carriage.

"Mr McNair did not strike me as a dangerous fellow, Holmes. I can't help thinking Scottish nationalism is a harmless cultural movement with few political ramifications."

"You might pop in to your tobacconist while we're here," Holmes said. "You are out of cigars and down to the last quarter pound or so of tobacco."

I did as Holmes suggested, and I took the opportunity to visit the *parfumerie* nearby. I returned with my packages and found our carriage outside the Coal Hole with Rankin on the box.

I climbed aboard, but Holmes was not inside or on the pavement. My pistol weighed heavily in my pocket, and I fingered the grip as I looked warily around me.

Holmes came out of a florist's shop holding a bunch of flowers at arm's length.

He lay his flowers on the seat opposite him. I showed him the bottle of rosewater I had purchased, and we exchanged wan smiles as we set off again.

"Are we too focused on the Scots?" I asked. "Could not someone else be behind the outrage? The Irish, or nihilists."

"That's possible," Holmes answered. "But two lines of enquiry stand out: the Scottish and the German connections. We will now focus on the latter."

Prince Albert, reigning Duke of Saxe-Coburg and Gotha and Duke of Edinburgh

## 6 LEGERDEMAIN

"There are public telephones in the Charing Cross Hotel," Holmes said. "We can make a call on our way."

"Our way where, Holmes? And call to whom?"

"To Baron von Feldberg's lair in Regent Street."

We stopped at the hotel, and I sat on an overstuffed sofa as Holmes stalked to the concierge and was allocated one of the carved wood and etched glass telephone cabins that lined one side of the lobby. Each had a writing desk and chair, a deep, buttoned armchair, a potted plant and a side table on which the apparatus stood.

Holmes disappeared into the booth and a short time later marched out, paid the fee at the concierge's counter and joined me.

"Less than two minutes of bawling at each other at a cost of a shilling, and no record of the conversation," Holmes snapped as we made our way through heavy glass doors and outside into the sunlight.

"Regent Street," I ordered Rankin, and we got back into our carriage.

"The baron conducts his wine and spirits importation business from offices in Regent Street," Holmes said. "He has a villa in Windsor to which he retreats at the end of each week. He is said to be an amiable fellow with a large circle of acquaintance – an Anglophile with a taste for English-cut suits, high play at the card table, horse racing and shooting. He is an aficionado of the soubrettes at the Gaiety Music Hall."

"Gaiety girls! They may be his Achilles heel," I suggested.

"The baron is interested in inventions and processes," Holmes continued. "Part of his remit is to inform Berlin of advances made by our scientists, especially in military affairs. He wrote an interesting piece for the *Illustrated London News* describing his outing at Windsor with the famous horseless carriage enthusiast the Hon. Evelyn Ellis. The other passenger was the Prince of Wales."

Holmes peered out of the window. "We will set down here and walk. Keep a little distance if you would and look out for crows. We may still be under surveillance."

Holmes stepped down from the carriage, walked to the corner and turned into Regent Street. I followed a dozen or so paces behind him, looking about me in a casual way and stopping now and then to peer into a shop window and use the plate glass as a mirror. I kept Holmes' angular figure in sight, and I saw him pause to buy an evening newspaper from a vendor with a stall outside a public house. He tucked the paper under his arm and walked on.

I followed him with something of a complacent feeling that no ordinary spy could dog John Watson. I had not spent over sixteen years in the company of the world's foremost expert in surveillance for nothing. I sauntered along the pavement with a nonchalant air, but my eyes flitted over my fellow pedestrians and passing carriages as I deployed my finely honed expertise in stealthy reconnaissance.

The weather was still oppressive, with not a hint of a cooling breeze. The upper-story windows of the houses we passed were all open, the occupants trying to catch the slightest waft of air to counter the relentless heat. I began to wish I had exchanged my bowler hat for a straw boater, and I was almost tempted to loosen my collar and undo the top button of my shirt, but saner counsels prevailed, and I merely mopped my brow with my handkerchief as every second man in the street was doing.

I narrowed my eyes against the glare and scanned the street as I walked. A group of soldiers in blue regimentals stood in the shade outside the public house, smoking, chatting and listening to the music of an accordion player who leaned against the wall, his dog at his feet, playing music hall tunes in a listless fashion. Omnibuses, cabs, carts and vans lumbered along the roadway, drivers and horses with their heads down, oppressed by the glaring sun.

A pretty girl danced across the pavement to me and held up a chain of daisies she said could be mine for a penny. I shook my head, but she smiled in such an innocent, appealing way that I detached one flower from the chain and allowed her to pin it in my buttonhole. I gave her a penny at which she grinned and, to my consternation, kissed me on the cheek. She tripped away, looking back and waving every few steps.

I smoothed my moustache and yanked at my constricting collar, my face reddening in the torrid heat. I turned, but the girl was gone, and I smiled and was about to continue on my way when I blinked at the street ahead of me and realised Holmes was no longer in sight.

I hurried forward, stopped at the newspaper vendor's cart, bought a paper as cover and carefully looked about me. I noted a dozen open doorways within a few paces into which Holmes could have ducked, and I felt a surge of annoyance he had not made a sign or otherwise let me—

"Second door after the pub, Doctor," said the newspaper vendor. "Above the dentist."

I gazed at the young man in astonishment. He was a knowing-looking fellow with a thin moustache, wearing a shabby jacket, a grey neck cloth and a checked cap. He winked at me and turned to a customer.

I flapped my paper open and peered over it at the doorway the vendor had indicated. The front door was ajar, revealing a hall in which a hat stand and a potted plant stood beside the entrance to the dentist's surgery. On the left, a set of stairs led to the upper floors. A boy sat on the steps whittling a stick with his penknife.

I squinted up to the first-floor bow windows and read 'S. Rains and Son, Stationery Supplies' in gilt lettering. Net curtains were drawn across the windows, and I could not see inside.

I folded my newspaper under my arm, ambled across the pavement and stopped at the front door. I looked casually about me, then slipped into the hall.

The dentist had his door open to allay the fierce heat, and although I averted my eyes from the scene inside, the jarring, grinding sound of the drill followed me across the hall and brought back awful memories. I passed the boy, who ignored me, and I hurried up the stairs.

I crossed the landing and peeked into the open door of the front room. It was sparsely decorated, with a couple of chairs and a round table. Two men stood silhouetted in the bow window, bending over a brass apparatus on a tripod.

One turned. "Ah, here you are at last," said Holmes. He smiled at the man with him. "A glass of lemonade for the Doctor, Harry."

"Wiggins!" I cried. The erstwhile leader of Holmes' band of ragamuffin street Arabs crossed the room and held out his hand.

"Very pleased to see you again, Doctor." Wiggins beamed at me, and I at him. He had grown prodigiously since the last time I had met him, and he now had a fine moustache.

"You're looking well, if I may make so bold, sir." We shook hands, and Harry gave me a glass of iced lemonade that was nectar of the gods.

Holmes indicated a large brass telescope mounted in the window alcove. "We have an excellent view of the baron's premises, better than we might have hoped for as all the windows are open. His rooms and private office are in the corner suite on the left."

He took a glass of lemonade from Wiggins. "When the telephone apparatus at the hotel was connected to Baron von Feldberg, Harry not only heard the ring of the telephone bell across the street, he saw the baron pick up the earpiece and answer my call."

He smiled. "I visited the shop on the ground floor this morning in the character of Mr George Pennington. I left my card and took one of the Baron's cards that listed the company telephone number."

Holmes passed me a card printed with a studio image of a dapper gentleman with luxuriantly curled moustaches wearing a straw boater.

"He does not look very Prussian," I remarked. "He seems a jolly fellow. I could see him selling me a gelato from an Italian ice-cream cart." I frowned. "What an odd notion, having one's portrait on a calling card."

"Here is mine." Holmes handed me a regular business card purporting to be that of Mr Pennington, a wine importer with an address in Philadelphia. I raised my eyebrows.

"You will recall Harry's Uncle Silas," said Holmes.

"The forger?"

"Tut, tut, Doctor," Wiggins said, gesturing at the gilt-lettering on the windows. "Master printer."

"When I connected with the baron," Holmes continued. "I asked him some nonsense about the availability of certain brandies. The baron said the line was bad, and he suggested I put my request in writing and he would have his clerks check his stocks. The fellow was affability itself, eager to please and apologetic with regard to the telephone problem."

He laughed. "In fact, I had a handkerchief over the mouthpiece of the telephone apparatus which muffled my voice and gave the impression of a fault on the line."

Holmes took me by the elbow and steered me to the telescope. "Look through the lens, and I will slip aside the net."

I bent to peer through eyepiece, and when the curtain was moved aside, the image was crystal-clear.

"You see the baron's office? Track left to just outside his window. The telephone wire is stretched from a pole in the street to his office, another line leads to his shop on the ground floor and a third to the warehouse where he stores his wines in modern, temperature-controlled storerooms."

I straightened and took a sip of lemonade. "What's the plan?"

"Did you spot any surveillance?" Holmes asked.

I shook my head. "None, we are clear. Apart from the newspaper vendor, who I suppose is your man."

Holmes winked at Wiggins, and they laughed.

"You think the hound has the royal couple in that building?" I asked, a little miffed at my friends' laughter, which seemed to be at my expense.

"It's a possibility," said Holmes. "We can say no more than that. With more time, we could have reconnoitred more thoroughly and set a watch. If a Fortnum and Mason's van had turned up at the door, we would have known they were there; I imagine that the grand duchess is a fastidious eater."

He strode to a round table in front of the empty fireplace. "As it is, and with our deadline looming, we must adopt more active measures. Come and look."

I joined Holmes at a table scattered with maps, lists and what looked like handwritten timetables. Holmes spread out a diagram, a representation of the building opposite. "The von Feldberg building is compartmented into offices, warehouse space for his wines and spirits, and extensive stables at the back for company carriages and delivery carts. The baron has live-in clerks on the top floor and watchmen on guard over his valuable stock day and night. There is no doubt he could sequester the royal pair here, possibly in the basement. Most of his staff are German and brought with him to this country; only two minor clerks and the drivers and stable hands are British."

"Could not the prisoners be held in the baron's apartments?" I asked.

"No, he has just three rooms: the office, sitting room and a small bedroom. The windows are open against the infernal heat, and Wiggins has been able to examine every inch of the interior through his glass. There is no nook or cranny in which von Feldberg could secrete a rabbit, let alone a heavily built prince and his ample wife."

"How do you intend to proceed?" I asked, with little hope I would get a sensible answer.

Holmes grinned. "You will see very soon. At one o'clock precisely (the baron has a Prussian attitude to time and a horror of tardiness) Baron von Feldberg will take his luncheon. He favours a French restaurant in Jermyn Street, a brisk walk from here. His dinners and suppers are gay affairs, but he prefers to eat his luncheon alone."

Holmes checked his watch. "We have eight minutes before the curtain rises."

He held up a newspaper. "I got a copy of the *Peoples Journal*, the Scottish paper, through the good offices of an ex-Irregular." He grinned. "Did you recognise Monty at the newspaper barrow?"

"Monty? Your young Irregular? I am very much afraid I did not. He was a chubby little boy, as I recall, and now he is a slim young man with a moustache."

Holmes nodded. "I'll study my newspaper while we wait."

I went to the window, moved the lace curtains aside and scrutinised the street below me, attempting to spot any crows. My companions' laughter earlier seemed to suggest I had missed at least one watcher. I looked hard, but I could see nothing out of the ordinary.

The street was busy with omnibuses, delivery vans, cabs and private carriages. The clip-clop of horses' hooves, the grinding of wheels and the jingle of harness came through the open windows, accompanied by swirls of dust from the roadway. The strains of the accordionist outside the public house were just audible over the street noises.

People thronged the pavement, hurrying across the bars of sunlight between the shops' awnings. Ladies hid under their parasols and gentlemen shaded their faces with newspapers or their hands. Many gentlemen I saw carried umbrellas, but naturally none would think of opening one to use as a sunshade.

Street sweepers cleared horse dung from the road and piled it into a handcart, creating eddies of noxious dust that augmented the billows created by the passing traffic.

I started from my reverie as a dapper gentleman in a grey jacket and straw hat with upcurved whiskers issued from the gate of the building opposite and set off along the street with a jaunty stride.

"I say, Holmes. Is that the baron?"

Holmes peered over my shoulder. "That is he."

"He is short, for a Prussian," I observed.

"We must not underestimate our quarry. He is accepted into Society at the most exalted level," said Holmes, "and he is accounted one of the finest marksmen in England."

Von Feldberg turned the corner. Wiggins appeared by the newspaper vendor and looked up at Holmes. He nodded, and Wiggins took out a large white handkerchief and blew his nose.

Holmes smiled at me, his eyes gleaming. "Our little drama begins."

A van loaded with ladders and other equipment pulled by a weary-looking horse plodded along the street and stopped outside the Feldberg premises. Three men in the uniforms of one of the London telephone companies got down and peered up at the building.

"The first act: telephone engineers," said Holmes. "Or an adequate simulacrum. One will present his repair docket to the reception clerk while the others assemble their ladder and await permission to examine the cable."

The engineers laid their ladder against the façade of the building, and one climbed to where the wire stretched from the pole to a window.

"You see? The baron's minions take no chances; a clerk is already at the window of his private office watching the work and making sure the engineers do not peer inside or attempt entry. Ah, he closes the windows and the curtains."

"Does that foil your plan?"

Holmes laughed. "Not at all. A twist of wire and all is done." He settled down once again with his newspaper.

The telephone company man climbed down, he and his colleagues disassembled their ladder, the van clattered off and the street went about its usual business.

A line of sandwich men marched past advertising patent electric hair tongs, and a cat's meat man drove by on a cart laden with horsemeat – I recoiled from the smell. I watched with interest as one of the new electric-powered cabs whizzed along the street, but aside from that nothing unusual occurred for ten or more minutes.

I knitted my brows as I heard the faint ringing of bells in the distance. The sound grew louder, then the noise burst upon me as first one, then another fire engine raced around the corner into Regent Street, horses straining, bells clanging and clouds of steam billowing from the boilers.

Holmes was beside me. "The fire station received a call from the baron's office reporting a fire in a store of flammable spirits in the cellars. *Eh, voilà!*"

"The telephone repair men called the brigade."

Holmes nodded. "And now for act two: the prestidigitation. Everyone watches firemen, Watson; they are an irresistible lure. While all eyes are distracted by the prancing horses, shining engines, gleaming brass helmets and steaming boilers, the crossing sweeper imps (Harry's latest swarm of Baker Street Irregulars) dart past the guard at the gate, as if in play."

The sweeper boys threw their brooms onto the handcart, grabbed what looked like batons and raced across the road. The gate guards were, as Holmes had predicted, outside on the pavement gawking at the fire engines.

I waited with bated breath and then blinked in astonishment as tendrils and then thick clouds of smoke issued from the entrance to the warehouse.

"They set a fire, Holmes?"

"Smoke, but no flames. A half dozen plumber's smoke rockets flung down the stairs to the wine and spirit cellars."

The ragged boys came racing out of the smoke and clustered around their cart cheering on the firemen.

"The Irregulars withdraw," said Holmes, "leaving a roiling cloud of smoke coming out of the warehouse and a most irrefutable reason for the firemen to enter the cellars."

Huge clouds of steam surged from the funnels of the pump engines as the firemen stoked the boilers and increased the water pressure. A brigade officer in a silver helmet barked orders, and his men unrolled their hoses and ran them through the gates to the door of the warehouse.

I frowned. "I can hear odd music."

Holmes smiled. "You saw and heard the accordion player outside the public house?"

"I did."

"His name is Igor, and he plays nightly at the Troika restaurant in Fitzalan Street, an establishment that, as you may surmise, specialises in Russian food. He has crossed the road, and he is serenading the firemen with Russian folk songs."

I frowned again.

"Her Imperial Highness Maria Alexandrovna is a determined woman with, by all accounts, a penetrating voice. If she hears music from her motherland, she will conclude friends are at hand. She will find a way to let us

98

know where she and the duke are incarcerated. Listeners are stationed nearby."

The opposite side of the street was almost masked by clouds of smoke and steam, but through gaps I glimpsed a scene of utmost confusion, with people running in all directions. I heard shouts in German coming from behind the billows.

"We must save the stock," Holmes translated. "Two men in my employ dressed as Feldberg employees and speaking German have joined the firemen. They will sound the walls of the cellar for secret doorways and chambers and call for the duke and duchess. They will collect the spent plumber's rockets."

I coughed as the smoke drifted across the street on a zephyr of wind I could not feel, and in a few moments I could make out more of the building and pavement opposite. Firemen lounged by their engine lighting cigarettes and pipes while others rolled the hoses up and stored them.

"The fire was a false alarm, of course," said Holmes, "but the chief officer on the scene will insist on checking the building thoroughly to find the source of the smoke. Indeed, he has a legal obligation to do so." He put his finger to his lip in a thoughtful pose. "If our German speakers have not found the royal couple, he may do so."

Holmes let the net curtain close, poured two glasses of lemonade from an iced jug and handed me one. "Let us await Harry's report with what equanimity we can summon."

BARON VON FELDBERG

# 7. SEDITION

"Not a sausage, German, Russian or otherwise, Mr Holmes," said Wiggins.

"Very well." Holmes nodded slowly as he opened a gap in the net covering the windows. "Here is the baron, returning from his luncheon. We should make ourselves scarce. Baron von Feldberg is not an idiot; the Prussians did not send us their second eleven. He will conclude he has been the victim of a conspiracy, but I hope I have muddied the waters by having my two German speakers liberate a case of champagne from the cellar if they did not discover the Duke and Duchess of Edinburgh incarcerated there. I wish to create the impression we had designs on his stock."

I stiffened. "You mean your men stole champagne from the baron, Holmes."

"A necessary cover, Watson. Remember, if the duke and duchess are not here, they may be imprisoned in the baron's villa near Windsor. We do not want him to divine our intentions and increase security there or move the prisoners to a new location. Or worse."

I nodded. "I see that logic, Holmes, and I trust the champagne will be restored to the baron if he proves to be an innocent party in this affair."

"That is my intention," Holmes said in a tone of patent falsehood.

Holmes handed Wiggins a leather bag that chinked agreeably. "Pay everyone off, Harry, and let's meet later in the day at Baker Street."

I followed Holmes down the stairs, past the boy and the screeching dentist's and into the street. "You didn't recognise Monty?" he asked as he nodded a greeting to the newspaper vendor. "He's joined Harry's uncle in the slum paper business; they do work of the highest quality."

"Slum paper? You mean forgery?"

Holmes smiled and took my arm. We sauntered along Regent Street, and I kept a lookout for the charming flower seller I had encountered earlier.

A young man in a bowler walking ahead of us stooped to pick up something from the pavement. He held the object to the light, and I saw that it was a gold ring set with a small diamond glinting in the bright sunlight.

"Coo," said the man, or boy, in fact. He was dressed as a clerk or messenger. Holmes and I and several other passers-by stopped to look at the ring.

"Coo indeed," said Holmes, peering at the jewel. "That is a fine piece."

"You must hand it in at the police station," I said.

"Bet there's a reward", said a shrill voice from the back of what was becoming a crowd around the boy.

"Bound to be," said another voice.

"Ring like that, worth a hundred pounds," someone called.

"Guineas," said another.

The boy frowned. "I dunno about any reward or police business. I've got my shift at the office starts in ten minutes. I can't mess about with rewards and such."

"I'll give you two bob for it," cried the shrill voice.

The boy turned to Holmes. "What shall I do, sir?"

"Watson," said Holmes, "lend me a sovereign, will you? I am out."

I frowned. "I say, old man—"

Holmes snapped his fingers.

"Very well," I said sharply. "If you insist, but I shall make a note and expect restitution." I lowered my voice. "And think, Holmes, this fellow may be not be as he seems—"

The young man gave me a cold look.

I handed Holmes the coin, and he held the sovereign up in front of the boy and raised his eyebrows. The boy's eyes gleamed, and he made to take it, but Holmes held it higher.

"Now, we don't want any funny business, young man," he said. "You tuck the ring into my waistcoat pocket, and I shall do the same with the money."

With the crowd cheering him on, the boy slipped the ring into Holmes' pocket. Holmes held up the gold coin for all to see and, with a flourish worthy of the Alhambra, he tucked it into the boy's waistcoat pocket, then grabbed the boy's hand and shook it. "A deal, young man? Are you satisfied?"

The boy grinned. "I am, sir, and now I must get along to my work." He pushed through the crowd and disappeared.

The crowd dispersed, several men patting Holmes on the back and wishing him well. I let go of my wallet, that I had held tight through the incident, and took Holmes' arm again as we walked on.

I chuckled to myself, and Holmes glanced at me and raised his eyebrows. "May I see your purchase?" I asked.

"Certainly." Holmes plucked the ring from his waistcoat pocket and gave it to me. It looked real enough. I had heard a sharper would show a genuine ring, and at the time of payment substitute a cheap fake. I handed it back to my friend. "I suppose we must stop at the police station. There's one – what?"

Holmes convulsed with laughter. "You must not think me such a flat, Watson," he said as he recovered and wiped his eyes with his handkerchief. He held out a coin. "Here's your sovereign. Thank you for the loan."

"And the ring?"

He held it up to the sunlight. "An obvious fake, but pretty. It is a spoil of war."

He passed it to me. "Give it to our maid with my compliments. Here's Rankin with the carriage."

He opened the carriage door and stopped. "You know, we have not done well so far. Perhaps we should stop off at a news agency and advertise in the evening editions – only the quality newspapers, naturally."

"What for?" I asked.

"A lost duke, a missing grand duchess and a large rock."

"Did you see the electric cab in Regent Street?" I asked as Holmes and I settled in our chairs in our sitting room and lit our pipes.

"Hmmm?"

"A cab service is starting next month using electric carriages."

I frowned. "I suppose horseless cabs are an inevitable innovation, practical and sensible and so on, but I can't help thinking of the potential danger to passengers and pedestrians. I read the cabs can reach a speed of fourteen miles per hour! Imagine two of them crashing together; it would be like a train collision. I recall a newspaper report earlier in the year of the arrest of the driver of one of the electric vehicles for drunkenness and endangering life. At least a horse would have the good sense to attempt to avoid a crash, but an electric carriage would go where the engineer directs it. I may be becoming something of an old fogie, but—"

I was interrupted by a long ring on our doorbell.

Billy brought up a brown-paper-wrapped package which I took without enthusiasm. "I am less and less enamoured of Scots poetry," I said as I unwrapped the package. "Was not the last assassination attempt against the Queen perpetrated by a Scottish poet? At Windsor Station as I recall."

Holmes nodded. "Roderick Maclean, he had a Scots pedigree, even if he was not born in that country. Another Scots poet immortalised the outrage in verse. I noted the poem at the time in my Index under 'M' for McGonagall."

He took down the heavy volume, flicked to a page and declaimed.

*"God prosper long our noble Queen,*
*And long may she reign!*

> *Maclean he tried to shoot her,*
> *But it was all in vain.*
>
> *For God He turned the ball aside*
> *Maclean aimed at her head;*
> *And he felt very angry*
> *Because he didn't shoot her dead."*

I sniffed. "Dear me, what sad stuff. The fellow could not compete with Tennyson, or even with the profligate Byron. I hope this Ossian chap can do better."

Holmes smiled. "Do you remember how Maclean was foiled?"

"It's a famous story. The madman aimed at the Queen's carriage outside Windsor Station, and a pair of Eton schoolboys beat down the pistol with their umbrellas. They were rightly feted by the Queen and by their school. It was a brave action."

"Yes, that was the headlined story in the press. A good tale, almost a believable one, but not at all factual."

"You are not suggesting the Eton boys lied," I asked coldly.

"Ha! The boys, understandably and patriotically, beat Maclean about the head with their umbrellas as he was dragged away by a pair of railway policemen. Their blows mostly landed on the constables rescuing the would-be regicide from a mob. The young heroes were, as you say, feted by Her Majesty and by the college, whose four hundred boys processed to Windsor Castle, gathered outside Her Majesty's apartments, sang patriotic songs and cheered her deliverance. They presented their two brave comrades for royal approval, with their bent umbrellas as proof of the ferocity of the conflict. I am surprised the boys weren't knighted on the spot."

I frowned. "Smith and Sons of New Oxford Street use the incident in their advertisements to prove the sturdiness of their umbrellas."

Holmes put his finger to his lips in a characteristic gesture. "Roderick Maclean was bullied at his school, like our Prime Minister, Lord Salisbury. Eton is no place for shrinking violets."

"I would hardly call Lord Salisbury that, Holmes," I said in a puzzled tone. I could not fathom where our conversation had come from, nor where it was going. I delved into the package and took out a sheet of paper. "A message from Mycroft. It seems this wreath was found on the Albert Memorial this afternoon.

It says,

> *I said I would cast off her rule.*
> *And would submit to her no more*

That is sedition, Holmes, if not treason."

I held the ribbon to the light from the window. "I believe the blue and white colours of the silk reflect those of the Scottish flag."

"The Saltire," said Holmes. "A white St Andrew's cross on a blue background."

"What of the poem?"

"More Ossian, I expect," said Holmes. "I'll bet the original says 'cast off *his* rule', meaning Finn's."

"Are not these verses getting more menacing, Holmes?"

"Certainly more direct."

"The Queen travels to Balmoral tomorrow," I said grimly. I looked again at the note. "Mycroft says an abandoned carriage has been found near Windsor. It fits the description given by the duke's footman of the carriage used by the kidnappers. The local police have been ordered to move nothing until you get there."

Holmes smiled. "Are you game?"

"Of course. But, I say, do I have to keep lugging my revolver about with me. It's deuced awkward and heavy. I mean, Windsor is not a dangerous place."

"I'm sorry, old man, but I must insist. I think you may be surprised what evils may lurk in Berkshire. I intend to carry my lead-loaded riding crop."

A police inspector and a trio of constables stood at the head of a narrow, grassy track that wound along the Datchet bank of the Thames. The inspector introduced himself in a faint Scots accent as Inspector Fraser of the Berkshire Constabulary.

"The carriage is where we found it, Mr Holmes," the inspector said. "I directed nothing should be touched, as per my instructions from the Home Office. We just unharnessed the nags and put them in the stable of a local pub. The poor beasts were in a bad state, what with the heat and all."

He consulted his notebook. "It's a hired vehicle, sir, belonging to the London, Brighton & South Coast Railway. The carriage is marked with the station code and an identification number. We sent the details to London Bridge, and the station master says the carriage was booked by telegram from Newhaven and picked up from Victoria Station by a young couple just arrived on the Boat Train."

"Victoria Station and the Boat Train, Holmes. A Continental connection!" I exclaimed.

Holmes circled the carriage, examining the ground below the doors and the track ahead of the vehicle.

"Tut, Inspector, hobnailed boots and horses' hooves have flattened the grass and obscured the trail. I cannot, ah—"

He stopped, pulled out his magnifying glass, knelt and glared at the path. He took a piece of string from his pocket and stretched it across the grass.

Inspector Fraser blinked at me.

"Holmes has found a set of wheel tracks from a second carriage," I explained. "He is measuring the distance between the front and back sets of wheels and across the wheelbase to determine the type of vehicle.

"A private Victoria," Holmes said, walking back along the track. "Two horses: the offside has a loose shoe."

Inspector Fraser frowned. "It has not rained for days, Mr Holmes. The earth is too dry for prints. How did you deduce the loose shoe?"

"No deduction was necessary, Inspector," Holmes said as he pulled open the carriage door. "The horse stepped in its own dung."

Holmes peered into the carriage. "There is no obvious blood."

"Thank God," I said fervently.

Holmes stepped carefully into the carriage and closed the door.

Inspector Fraser sniffed. "Did I hear Mr Holmes mention blood?"

"Yes, that is significant," I answered.

The inspector gave me a cold look. "I checked the carriage, Doctor. I saw no blood."

I smiled at him. "That is what is significant."

He gave me another look I could only describe as frosty, and he turned away as the carriage door opened and Holmes leapt down.

"Is there anything to link—" I glanced at the inspector and hesitated. "To connect the carriage with the case at hand?"

Holmes held out his fist and opened it to reveal a gold ring and a diamond bracelet with a hanging locket. "They were slipped down the side of a cushion." He handed me the jewels.

"A signet ring," I said, "and a bracelet and locket holding a Russian icon. The ring shows two letters intertwined, 'M' and 'H', for Maria and – who do we know with a name that begins with H? It should surely be 'M' and 'A' for Albert—"

I glanced up and realised the inspector was leaning forward and listening to our conversation with interest.

Holmes smiled. "Maria had the presence of mind to tuck these trinkets down the edge of her seat. She is a formidable lady."

I looked around at the high grass fringing the lane. "Should we search for bodies?" I asked softly.

Holmes shook his head. "No, no. The couple were transferred to a private four-wheeler. But your question raises an interesting point. If the abductors intended to do away with the duke and duchess, what better place than this overgrown and tranquil lane?"

We thanked the inspector, who was the very picture of frustration, and walked back to our carriage.

"Do you now discount the possibility of Prussian involvement in the outrage, Holmes?"

"I do not. The Baron's villa at Datchet is no more than a mile or so from here."

I frowned. "I still cannot accept the Kaiser would lay a violent hand on his own uncle!"

"It is not unknown in dynastic matters for uncles and nephews, brothers and even fathers and sons to fight. Our own history is replete with examples."

"But hardly in modern times, Holmes." I considered. "Or at least not so often."

"I can't be sure the Kaiser had a personal hand in this affair," Holmes said, "but what might be done by proxy, by an over-zealous subordinate?"

"Who will rid me of this turbulent duke?" I suggested.

"Exactly."

We climbed back into our carriage and set off. "You know, a private carriage is very convenient," I said. "We might look into prices and so on when we have leisure."

Holmes called up to Rankin. "Simpson's in the Strand." He smiled at me. "An early dinner, and then to the music hall."

Angus MacDonald, illusionist

## 8. REPENT!

We stepped down from our carriage outside the newly rebuilt Alhambra Music Hall in Leicester Square. I gave Rankin three shillings for his supper and feed for the horses, and I followed Holmes past a crowd of gentlemen and a few ladies queuing at the kiosk. Holmes produced a ticket from his waistcoat pocket and presented it to an usher at the door of the hall.

"I had Billy book a private box at the theatre this morning," he said. "I do not care to queue."

We were shown upstairs and into a box above stage right. I settled into my seat and looked with some complacency at the crowd in the stalls below me. Holmes purchased programmes, rented two pairs of opera glasses and ordered a bottle of the house red.

I removed my gloves, took a programme and leafed through it. "You are in a free spending mood, Holmes. A bumper dinner at Simpson's and now this."

Holmes smiled. "We are on expenses. I made that clear to Mycroft. One should not skimp when on government service; it looks mean and shabby and does the country no credit."

I flicked through my programme. The bill was the usual mix of song and novelty acts, spiced with comedians, strongmen and performing animals. I turned to Holmes.

"Why are we here, Holmes? A straight answer now, if you please."

Holmes considered. "For two reasons. Mr McNair suggested we talk with his friend and colleague Mr Angus Macdonald, who appears here tonight. The other is (don't look) Baron von Feldberg is in the box opposite us. He is an aficionado of the music hall."

"He is not the stiff-necked, humourless prude we expect a Prussian to be," I said, keeping my eyes on my programme.

Holmes smiled. "His motive for visiting the Gaiety Music Hall is clear. The baron's interest is directed towards one of the performers there, a Miss LeBeau, a chanteuse. He showers her with chocolates, flowers and trinkets, as is the custom, but until now she has not been amenable to his attentions."

I looked up at Holmes. "Until now?"

"He also comes here," Holmes continued. "He attends the Alhambra twice or more in a month. Why? Miss LeBeau does not perform here, and he does not seem interested in the Alhambra's ladies. That is odd, is it not?"

Holmes picked up his programme. "Let's see if we can determine which of the acts might tickle the baron's fancy."

I leafed through my programme. "Should we exclude the animal acts, *lions comiques*, singing tramps, dwarves and jugglers, Holmes? I hardly think a Prussian baron would be interested in those."

The lights dimmed, and the orchestra began a sprightly overture that soon had my foot tapping. I turned to Holmes, but his hat was over his eyes and his attention was elsewhere.

The music ended, and the chairman banged his gavel for silence as he introduced the first act, a birdsong imitator dressed in a parrot costume. I chuckled and was about to make a deprecating remark to my companion when I saw that Holmes' interest was fixed on the performer. After a few moments, he frowned and shook his head. "A dead duck."

I blinked at him in confusion. "How did you know Baron von Feldberg would be here tonight, Holmes," I whispered over the tweets and warbles. "Or is it a coincidence?"

"The lady in the theatre box office is my crow," Holmes murmured. "She sent me a note as soon as the baron booked his box."

Holmes and I endured a succession of novelty performances, including the inevitable dancing dogs, and although he ignored most of the acts, he took great interest in others that seemed no more entertaining.

He perked up as an easel was placed on the side of the stage with the legend 'Angus MacDonald, illusionist' on a card.

The curtains opened to reveal a snowy landscape, a moorland perhaps, with a neat cottage. The wind howled, blowing snow across the moor, and thunder, lightning and dark music from the orchestra added to the dismalness of the scene.

A great organ chord sounded as the door of the cottage flew open and a young woman stumbled out. She held a baby in her arm and a pretty little girl in a flowery dress by the hand. They staggered across the stage against the wind and fell to the ground. A man in a frock coat, cloak and top hat twirled his upturned and waxed moustache at the cottage door. In a cliché of melodrama, the wicked landlord had cast a mother, baby and infant out of their home for non-payment of rent.

The young mother heaved herself from the ground and sang a mournful song in which she explained that her husband was a sailor feared lost in an engagement with the French. For those who did not follow the lyrics, the pageboy posted a card that said 'A Hero Slain'.

I yawned. The sailor husband would no doubt turn up in the second act and make all right. I thought melodrama an odd style for a performer who promoted himself as an illusionist.

In fact, it did not take long for mother and children to succumb to the cold, no doubt encouraged by the sepulchral music played by the orchestra.

A swift scene change, and we saw the inside of the cottage and the wicked landlord lounging before the fire drinking a large glass of whisky and ignoring both the hisses and boos from members of the audience and the card on the easel which read 'The Demon Drink'.

The villain frowned when a loud knocking noise was heard, and the audience went quiet as he looked nervously at the door. It was an isolated dwelling, one gathered, and he did not expect visitors.

After some stage business, peeking through the storm-lashed windows and biting his nails, the landlord opened the door, letting in a blast of snow. He fell back in horror. Standing in the doorway and pointing an accusing finger at him was the little girl we had seen die in scene one. The ghostly apparition was dressed in the tattered remains of her flowery dress and chalk white in face and limbs.

"Repent!" she cried.

"Oh dear," I murmured.

The landlord slammed the door and went back to his chair. He picked up the whisky bottle and shook his head, obviously thinking the strange vision had its origins there. He poured another glass and warmed his hands at the fireplace.

A second sharp knock came from the cabin door, and the landlord stepped fearfully to the front of the stage as the cottage door creaked open again to reveal the same ghostly girl.

"Repent!" she screeched.

With a clap of thunder and a puff of smoke, the door slammed shut and a powerful stage light swung to the box opposite ours. The little ghost stood among the seated gentlemen; again she pointed at the landlord and called on him to repent his evil ways.

He fell to his knees and clutched his throat with his hands. Another thunderclap and more smoke and the girl disappeared. I turned to make a remark to Holmes, and I was suddenly blinded by light. I lifted my hand to protect my eyes and saw through my fingers the ghastly form of the apparition standing not a foot from me.

"Repent!"

I sprang to my feet and stepped back to the wall of the box, holding my hands up against the glare. More thunder, and the light swung to the stage. The girl was gone, leaving us once more in darkness.

A roll of drums, and the door of the cottage swung open again and the little ghost stalked in. Glowering at the landlord, she advanced towards him repeating her injunction in time with her steps. The landlord knelt, squirming in terror at the front edge of the stage. He clutched at his throat, then at his chest and at last fell to the floor as a long roll of thunder shook the theatre and the curtain came down.

A final card read 'Landlord played by Angus Macdonald, Illusionist'. The audience erupted with cheers and with applause in which, I have to admit, I joined.

I sat again in my seat, drew a breath and turned to Holmes.

He smiled and stood. "Smoke and mirrors, my dear fellow. Come, we have work to do."

I followed Holmes downstairs to the ground floor of the theatre, through a green baize door and along dusty unpainted corridors to the back of the stage. We stopped outside a door with the name Angus Macdonald printed on a label pasted above a faded star.

Holmes knocked, and an unintelligible cry came from within. Holmes swung open the door to reveal a brightly lit dressing room. The landlord sat at a mirrored table, without his waxed moustache. Beside him stood three little girls with chalk-white faces in identical ghost costumes.

"You'll be the detectives," the landlord said in a thick Scots brogue. "I've been expecting you."

"Good evening, Mr Macdonald," Holmes said. He introduced us, and Mr Macdonald indicated a couple of dining chairs against one wall of the room.

"Sit yourselves down, gentlemen and have a drink." He poured three measures of whisky, took one himself and handed a glass each to Holmes and to me.

"To the king across the water!" Mr Macdonald said, draining his glass.

I waited a moment to dissociate myself from the toast and took a sip of whisky; it was surprisingly good.

"Meet my wee cherubs, gentlemen. They are Fiona, Malvina and – the other one." Mr Macdonald frowned. "I shall not particularise as I am almost sure they swop names to fool me." He placed a shilling in the outstretched hand of each of the girls.

"In fact, the little darlings are not mine. I rent them from an agency in the Strand for twelve shillin' a week and a bob each per performance direct into their grubby, grasping hands." He jerked his thumb over his shoulder. "Awa' with you now, to your mothers."

The girls left, the last unnamed turning at the door and poking her tongue at Mr Macdonald in an unseemly manner.

He faced the mirror, dipped a handful of cotton waste into a bowl of unguent and began cleaning off his make-up. "How may I be of assistance to you gentlemen?"

"I spoke to Mr McNair, who represents the *Peoples Journal*," Holmes answered. "He mentioned you have a knowledge of Scottish history."

"He told me of your visit." Mr Macdonald indicated a small stack of books that stood with a pen, an ink pot and a sheaf of stationery on a blotting pad on a corner of his dressing table. "I consulted my authorities to refresh my memory of certain events that might interest you."

Holmes nodded. "We are focused on any evidence of a movement advocating political separation from England, and on symbols or icons important to that cause."

Mr Macdonald smiled. "You must understand that for many in Scotland, England is the old adversary and ever has been. More than enough blood has been spilled by both sides to make Scotland and England eternal enemies. In what we Scots call the rough wooing, your Henry the Eighth sent an army to invade Scotland. I have his instructions to his troops." Mr Macdonald wiped his hands on a towel, picked up a book from the stack in his table and handed it to me. "The passage is marked, Doctor."

I held the book close to the gas lights and read. "Put all to fire and sword, burn Edinburgh town so used and defaced that when you have gotten what you can of it may remain for ever a perpetual memory of the vengeance of God lightened upon it for their falsehood and disloyalty."

I returned the book, and Mr Macdonald continued wiping off his make-up.

"Might we consider more recent events?" Holmes said, a shade impatiently.

"What of symbols of Scottish nationalism, the Stone of Destiny, for example?" I asked.

"This Stone shall be God's house (Genesis 28; 22.)," Mr Macdonald answered. "When the Stone is lodged in Scotland, the Scots will once more possess the land. There is a verse of Walter Scott's that puts it well."

"This one?" I passed Mr MacDonald my notebook open at the page in which Canon Blood had written the verses on the original wreath. Mr Macdonald reached for his spectacles and read.

> *"Where'er this monument be found,*
> *The Scottish race shall reign"*

He nodded. "A Latin epigram based on an ancient prophecy." He held up the whisky bottle. "Another dram, gentlemen? No? But you'll not mind if I do."

"What of the Golden Crown of Scotland?" Holmes asked.

"The lost Crown? Aye, that would be something. If the Crown were found that would be something. Its recovery might inspire Scotsmen to redeem themselves once and for all from English domination."

Holmes sniffed. "The so-called Scottish Honours at Edinburgh castle were worn or carried by Scottish kings. Are they not equally revered?"

Mr Macdonald gave Holmes a cold look. "You say 'so-called' in that sneering tone, sir, as if the Scots' desire to retain their national symbols is provincial and immature, but English patriotism may be properly expressed in traditional emblems like the Crown Jewels, the Garter and St George."

"I apologise," said Holmes. "Pray tell me more of the Golden Crown."

"You will know that John Balliol, King of Scotland was deposed by your Edward the First?"

"We do." I said. "And King Edward took the Stone of Destiny from Scone Abbey."

Mr Macdonald laughed. "So they say." He gulped his whisky. "Edward stripped King John of his kingdom, imprisoned him in London for three years, and then let him go into exile in France. When John attempted to leave England following his release, his chests were searched at Dover, and the Great Seal of the Kingdom of Scotland, with vessels of gold and silver and a considerable sum of money were found. Hidden in one chest was the ancient Royal Crown of Scotland."

"The crown is older than the current 'Honours'?" I asked.

"Its origins, like so many things in Scotland, are lost in the mists of time. We have a good deal more mist in our glens than you do in your English dales, but you have more historians, and history is not written by the conquered."

"Conquered!" I exclaimed. "Your Scottish King James became our monarch! Our nations were joined by a union of crowns and then of parliaments, not by force."

Mr Macdonald took a sip of whisky and considered me for a moment over the rim of the glass. "You are vehement, Doctor. Is there no' a drop of Celtic blood running in your veins?"

I smiled. "As a matter of fact, I may well—"

"The Crown, if you please," Holmes said.

Mr Macdonald refilled his glass. "King Edward ordered that the Crown and Great Seal be confiscated, the Crown sent to the shrine of Thomas à Becket at Canterbury and the Seal held in his private treasury. The money he returned to King John for the expenses of his journey. The Crown never reached Canterbury; it was probably lodged with the English jewels in Westminster Abbey."

Mr Macdonald lifted his glass in a toast. "To the ancient crown of the Kingdom of Scotland, gentlemen. Its discovery would be a momentous event for those who long for freedom."

"Might it still be in English hands?" I asked. "Could it be secreted somewhere, or stored and forgotten?"

Mr Macdonald laughed. "We shall never know. You'll forgive me, I hope, Doctor if I agree with the opinion of most of the world that the English are a tricky race." His tone hardened. "'For so long as a hundred men survive, we will never in any way submit to the domination of the English. It is not for glory or for riches or honours we fight, but simply and solely for freedom, which no good man surrenders but with his life.' That was written in Arbroath in 1320."

Holmes stood. "Good evening to you, Mr Macdonald."

We left the Alhambra through the stage door and made our way along an alley at the side of the building to the mews where our carriage waited.

I frowned "Fiona and Malvina? What odd names for girls."

"Mr Macpherson, the forger of the lays of Ossian, coined them."

"I doubt they will catch on. You know, I am getting the hang of the Scottish dialect, Holmes. I understood much of what Mr Macdonald said despite his thick accent."

We climbed into our carriage and set off for home.

"Was our excursion worth our time and trouble," I asked my companion as we clattered along Piccadilly. "I mean, we received a lesson in Scottish history that is frankly irrelevant and dated. Mr Macdonald is an unlikely seditionist. And his is a strange sort of magic, or illusion rather. Relying on triplets, as he does, is (how shall I say?) mere trickery, or almost fraud. As an act, it does not stand comparison to the great feats of legerdemain we see from artists like Maskelyne at the Egyptian Hall."

Holmes laughed. "My dear fellow, when you jumped out of your seat, your face was as white as that of the apparition."

"Hardly so," I replied stiffly. "I was blinded by the light."

"And Macdonald is indeed an illusionist," Holmes said in a darker tone. "His accent is assumed; I recognised him, despite the absence of his once ample beard, as Albert Meecham, born and bred in the workhouse at Wapping, who made a living as a bruiser for an extortion gang until he was discovered dipping into the collection money to finance his drink and gambling.

"Meecham is the Lavender Pond Strangler. He despatched his wife and two of his three children for the burial club insurance during the cholera epidemic of the sixties. People were dying in such numbers that post mortems were not practicable (and very dangerous to the doctors). Only when Meecham disposed of his third child a few months later in the Lavender Pond was foul play suspected. Meecham disappeared, and supposedly fled to America. In fact, he assumed a fake Scottish accent and a new profession."

"My God, Holmes. We must inform the police."

"Mmmm? Not quite yet. I am intrigued by his relationship with Baron von Feldberg."

"They know each other?"

Holmes smiled. "They communicate, but very discreetly. I watched all the acts that might have involved a coded transmission of information – the bird warbler was an obvious possibility. In fact the method was simple. One of the little girls in Macdonald's performance appeared in von Feldberg's box, pointing at the stage, yes?"

"Then in ours, another of the girls, I mean."

"Indeed. You were blinded by the light as it switched from the baron's box to ours. I was not. I held my programme up to shield my eyes while I kept close watch on the opposite box."

Holmes smiled. "I saw the baron exchange packages with the girl."

"What can be in them?" I wondered aloud. "You say the baron buys information."

"The packets are a substantive link between the Scots and the Prussians. We have been thinking either or, when the truth may be both. It could well be, my friend, that these cases are connected. The theft of the Stone, the ducal kidnapping and the veiled threats against Her Majesty could be a coordinated attempt to wrest Scotland from the Empire and force Saxe-Coburg and Gotha into Prussian hands."

"The Scottish Nationalists are hand-in-glove with the Prussians," I exclaimed. "We must act. They may threaten other members of the Royal Family. Perhaps even the Queen! She is among Highlanders even at Windsor. Balmoral must be teeming with them!"

Holmes waved my fears away. "Our focus is now on Baron von Feldberg. We have less than twenty-four hours until Lord Rosebery's dinner, when the absence of the Duke and Duchess of Edinburgh will occasion concern and speculation."

"What of the servants, Holmes? The Russian maid was very forward, and that priest had a shifty look about him. They may speak out."

"Mycroft has seen to them."

I blinked at Holmes.

"No, no, my friend, we are not in Berlin or St Petersburg. The servants are in comfortable seclusion until they are cleared of involvement in the abduction. That investigation will take at least two more days. We can therefore discount a leak from them for that long and no longer."

Holmes banged his gloved fist into his palm. "We cannot keep the matter quiet after tomorrow, and we cannot calculate the consequences of exposure. We must get to the root of this affair before then or the government may be forced to adopt a position on the abduction without sufficient data to lay the blame in its right quarter. Wars start so."

He turned to me. "Did you notice anything when Mr Macdonald lifted the Bible from the blotter?"

I shook my head.

"There was a line of print, freshly blotted, upside down, and in mirror-writing. It said, 'Sons of the Thistle'."

DAIMLER GRAFTON PHAETON 1897

# 9. VILLA OF MYSTERIES

The next morning, enduring another meagre breakfast, Holmes and I set off again in our official carriage. We borrowed Billy and put him on the box with the driver.

A weary journey across London and then west through Berkshire, led us to a house agency in Windsor, where Holmes wreathed me in blankets, wrapped a woollen muffler around my neck and set a wide straw hat on my head.

"Holmes, I melt under these infernal covers."

"You are an invalid who requires warmth and complete peace and quiet; any noise or excitement might have fatal consequences."

Holmes spent ten minutes inside the agency while I baked in the carriage. Not a whiff of air, nor puff of wind came through the windows.

At last Holmes emerged with a young man who had the look of an assistant in a draper's or a stockbroker's clerk, obviously the house agent.

"We will take the property for a week, on trial," Holmes said as he opened the door of the carriage, letting in a little welcome air. "I imagine twenty guineas in gold will cover the deposit." Holmes held out a small leather bag.

"That is not at all necessary, Mr Wainwright," the clerk said with a bright smile, slipping the bag into his satchel with a practised air. "But it is the usual thing, and business is business as my employer frequently avers."

Holmes turned to me. "My father prefers to do things in the proper manner," he said, patting me on the knee. "He has a horror of appearing singular, don't you, Papa?"

I grunted a reply and pulled my scarf further over my nose as Holmes and the young man got into the carriage. Holmes sat with me and the clerk opposite him, and we set off at a walk.

"Papa, this is Mr Rutland," Holmes said in a loud voice. "He'll tell you about your nice new house."

Mr Rutland beamed at me. "The house stands on gravel," he said. "It consists of twelve rooms furnished in the modern style, ah—"

"You'll have to speak up," Holmes said. "Papa is a little deaf."

"It is a select neighbourhood, sir," Mr Rutland yelled. "Your nearest neighbours are but two. One is the Hon. Evelyn Ellis, the horseless carriage enthusiast. He drives a motor carriage which he brought over a short time ago from Paris. I understand they are in frequent use there. Mr Ellis condescended to invite me on a trip from his house to Old Windsor last Sunday. We whirled up Priest Hill, down the steep road on the opposite side, past the workhouse and through Old Windsor. We returned home in just under an hour!"

"My father does not approve of innovation," Holmes said coldly. "And he has strong views on Sunday travel."

Mr Rutland subsided into silence as we continued along pleasant lanes and through country that would have delighted me had I not been encased in my personal Turkish bath.

"You mentioned two neighbours?" Holmes said.

"The only other villa within half a mile of 'The Oaks' belongs to Baron von Feldberg, the wine and spirits importer."

My woollen shawl tickled my nose, and I sneezed. Holmes threw up his hands in horror. "My father is appalled! One of our neighbours is an importer of the devil's spirits! And a foreigner!"

"I can assure you, sir," Mr Rutland said, blinking at Holmes, "the baron is a gentlemanly person, and his house is very quiet. He spends most of the week in London, and he comes to his villa only on Thursday, staying until Monday morning. You will hear hardly a peep from him, except perhaps a little music from his occasional evening entertainments."

We travelled on in silence. I stifled under my wrappings, and I was pleased to see that Mr Rutland was also uncomfortable as he made several attempts to yank his high collar open and allow himself to breathe. "We are near," he said in a strangled tone. "The baron's villa is just visible through the trees."

"What are those strange constructions at either end of the house?" Holmes asked.

"I understand that they are lightning conductors. Baron von Feldberg has a morbid fear of lightning."

A little past the baron's house, Mr Rutland directed Rankin to turn through a set of gates and we approached a fine-looking villa along a gravel path.

I was helped from the carriage and into a chair on the veranda where I was revived with a glass of iced soda water from a large hamper of provisions Billy unpacked. I gulped the delicious drink while Mr Rutland showed Holmes through the house.

After ten minutes or so, he ushered Holmes to the terrace. "There is a fine, mature garden for your father to gaze upon."

I growled at him.

"Father's spirit is urban," said Holmes. "He derives no pleasure from the plant kingdom."

"Oh," said the discomfited Mr Rutland. "What of staff, Mr Wainwright? We can provide a full staff, if you require them."

Holmes considered. "No, I should not like to engage more servants until we make our decision on the property. We will stay tonight at the Royal Stag public house and move in tomorrow when our baggage and attendants arrive from London. My father's wants are simple: a cook and a half-dozen servants can fulfil them adequately. His personal doctor will come down today or tomorrow."

Holmes wished Mr Rutland good day, and our carriage took him back to his office.

I flung off my covers the moment the carriage was out of sight, and I shrugged off my frock coat and waistcoat and stood on the porch in my drenched shirt waggling my arms and fanning myself with a copy of *The Times*. "Was this charade necessary, Holmes?" I asked.

"I could have wished we were in Town," Holmes mused. "It would have been a simple matter to conduct a surveillance there using common loafers and the Irregulars. In a quiet suburb like this we must be circumspect; strangers are questioned if they loiter."

He turned to me. "When we liberate the duke and duchess from the baron's clutches we will need a haven where you can minister to them after their ordeal. A story was essential. Our presence here will be known throughout the village before nightfall. Instead of wondering who the people who have taken The Oaks on liking are, the gossips will exchange their views on what ailment might necessitate a sojourn in the country for the old gentleman. They will settle on gout and be satisfied."

Half an hour later, our carriage turned through the gate with Rankin on the box. It was followed by a light trap with Billy driving.

"When the horses are rested, I go about my business," Holmes said, "and you can take your luncheon and metamorphose back into Doctor John H Watson, personal physician to my father, General Wainwright."

"What shall I say if any of our neighbours call?" I asked.

"As our present sojourn is in Berkshire, rather than Tuscany or San Moritz, they will not call. Happily, we English, particularly the country-dwellers, are a morose and misanthropic race who gossip about but do not cultivate the acquaintance of our neighbours. We will not be molested." Holmes took a brown-paper-wrapped parcel from Billy and disappeared into one of the ground-floor rooms.

I helped Billy unpack the delicacies from the Fortnum's hamper, and I was delighted at the cornucopia revealed. Billy fetched a block of ice he had kept wrapped in sacking under the box of our carriage, and he cracked ice into a wine cooler containing a bottle of rosé.

Holmes reappeared wearing a disguise I had not seen before. "I am a salesman; I travel in electric hair tongs." Holmes held up a contraption of steel and wires. "These were designed by Mr Hiram Maxim, of machine-gun fame. I borrowed them from Mrs Hudson."

I frowned. "I'm surprised she let you have them, Holmes. They are dear to her."

"She has no need of the apparatus until the end of the week. She frizzles her hair on Saturdays. Surely you must have noticed the acrid smell that taints the house on Saturday afternoons?"

"I put that down to your chemical experiments."

"Ha!" Holmes pirouetted in front of the hall mirror. "What do you think?"

I considered. "One of your better efforts. You have just the right not-quite-seedy, rakish look of the travelling salesman. The Macassar-oiled hair and centre parting are characteristic of the type."

Holmes put on his straw hat. "I hired a light trap from the station as the final touch of authenticity. *Au revoir.* Do not allow the boy to lay waste to the entire hamper before I return."

Billy and I took our luncheon, picnic fashion, on the terrace. The Fortnum and Mason's basket was a treasure trove of roast chicken, tinned ham, bottled tongue, jars of pickles, mustard and relish, fresh vegetables and crusty bread wrapped in paper. We shared a pineapple and a bottle of apricot halves in syrup for pudding. I had a couple of glasses of a pleasant rosé that I allowed Billy to drink half-and-half with soda water. I sat back in my chair, perfectly replete, and I lit a cigar.

"He's a sour one, Doctor, that Mr Rankin," Billy said as he leaned back in his chair and lit a cigarette. "I didn't get a peep out of him all the way from London."

"It's a Scots trait, Billy. They admit themselves that they are a dour race."

I heard a growl from behind us, and Billy and I turned. Rankin was framed in the doorway of the drawing room wearing his battered top hat. "The worrrd in Scots is 'dour', Doctor," he said, "pronounced in the French manner as *dur*, meaning hard. We Scots have to be tough, else we'd no' have survived the enmity of our larger neighbour. We can also be *pawkie* if we've a mind, and *fasht* if we have to wait too long for our dinner."

He held out his hand. "I'll take mine at the pub we passed, Doctor. The young lad and yourself are welcome to join me there for a wet if ye've a mind."

I stood and gave him a half-crown. "Billy and I are content to remain here, thank you, Rankin."

He nodded. "Then I'll leave you."

Rankin turned away, and Billy and I looked wide-eyed at each other.

"I'd not like to meet Mr Rankin when he's *fasht*, Doctor."

I blinked at the boy. "Indeed not."

I dozed in my chair on the terrace until I was awakened by the sound of wheels on the gravel path. Holmes sat hatless and dishevelled on the box of his trap. He jumped down, climbed the steps to the porch and slumped into a chair. "A whisky soda, Billy, quick as you like. I need something strong and recuperative."

I looked a question.

"It is infernal warm," Holmes said. I smiled a not altogether sympathetic smile as Billy handed Holmes a glass, and he emptied it in a single gulp. "Another!"

"All went well at first," he gasped. "I approached the Baron's house by the service road at the rear and was let in to the servants' hall. The maids were much taken by the electric tongs, so much so I was required to demonstrate the apparatus on Cook." He held out his hands, revealing scorch marks on his fingers. "I wish it had been a Maxim machine gun."

After another long whisky soda, Holmes was sufficiently himself to give me the details his adventure.

"It is a villa of mysteries, Watson. Baron von Feldberg lives, when he is in residence, in the central part of the house. His bedroom is directly above the portico. The staff occupy the top floor of the west wing, with a basement kitchen, ground-floor reception salon and dining room. Guest rooms are on the first floor."

Holmes picked a chicken leg from our feast and nibbled it. "Close to, the lightning conductors on either side of the house are on the grand scale; they must be fifty feet high and built of a lattice of the strongest steel anchored into deep foundations. Pass the wine, old man."

I poured Holmes a glass of rosé.

"The servants were loquacious for an interesting reason, but of the east wing they know little; they are not allowed, under pain of dismissal, to pass the locked door from the central hall into the eastern part of the house. They surmise the baron's private office is on the ground floor and the first floor houses a library, but of the other floors they know nothing. Only the two German members of the baron's staff are allowed into the secret wing. They are the gatekeeper and a valet who travels to London with his master on Mondays and returns here in his company on Thursdays."

Holmes sipped his wine. "The grounds are tightly secured. Walls and gates are fitted with revolving spikes of a patent design I have never encountered, and an electric wire is drawn along the top of the wall. Its charge is lethal."

"Dogs?"

"Two hounds are let out at night. The servants are terrified of them; only the baron and his gatekeeper may command them. Mustard?"

I handed Holmes the jar and a spoon.

"It is supposed the reason for this security is that valuable wines and spirits are stored in the east wing," Holmes continued. "Large crates are regularly delivered by the baron's London staff."

"Aha!" I said. "A person may be concealed in a crate." I passed Holmes the remains of a crusty loaf which he broke and lathered with butter.

"There are more curiosities," he continued. "The house draws electrical power from a generating apparatus kept in an outhouse. It was built last year, at the same time as the lighting conductors, and engineers travel from Berlin every month to tend it. Two large buildings were constructed behind the house. One is a toilet and bathing facility on a scale far beyond the needs of the house, the other a meeting or dining hall."

Holmes peered at the food laid out on the tablecloth. "Where is the *foie-gras*? I distinctly ordered a slab of *foie-gras*." He sighed. "There, I told you the telephone is useless for precise communication. I'm surprised at Fortnum's; they are not usually so sloppy."

I smiled. "I didn't know you were a regular customer of Fortnum's, Holmes. Mrs Hudson favours our local market and butcher."

Holmes reached for the bottled ox-tongue. "The servants imagine the villa is haunted. Strange lights have been seen over the countryside at night. Mechanical sounds and high-pitched voices issue from the east wing, even when it is apparently unoccupied. That is quite apart from the shrieks of female laughter they hear from the baron's guests at his Friday and Saturday evening soirees. I fear our Mr Rutland was equivocal about the noise we might expect from our neighbour."

"High-pitched cries during the night, Holmes. Could those belong to the grand duchess, calling for help?"

Holmes tapped his finger to his lip. "The most intriguing fact is that Baron von Feldberg gave his entire British staff a month's notice of dismissal. He intends to marry, and his wife will bring her own staff from Germany. The term expires today, and the servants, some twenty in all, are packing their possessions. They are not sorry to leave a house with so many mysteries and ghostly noises, and the baron's severance terms are generous."

Holmes finished his luncheon, and we left Billy to clear up as we took a stroll along the lane towards the village. We stopped for a moment at the gate leading to Baron Von Feldberg's villa, and I glimpsed the tips of tall latticed towers through the trees.

The blast of a horn startled me, and Holmes and I spun around. A horseless vehicle with an elderly, bearded gentleman in a bowler as passenger and a younger man in leathers and a flat cap at the tiller careered along the lane towards us at an alarming speed.

The gentlemen raised their hats as they passed, gave another toot on their horn and disappeared in a cloud of dust and smoke, leaving behind the stink of burnt lamp oil.

I flicked motes of soot off my coat and muttered certain imprecations to myself.

"Fit a Maxim gun to one of those and you would have a formidable engine of war," Holmes said as he passed me a cigarette from his pack.

We stopped at the Royal Stag public house. Holmes brought out a pint of cool ale and left me while he chatted with the landlord and his wife.

The horseless carriage was parked outside the door, and I took a walk around the machine. It had the dimensions of a neat and compact four-wheeled dog-cart and was painted a pleasing blue, edged in brass. The carriage was heavily built, with ample accommodation for a driver, three passengers and two portmanteaus. Its power was provided by an engine under a curved metal cover at the front of the vehicle. The cover was hot to my touch, and the machine emitted tendrils of lamp-oil fumes and made faint clicking and hissing sounds as it cooled, almost like a thing alive.

A white-haired gentleman I recognised as the passenger on the vehicle came out of the public house holding a glass of ale. I introduced myself as one of the pedestrians he had passed, and Mr Evelyn Ellis, for it was he, gave me details of his Daimler Grafton Phaeton horseless carriage, built in Coventry under licence from its German designers. Mr Ellis was a true enthusiast and promoter, and I listened in fascination as he described the intricacies of the machine. In no time at all we had finished our pints of beer, and Mr Ellis suggested we go for a spin.

We climbed aboard, and to my astonishment Mr Ellis invited me to take the steering tiller while he operated the throttle. I accepted with not a little trepidation, but I found the machine no more difficult to control than a steam launch, and our short journey along the lane behind the Royal Stag and back, although bumpy, was extremely exhilarating.

I jumped down and thanked Mr Ellis. He introduced me to his usual driving companion, his young daughter, who I was surprised to discover was the leather-clad steersman of the vehicle. She helped her father back aboard, and they set off along the lane with a cheerful 'parp, parp,' from their horn.

I sat on a bench under a giant elm and watched the locals playing bowls while I contemplated my first close-up encounter with a horseless carriage. It was an invention very appealing to a doctor, allowing him to attend his patients at a moment's notice without the need and expense of horses, grooms and stable hands. A firm grip of the steering-handle and a keen eye were necessary for the safe guidance of such a powerful vehicle, but I was sure I would soon get the hang of it, as I had my Humber tricycle.

Holmes joined me, bringing two fresh pints of ale. "Rankin is at the bar telling droll stories about English perfidy towards the Scots. The locals roar with laughter as he portrays us to be a nation of ignorant and untrustworthy rapscallions. It must be irritating to our neighbours on these islands that we are secure enough in our superiority to laugh readily at our depiction as knaves."

He beamed at me. "The flashing lights above the baron's villa and strange sounds at night are confirmed. The view in the village is that Baron von Feldberg is a mad scientist, like the Hon. Evelyn Ellis who careers through the lanes in his horseless carriage with no thought for the lives of his neighbours. They say Mr Ellis boasts of reaching twenty or more miles an hour."

I frowned. "Surely not. That is above the legal limit."

Holmes took a sip of beer. "The landlord's wife told me she was at Windsor Station when a consignment of crates marked for delivery to the von Feldberg villa were unloaded and stacked on the platform. The contents were stamped in German and English."

He smiled at me.

"Well?" I asked.

"Tinned sausages," he answered. "Enough sausages to feed the household till the crack of doom. Did you enjoy your ride?"

I considered. "I was a little nervous at first, but in fact the machine was perfectly under control, and the sensation of being whirled rapidly along is decidedly pleasing. Mr Ellis told me one might pay two hundred guineas for a similar carriage, and for long journeys its maintenance would be from tenpence to a shilling an hour. He claims it's a splendid climber, able to go uphill at a faster pace than a pedestrian can walk."

I leaned forward. "I have to say, Holmes, that using Mycroft's private carriage has not proven as economical as I'd hoped. Rankin and the horse require regular feed and maintenance, and the cost is not insubstantial."

Holmes stood. "Let's enjoy a pleasant stroll back to the house, then we may return to London."

We arrived at our villa just after Rankin, and Holmes gave him his instructions as Billy loaded the carriage and I checked the house and locked up.

Rankin took Holmes and me to the station with Billy following in the trap, and I bought our tickets while Billy returned the trap to the mews and reclaimed our deposit.

"You understand everything, Rankin?" Holmes said as I joined him and our driver on the forecourt.

"I do, Mr Holmes."

Holmes handed Rankin a heavy leather bag of coins and smiled at me. "There will be certain unavoidable expenses."

Holmes, Billy and I boarded our train and settled in a private carriage. I buried myself in the evening paper, and Holmes packed his pipe with strong tobacco and lit it, filling the compartment with smoke. I motioned to Billy to open the windows as the train clanked, shuddered and set off for

London. He put our bags up on the rack. "Shall I put the tongs away, sir?" he asked Holmes.

"Eh? The hair tongs?" Holmes looked about him. "They are in a leather box." He blinked at me. "I am sure it was by me in the trap. Well, almost sure. Perhaps I left it under the driver's seat."

Billy gaped at him wide-eyed.

Holmes stood and straightened his cravat in the compartment mirror. "Never mind, we can telegraph the station when we get home. Saturday is curling day. Mrs Hudson will not miss the instrument until then."

I narrowed my eyes. "Holmes, you say you borrowed the hair tongs?"

Holmes waved away my question, but I detected an anxious gleam in his eyes as he frowned at his reflection in the mirror. "No, no, we have four days to replace the apparatus; it will not cause us the slightest disquiet."

I came down to breakfast and found Holmes already at our breakfast table and Billy in his tight buttons uniform leaning against the mantel with his arms folded and a sour expression on his face.

"Kippers!" I exclaimed. "We are forgiven at last. The flowers and rosewater did the trick. I might open the windows a little wider; there is no smell more enduring than that of a well-cured kipper." I flung our windows open and drew in a long breath of air. "Not a cloud in the sky, I'm afraid. We are in for another scorching day."

I took my seat opposite Holmes and reached for the coffee pot.

"The condemned men ate a hearty breakfast," Holmes said with a wry smile. "Make the most of it, we may not see kippers again for a while."

I raised my eyebrows. "Has that which will not cause us the slightest disquiet caused disquiet?"

Holmes nodded. "Mrs Campbell from number ninety-seven wanted to borrow the hair tongs, and Mrs Hudson owed her a favour because of the oats from Clackmannan."

"Mrs H says she's very welcome to borrow the tongs (Mrs Campbell, that is), only they're not to be found," Billy added, rolling his eyes.

Holmes poured himself a coffee. "Billy is the obvious suspect in the theft owing to his villainous appearance and his previous form. Although what reason he would have for taking the tongs is beyond me."

"Because a certain person ordered me to *borrow* them," Billy said in a severe tone. "And promised on the tears of his granny to have them back the next day."

"Oh what a tangled web—" I said in faux Scots and with more than a hint of complacency, which was punctured when I realised that we were again in for austere meals and cold comfort.

We ate our breakfast in silence.

Holmes drained his coffee cup and stood. "There is only one thing for it." He went to his desk and gestured for Billy to join him. They had a whispered conference, and Holmes took some coins from our cashbox and passed them to the boy. He scampered off downstairs.

Holmes sighed, picked up his magnifying glass from his desk and, shoulders stooped, shuffled to the sitting-room door. "I shall speak to Mrs Hudson."

"Good for you, Holmes," I exclaimed. "The truth will out, as they say, and confession is good for the soul."

"I would be grateful if you would second me, old man," Holmes said softly.

I stood. "Of course, my dear fellow. Should I get my service revolver?"

We found Mrs Hudson sitting at the table in the kitchen with our maid Bessie and another lady I presumed was Mrs Campbell from number ninety-seven.

"Now, Mrs Hudson, my dear lady," Holmes said in an unctuous tone. "I am here to help. Kindly show me where the apparatus was kept."

Mrs Hudson stood and grasped Holmes' hands in hers. "Oh, it is so good of you to trouble yourself on my behalf, sir. I was just saying to Mrs Campbell what a treasure you are as a lodger (apart from one or two tiny peccadillios)." She looked teary-eyed at me. "And the good doctor here as well."

I gave Holmes a reproachful look.

"Yes, yes, my dear lady," said Holmes, extracting his hands and stepping back out of range of her attentions. "Where are the tongs usually stored?"

Mrs Hudson's expression hardened. "I had thought in a Christian household there would be no need of lock, keys and the like, but I was wrong, sirs. Come, Mr Holmes and Doctor Watson, and I will show you the scene of the crime."

"I can see the headlines, Holmes," I said as we climbed the stairs to our sitting room. "We'll see 'Hair tongs stolen from home of Sherlock Holmes' in the *Police Illustrated News*, and 'Curling apparatus filched from under detective's nose' in the *Barber's Weekly*. Ha ha."

Holmes crossed to the fireplace. "This is not the moment for levity, Doctor. And you are out of cigars." He scrabbled through the stack of opened envelopes, neglected bills and other detritus.

"Ha! It is indeed not a time for levity. You should be ashamed of yourself, Holmes, deceiving that good woman with your 'Will you leave the matter in my hands?' and your 'Can you trust my judgement in this affair?' nonsense, and your talk of cat burglars in the neighbourhood. There is a new pack of cigars in the coal scuttle (though why you put them there, I cannot fathom)." I sat at my desk, took out my notebook and turned to a fresh page.

"What are you doing?" Holmes asked.

"I am writing up the case. I shall call it 'The Mysterious Disappearance of the Maxim Electric Hair Tongs'. I don't think the *Strand Magazine* will take it, but *Punch*, or *Fun* might."

Holmes slumped into his chair in front of the fireplace and lit his cigar. He perked up as the door opened, and Billy slipped in holding a brown-paper-wrapped package.

"There," said Holmes. "A simple matter, a storm in a teacup; I knew—"

Billy shook his head. "Not to be had, sir." He handed me the package and gave Holmes a large envelope adorned with a printed crest.

Holmes sighed as he opened the envelope. "I suppose it was too much to hope the local ironmonger would carry such esoteric items as electric tongs. We must try farther afield. Pass me a notepad, would you?"

He took a sheet of paper and scribbled a note. "Give this to Peterson," he ordered Billy. "With five bob the doctor will give you."

I gave Billy the coins, and he scampered off.

Holmes waved the crested envelope at me. "You must dig out your best bib and tucker: we are invited to dinner by Lord Rosebery."

"When?"

"Tonight. At number forty, Piccadilly. It is the anniversary of the death of Robert Burns, the Scots poet."

I frowned at my friend. "It seems an odd coincidence that we are investigating a case with strong Scottish connections, and we receive an invitation from our ex-prime minister, a Scotsman."

"Coincidences are always odd; that is why we remark on them."

I opened the brown paper packet and read the attached note.

"What's this?" asked Holmes. "More wreaths?"

"Discovered yesterday evening and this morning on the statue of Edward the First in Westminster Abbey." I smiled. "The Hammer of the Scots, as you will recall." I picked up the second wreath in the packet. "And this one was left at the foot of Nelson's Column."

Holmes sighed. "More Ossianic drivel. I am more than replete with Scots poetry."

"No, Holmes," I said as I read the poems printed on the blue and white ribbons. "The pace is quickening. No more Ossian allusiveness, we now have direct reference to rebellion.

> *Avaunt! thou caitiff, servile, base,*
> *That tremblest at a despot's nod,*
> *Yet, crouching under the iron rod,*
> *Canst laud the hand that struck th' insulting blow!"*

I threw the wreath onto the table. "What infernal cheek, Holmes, calling the Queen a despot. It is not only seditious, it is indecorous."

I frowned at Holmes. "Her Majesty travels to Scotland this morning, Holmes. An outrage may be planned against her!"

Holmes nodded. "I have formed certain conclusions regarding the threat posed by the authors of these writings, and I agree it is my plain duty to add my efforts to the official measures to protect Her Majesty during her stay in Scotland."

I stood and stiffened to attention. "I shall accompany you, Holmes."

He nodded "Come, let's pack." He stood and glanced at his watch. "We'll have to hurry, the Royal train leaves Windsor for Balmoral in less than three hours."

"What about Lord Rosebery's dinner, Holmes? We must send our apologies."

"I'll deal with that." he answered. "You'll need to pack evening dress – don't forget your pistol."

I ran up to my room and flung clothes and my wash bag into a valise. I carefully checked that my pistol was not loaded and put it in one pocket of my frock coat with a handful of cartridges in the other. I came downstairs and found Billy talking with Holmes and a package open on the table disclosing another wreath.

"Let me have a telegraph form, would you, Watson?"

"If you are still after hair tongs, why don't you telephone Whiteleys or Harrods and order a set?" I asked. "There are public telephones at the Post Office and at Paddington Station."

Holmes nodded. "A very good idea. Call a cab, will you, Billy?"

I opened the latest package and picked up the wreath and attached note from Mycroft. "It was fixed to the doors of the Bank of England.

> *The English steel we could disdain,*
> *Secure in valour's station:*
> *But English gold has been our bane*
> *Such a parcel of rogues in a nation."*

Holmes frowned. "Does the last line even scan?"

THE QUEEN

## 10. TO THE NORTH

I bought our tickets, secured a compartment on the Windsor Express with ten minutes to spare, leaned out of the window and watched for Holmes.

At one minute to departure time, the engine let out a cloud of smoke and steam and a long, low whistle, but I still could not see him. I was about to grab my valise and step out of the carriage when Holmes appeared from a billow of steam, running hard.

The guard's whistle blew, couplings clanked and the train shuddered and began to move. I flung open the door, and Holmes jumped in and slumped onto the seat. I slammed the door shut and sat opposite him.

"No hair tongs in stock, and would I like a patent mousetrap. Damn the telephone and damn Hiram Maxim and all his works."

I smiled. "Language, old chap."

Holmes tipped his hat over his eyes, and I settled back in my seat. I was very glad we were, at last, making a direct effort against the monsters who had designs against Her Majesty. Our engagement in the affair thus far had seemed peripheral or reactive rather than active. The danger was now clear, or clearer at least: the threat was to the Crown, and it was our duty to rally to the protection of the Queen.

These morbid thoughts occupied my mind as the train raced through the west of London, then past green fields and once again through the pleasant pastures and water meadows of Berkshire. We arrived at Windsor Station on time, the dramatic profile of the castle rising above us as the train came to a halt.

The platform was thronged with people, many of them in military uniforms or that of the railway company. A tall, portly gentleman stood alone outside the Royal Waiting Room leaning on his stick.

"I telephoned the Castle and offered our services to Mycroft," Holmes said as I followed him along the platform. The two brothers faced each other, but did not shake hands.

"Well, Mycroft?"

"Do I detect a note of interrogation in your tone, Brother?"

"Smoke and mirrors, Brother. I am engaged to find the duke and duchess and the Stone of Destiny, yet you withhold from me what I need to know to perform those tasks successfully."

Mycroft gave his brother a cold look, then he drew us into the Royal Waiting Room and closed the door. "I know little more than I have told you," he murmured, "and that little is mere rumour and speculation."

Holmes folded his arms. "The Sons of the Thistle."

Mycroft bent towards us. "Very well, but this is in the strictest confidence."

Holmes sniffed.

"We intercept the Prussian diplomatic traffic at the cable office," Mycroft murmured.

"I would imagine it is in code," I said.

"What one man may veil in mystery, another may with great difficulty attempt to reveal," Mycroft replied. "Of course, all diplomats on foreign postings suspect their host countries are monitoring the mails, that is why we have the system of diplomatic bags and couriers, but the diplomatic bag is a cumbersome method of communication, depending on railways and in our case steam ferries to reach the chancelleries of the Great Powers. This is a time of upheaval and grave danger, gentlemen. Opinions must be formed and decisions made with a speed that would have astonished statesmen of even a decade or two ago. The days of gentlemanly discourse and the elaborate exchanges of diplomatic notes are over."

Holmes sniffed impatiently. "To the point, if you please."

Mycroft coloured. "The information we obtained from certain measures of interception I need not describe in detail is so faint, so much a will-o'-the-wisp, that I hesitated to offer it to you lest your focus on the abduction be warped."

Holmes raised a disdainful eyebrow.

"There was a mention of the organisation called 'The Sons of the Thistle'," Mycroft murmured. "It was whispered in the ear of a lady in our employ by a clerk in the telegraph room of the German Embassy. He asked her what a 'thistle' was, as he often had occasion to telegraph the word to Berlin and it had piqued his interest. The lady asked for context, and he offered 'Sons of the Thistle', something to do with the Scottish Army."

Mycroft shrugged. "This would not have been flagged for my attention, except that a pair of gentlemen of military bearing appeared at the house of ill-fame where our *employée*, who I shall call Sally, plied her trade. They asked for her in German-accented English; no other lady would do. When they were told Sally had gone home to her mother's and would be back in a week, they left."

I heard a low rumble and Mycroft massaged his stomach.

"The clerk did not visit the brothel again," he continued. "He fell suddenly ill and had to return home. He was taken on board a German merchantman at Folkestone on a stretcher. The ship had been diverted from Rotterdam to pick him up."

"This for a lowly telegraph clerk?" Holmes asked.

"Just so," Mycroft said with a tight smile. "The two gentlemen returned to the bordello exactly a week later. They were told Sally was stayed at home by her mother's illness. They asked for her address, and when it was refused, they laid twenty gold sovereigns on the desk of the Madame. It would have been highly suspicious to decline such a stupendous bribe, and the quick-witted lady gave an address, that of her auntie in Carmarthen. We just had time to arrange a welcome when the two indefatigable admirers arrived on Auntie's doorstep with flowers, fruit and jars of beef tea."

Mycroft smiled. "Alas, according to Auntie, Sally's mother had died and the girl had left for Liverpool, address unknown and good riddance to her as a trollop."

Holmes considered. "What measures have you taken to discover more on these 'Sons of the Thistle'?"

Mycroft shrugged. "What can we do? We have no target for active measures, and if we instruct our agents on the Continent to nose about, that will inevitably come to the ears of the Prussians."

"Have you any link between von Feldberg and this organisation, if it exists?"

"None."

"I may have something." Holmes recounted our experience at the Alhambra Music Hall.

"Interesting," said Mycroft. "It is another indication that, despite his gaudy connections, Baron von Feldberg is not the fellow he appears to be."

Holmes described the strange arrangements at the baron's villa, the massive gantries and the lights and noises at night.

"Deuced odd, Sherlock. Should we stage a police raid? I have a coiners' press and a hoard of fake sovereigns we could plant in an outhouse to justify the intrusion."

I blinked at Mycroft in consternation, and he smiled. "My little joke, Doctor."

I looked to Holmes, but he had his finger to his lip and was deep in thought.

"Do they have designs against Her Majesty?" I asked. "The poems in the thistle wreaths are now openly seditious. Should not her visit to Scotland be called off?"

"There is no obvious connection between the Sons of the Thistle and the wreaths," Mycroft said. "The Thistle organisation has clearly been at pains to remain underground, and the Prussians have gone to extraordinary lengths to keep their connection with them secret. The poems and wreaths, whether they be warnings, or threats, are unsigned. They may be the work of the Daughters of the Unicorn for all we know."

"Well," I said, perhaps a little sharply. "What do we know? And more important, what can we do?"

"We know a faux-Scots illusionist is in secret communication with Baron von Feldberg," said Holmes. "We know the baron visits his embassy regularly; he attends receptions, balls and meetings with the officials who promote commerce with England. Thus the path to Berlin of whatever information Mr Macdonald, or more properly, Meecham, has access to is clear."

"We should have Meecham dogged to see who he meets, and thereby uncover any connection he may have with the Sons of the Thistle," I suggested.

"I have the Irregulars on him and on Mr McNair," Holmes said. "So far, Meecham leads an exemplary life for a drunken, murderous illusionist."

"Then we must apply your methods to the little girls who assist him," I said.

Holmes frowned at me, and his brother raised his eyebrows in astonishment.

"A bribe, gentlemen, well three bribes unless we can tell which of the girls is the go-between. Meecham described them as avaricious. They must pass the next packet of information to us."

Holmes held out his hand to his brother. "The document I requested?"

"I cannot think why you would require such authority, Sherlock," Mycroft said primly, "Or where or in what circumstances it might be applied."

Holmes smiled his jaguar smile and snapped his fingers. Mycroft took a long, elaborately sealed envelope from a valise at his side. "Your request is granted, most reluctantly granted, within a strict limit of twenty-four hours from this moment."

Mycroft handed Holmes the envelope which he slipped into his inside pocket. Mycroft checked the time, made a note on his shirt cuff with a silver propelling pencil and wagged a pudgy finger at Holmes. "Do not lose that authority, or it will be the Tower for you, not Windsor Castle."

A clanking and hissing came from the platform as the Queen's carriage was shunted to its position opposite the waiting room door.

"Lord Rosebery's dinner is tonight," Mycroft continued. "The Duke of Edinburgh and his wife are the guests of honour. If they do not attend, tongues will wag. We have our newspaper editors on a short leash, but tomorrow's Continental papers may indulge in dangerous speculation on the matter."

I heard another low rumble and Mycroft excused himself. "It is time for my apple. Mr Ponsonby, Her Majesty's private secretary, will brief you on security measures for the royal journey north."

Holmes and I left Mycroft in the waiting room and went on to the platform to examine the train. Holmes smiled at me. "Well, Watson, I see your scruples about bribery have evaporated."

"We act for the Queen, Holmes."

"Indeed we do," said Holmes. "Let us tour Her defences."

Mr Ponsonby folded his arms and peered at us over his huge white spade beard. "We already have the railway police, the Windsor Castle police, 'A' Division of the Metropolitan Police and Scotland Yard, and now I am obliged to find room for you, Mr Sherlock Holmes and your companion. That's on top of a company of Scots Guards for whom I do not have accommodation. I informed their captain he could stow his men on the roof of the baggage van, or he can find cattle trucks and couple them to the rear of the train."

He mopped his brow with a large white handkerchief. "In fact, I've had borrowed a pair of third-class coaches from the Great Western Railway." He turned away as a blue-uniformed messenger appeared with a note.

I grasped Holmes arm. "*Scots* Guards!" I whispered anxiously.

Mr Ponsonby dismissed the messenger. "The carriages of the Ladies and Gentlemen of the Royal Household are on their way. Her Majesty is about to leave the castle. I can give you only a few moments of my time."

Mr Ponsonby frowned over his beard at us. "You have seen the Royal Waiting Room where the Queen makes herself comfortable after the carriage ride. Half an hour before the train is due to start, the Queen's pages, upper servants and maids arrive and occupy their seats, then come the Ladies and Gentlemen of the Royal Household, the equerries and the Lords-in-Waiting and, finally, the Queen."

He gestured to the train. "As you can see, the royal saloon is opposite the door of the waiting room. The Queen crosses the platform and enters her carriage. After Her Majesty has taken her seat, the train is drawn forward, and halted for two minutes for the rear section with baggage and electrical vans and now the Scots Guards carriages to be attached. It then begins its journey north."

"Might we see inside the Royal Saloon?" Holmes asked.

"Certainly, but I must ask you not to touch anything. Her Majesty likes things just so."

A murmur came from the crowd at the front of the station, and Holmes and I turned and watched a procession of carriages turn in to the station approach and stop. A crowd of formally dressed ladies and gentlemen carrying bags and cases got down and hurried through the station entrance and towards the back of the train.

"The Ladies and Gentlemen of the Household," said Mr Ponsonby. We followed him across the platform, through the door of the Royal Carriage and into a sumptuously decorated saloon. The walls were quilted with royal blue silk that contrasted with the elegant bird's-eye maple pelmets. The ceiling was quilted in white with gold daisy buttons. A pair of heavily carved sofas and several armchairs and occasional tables furnished the saloon.

I noticed a cord with an ivory pull hanging by the door of the compartment, and Mr Ponsonby followed my gaze. "The Queen insists the train must not exceed forty miles an hour, and she does not care to walk across the vestibules between the carriages while we are in motion. One of her Ladies-in-Waiting pulls on that cord to stop the train each time Her Majesty wishes to move between carriages. The signal tells the driver to slow, stop immediately, or stop at the nearest station so the Queen may take refreshment. Her Majesty declares that eating on a moving train is quite unnatural."

Another messenger ran up and called to Mr Ponsonby from the door of the compartment. He nodded. "And now, gentlemen, I must be about my business and you yours. Her Majesty has left the Castle."

Holmes and I made our way out of the station and joined a throng of onlookers on the pavement outside. The crowd had grown into a sea of spectators, and the road was lined with children waving Union flags. A cordon of policemen kept the space before the entrance to the Royal Waiting Room clear, and the doorway was guarded, I was concerned to see, by a pair of tall men in Highland dress.

An open carriage appeared flanked by mounted lancers in bright-coloured uniforms and Indian turbans.

I turned to Holmes. "The lancers look fine, do they not?"

He smiled, but I saw that his attention was wholly on the crowd. I stiffened with apprehension, and I too scanned the mass of people for suspicious characters. My gaze met that of Mr Ponsonby, and he nodded gravely to me.

The carriage stopped before the waiting room and a tiny, bent figure swathed in black and with her head and face covered in black net topped by a white veil of lace was helped down. She hobbled through the door of the Royal

Waiting Room, followed by a pair of ladies-in-waiting, one leading a Pomeranian dog.

The instant she disappeared inside, the crowd surged through the station entrance, and I held tight to my wallet as I was dragged with them. They jostled for positions behind the silk ropes separating the onlookers from the platform-side door of the waiting room and the red carpet laid to the door of the Queen's carriage.

Mr Ponsonby stood by the Royal Saloon with a group of elderly gentlemen, some with silk sashes of office in gaudy colours over their coats, others in elaborate military uniforms. Beside him was a gentleman with drooping grey side-whiskers in a frock coat covered with orders and decorations. Mr Ponsonby beckoned to Holmes and me, and we ducked under the ropes and joined them.

"This is Colonel Fortescue, gentlemen," Mr Ponsonby said. "He is in charge of measures for the Queen's protection. May I present Mr Sherlock Holmes and Doctor Watson?"

"The author?" the colonel asked in a faint Scottish brogue, holding out his hand.

I mumbled a deprecating reply.

Colonel Fortescue frowned as he held out his hand to Holmes. "Mr Holmes, I have heard your name in connection with a certain department of the Government."

"You are thinking of my brother."

"What? Speak up, man, don't mumble."

Holmes sighed and shook the colonel's hand.

"I am reasonably sanguine, gentlemen," Colonel Fortescue said. "For close protection of Her Majesty's person, we have three detectives from Scotland Yard in the Queen's coach, all armed and reputed crack shots. They are dressed as footmen."

He took an enamel snuffbox from his waistcoat pocket and sniffed a pinch. He offered snuff to Holmes, Mr Ponsonby and me, but we declined.

"A fourth detective is on the footplate disguised as a railwayman. I and two of my aides are in the next but one carriage with the Gentlemen of the Household. We are armed with heavy pistols and an elephant gun. We drew a company of Scots Guards from the Castle, and they protect the rear of the train and act as a reserve. They are accommodated in the last coaches before the baggage and electrical vans."

"Police and railwaymen are posted every hundred yards along our route to Scotland," Mr Ponsonby said. "All other traffic on our line has been cleared for twenty miles before and behind, and a pilot train filled with sharpshooters runs five minutes ahead. All down trains must stop or slow near us, and no passing train may match our pace. Troops of cavalry are on hand at the stations the Queen regularly stops at for luncheon etcetera." He mopped his brow with his handkerchief. "If only it weren't so confounded hot, and I could think straight."

Colonel Fortescue turned to me. "Is the attempt likely to be to capture Her Majesty, or are the fiends bent on assassination?"

"We do not know," I answered. "The messages we have received are harshly worded enough to suggest the latter."

The colonel struck his fist into his hand. "I believe we are covered to the border. The devils will strike after we cross into Scotland." He let out a string of what I imagine were Scots oaths. "I'll tell you my fear, gentlemen," he said, his accent thickening as he grew more heated. "A lunatic wi' an inferrrnal device. Could we no persuade Her Majesty to—" He sighed. "I know the answer to my ayn question."

Mr Ponsonby patted the colonel on the arm "We will do our best, Fortescue, and we can do no more,"

Holmes picked up his bag. "My companion and I will take our stand in the first luggage car."

"Aye," the colonel said in a dismissive tone. "You'll be well oot of the firing line there." He turned away, then stiffened to attention as the door of the waiting room opened and, with the crowd cheering and waving their flags, the diminutive figure of the Queen-Empress appeared, leaning on the arm of one of her Indian servants. She walked slowly and with obvious difficulty to the open door of her carriage where she was helped inside by two of her ladies.

"Come, Watson." I followed Holmes along the platform to the luggage cars at the rear of the train, and we climbed into the last one.

"Is it not a piquant irony that the Queen's protective company is provided by the Scots Guards?" I asked.

The car was piled with portmanteaus, cases, crates, rolls of carpet and even pieces of furniture. Large, sealed pottery jars stood in straw-filled containers. I frowned at Holmes.

"Judging by the aroma, they hold a stew for luncheon," he said.

A whistle blew, and the train clanked into motion. Holmes instantly jumped up, grabbed his bag, opened the farther door of the carriage and dropped onto the track. His head appeared in the open doorway as he jogged beside the train. "Come on, old chap."

I took up my valise and dropped beside Holmes. He softly shut the carriage door behind us and the train drew away, picking up speed. He gestured for me to keep silent as he led the way across the up railway line, over the low fence marking the limit of railway property and through a patch of scrub to a narrow lane where a four-wheeler cab waited with a burly figure in a bowler on the box.

He took no notice of us as Holmes opened the cab door and we threw in our bags and clambered inside. The cab moved off and Holmes hummed a merry tune. He offered me a panatela from his cigar case.

"No, thank you. What I would like right now, my dear fellow, is a word or two of explanation."

Holmes frowned. "You thought we were going to Scotland?"

"The Queen is in danger," I said coldly. "What else were we to do?"

"Think it through, old chap. As you say, the Queen may be in danger from the Sons of the Thistle or other Scottish Nationalists, with or without Prussian backing. It is publicly known she is visiting Scotland, travelling by train at her usual stately pace and stopping for luncheon and other refreshment on the way."

Holmes lit his cigar. "The authorities have increased her guards, alerted stationmasters, posted watchers along the track and arranged for a squadron of cavalry to escort the royal entourage as they travel by carriage and on horseback from Ballater Station on the River Dee to Balmoral Castle."

He puffed on his cigar. "They have also—"

I held up my hand. "The Queen is not aboard the train, Holmes."

"Exactly. The Queen is not aboard the train. She is represented by one of her ladies-in-waiting, who, in the circumstances she thinks obtain, with Jacobites or even Jacobins behind every bush, is a brave person."

Holmes blew a stream of smoke out of the open cab window. "Her Majesty was persuaded to postpone her trip to Scotland on the grounds that certain Diamond Jubilee obligations are not yet fulfilled. She left for the Isle of Wight early this morning. She will perform local ceremonies connected with the Jubilee from her home at Osborne House while her shadow journeys north and takes up residence at Balmoral, with what consequences we shall see. We now leave the safety of our sovereign and her simulacrum to the authorities and concentrate on our own affairs."

"What was that jumping from the train about?" I asked. "Who were we trying to hoodwink?"

"You know we are dogged. You saw the crowd of well-wishers outside the station to see the Queen off. Can you recall any of them?"

I frowned. "A knot of clergy, the station master and his staff, let me see, ah, some obvious foreigners, probably visitors to Windsor, with several gawking Americans. A group of Indians, well very likely Indians in their gaudy silks.

Soldiers in scarlet and blue. A cluster of Eton boys waving their umbrellas, Windsor townsfolk, of course, and groups of young children with their teachers. I would guess they are from local schools with Castle connections."

I considered for a moment. "I looked twice at that group of heavily bearded gentlemen in frock coats and gaudy uniforms on the platform, and the elderly hussar in the frogged jacket and fur hat—"

"The diplomats?" Holmes asked. "They attended a Jubilee dinner last night and stayed at the Castle. I believe the old gentleman in the hussar uniform represented Prussia." He smiled at me. "You looked, but you did not see."

I pouted. "I'm not sure there was anything *to* see."

ROBBIE BURNS

# 11. EAT YOUR NEEPS

The carriage stopped, and I blinked awake and peered out of the window. We were passing along a busy street thronged with omnibuses, cabs and private carriages. I glimpsed Apsley House, and realised we were almost at Piccadilly.

Holmes lifted his hat brim and bent towards me, his eyes glittering. "You have your service piece with you?" he murmured.

"I have," I answered, opening my coat to reveal the revolver tucked in its holster. I gripped the butt of the weapon and gazed out of the cab windows, narrow-eyed and alert. "Where are we going?"

"To the Criterion Grill. I have booked a private room. We may pass the time till the dinner hour with a game or two of billiards; it would not do for us to be seen at our usual London haunts, but we have an appointment tonight."

"Lord Rosebery's invitation!"

"Exactly, I accepted in my and your name." Holmes leaned towards me and smiled. "If I am not mistaken, we are one step ahead of Mycroft, and in for a lively evening

"Adam Smith and David Hume," I said as Holmes and I sauntered along Piccadilly in our white-tie finery.

Traffic was jammed tight in the usual early evening congestion of carriages, and the pavement was thronged with gentlemen and ladies taking the air or heading for refreshment at one of the restaurants and hotels in the area. The dazzling sun was low and in the eyes of people moving towards us.

"And Doctor Livingstone," I added. "They were all Scots."

"Burke and Hare, Captain Kidd, your *bête noire* Doctor Lister," Holmes retorted.

"I greatly admire Doctor Lister," I said stiffly. "His germ theory may be overrated, but it is a valuable insight." I wagged my finger at my companion. "And body snatchers Burke and Hare were not Scots, they were Irish."

"They went to the bad in Edinburgh. We are here."

We stopped at a fine mansion a short distance from Piccadilly Circus and joined a line of people outside the open door of Lord Rosebery's London home, one of several he and his wife, sadly deceased, had in the capital.

"Holmes, look!" I indicated a wreath of thistles hung around the lion's head knocker of the front door. "It is identical to the ones scattered about the city."

Holmes peered closely at the ribbon. "The sentiment is in prose and in English. On one side, 'Burns exalts our race'. On the other, 'Burns reasserts Scotland's claim to national existence, and he has thus preserved the Scottish language forever'."

"Could our ex-prime minister be involved in this affair, Holmes?" I frowned. "No I cannot believe it."

"He is a Scot, though born in London, as I recall."

We were shown to a cloakroom by a pageboy, and an attendant murmured that we might divest ourselves of our hats and gloves. He did not blink when I laid down my service revolver in its holster, together with a packet of cartridges.

I straightened my bow tie in the mirror. In the harsh light of the electric globes, my face showed every one of my forty-odd years. What had been a tinge of dark grey in my hair was now a series of grey and even white streaks. I sighed as I recalled the lines I had heard from Mr McNair in the Coal Hole public house. Then I smiled as I met Holmes' eyes in the mirror, and he winked and declaimed,

> *"When shall Ossian's youth return?*
> *When his ear delight in the sound of arms?"*

We grinned, and I took my friend's arm. "I do wish you wouldn't perform your mind-reading nonsense in public, Holmes."

We followed other guests through palatial reception rooms and into a smaller drawing room where a score or so of men and women clustered in groups. We accepted champagne from a waiter, and Holmes nodded to a corner in which several gentlemen stood in a huddle drinking whisky. I recognised Lord Rosebery as one of their number from caricatures I had seen in *Vanity Fair* and drawings in the newspapers. The earl had the appearance and bearing of a patrician, as one would expect.

"Come, we must meet our host," said Holmes.

I followed Holmes across the room, and we introduced ourselves and shook hands. Lord Rosebery mentioned Holmes' brother Mycroft, and as they spoke of him, I examined our ex-prime minister. He was of average height, his face was slightly elongated, smooth shaven, ruddy and surmounted by an abundant growth of hair parted on the side and silvery white. A mourning band was on his arm, and his bluish-grey eyes had a tinge of sadness about them. I had heard Lord Rosebery's disposition had been darkened and his health broken by the death of his wife some years previously.

I started as I realised that I had been staring, and that Lord Rosebery had asked me a question. "I'm sorry—"

"I wondered whether you are any relation to the Kinross Watsons, Doctor."

I smiled "I cannot be certain, but I have always had a feeling that—"

A piper in magnificent regimentals appeared in the doorway playing a stirring tune. He processed around the room, our host and guests formed up behind him and we trooped into the dining room.

Footmen showed us to our places, and I found myself between a glitteringly bejewelled and very deaf old lady with a huge ear trumpet who ignored me, and a vivacious girl with a bonny smile in a thistle-flower-sprigged dress and a tartan sash.

The piper finished his tune, and Lord Rosebery took his place at the head of the long flower-bedecked table and bade us sit.

He welcomed his guests to the dinner with few words explaining that we were celebrating the hundred and first anniversary of the death of Robert Burns. His Lordship lauded Burns as a champion of democracy and as an individual who harboured what he called the essential quality of man. He went on to inform us that Burns' birthday was celebrated more universally than that of any human being on Earth, and to suggest the poet's popularity was a testament to the endurance of the British Empire as a force for moral good.

"We venerate Robert Burns for his verse, but also for his life. He was a 'lad o'pairts', showing that personal ability was enough to succeed in life. And when we thank heaven for the inestimable gift of Burns," he concluded, "we do not need to remember wherein he was imperfect. We cannot bring ourselves to regret he was made of the same clay as ourselves."

With the faint clink of a spoon on his glass, he declared the dinner open, and grace was said by a white-haired military officer in Highland dress.

> *"Some hae meat and canna eat,*
> *And some wad eat that want it;*
> *But we hae meat, and we can eat,*
> *And sae let the Lord be thankit."*

Supper started with the soup course, Cock-a-Leekie according to the young lady on my left, a Miss Roberts from Fife. The soup was garnished with odd wrinkled, sweetish lumps Miss Roberts identified as prunes. It was a fine, tasty soup, and I thought I might ask for another plate, but Miss Roberts nudged me as the company stood, and the main course, a haggis on a large dish, was brought in by the cook and led to the host's end of the table by the skirling piper.

The haggis, a glistening brown object, much like a damp and overstuffed silken pillow, was laid before Lord Rosebery.

"A man's a man for a' that," Miss Roberts murmured.

"I'm sure he is," I answered frowning. "I don't doubt it for a moment."

She giggled, putting her hand over her mouth in a pretty way. "It is the name of the tune, Doctor, and a Burns poem."

Lord Rosebery stood, lifted a carving knife and recited another Burns poem, the 'Address to a Haggis'.

> *"Great chieftain o' the puddin-race*
> *Fair fa' your honest, sonsie face,*
> *Great chieftain o' the puddin-race!*
> *Aboon them a' ye tak your place,*
> *Painch, tripe, or thairm:*
> *Weel are ye wordy o' a grace*
> *As lang's my arm.*
>
> *The groaning trencher there ye fill,*
> *Your hurdies like a distant hill,*
> *Your pin wad help to mend a mill*
> *In time o' need,*
> *While thro' your pores the dews distil*
> *Like amber bead."*

The worthy young lady beside me whispered a translation in Scots-tinged English as the poem continued and Lord Rosebery ceremonially cut into the haggis, but I have to say I could not follow the sentiment beyond the amber bead. I smiled and thanked her as we were served with plates of what looked very much like the grey gruel of Mrs Hudson's porridge flanked with white mashed potato and an orange mashed vegetable. I regarded my plate with some trepidation.

"Eat your neeps," Holmes said across the table. "Turnips, as I understand, or perhaps swedes."

I was hungry, having had a salad luncheon at the Criterion, and although I was uneasy about my digestive capacity given the strangeness of the meal, I stiffened my upper lip and set to. I took a sip of wine, a full-bodied red with enough vigour to hold its own with the rich food, and as I turned to my comely neighbour to make a polite remark, I frowned.

A gentlemen with a spiked moustache farther down the table on Holmes' side met my gaze and bowed, rather coldly, I thought, as he raised his glass. I returned the compliment, but I was puzzled as to who he was. I tried to catch Holmes' eye, but he was chatting merrily with the lady on his left.

I found the meal tasty, but I was glad when, after a sweet course of whisky trifle, we were presented with cheese, biscuits and fruit and I was on familiar culinary ground.

After a series of speeches ending with the loyal toast to the Queen, the ladies retired, and the gentlemen gathered in an adjoining anteroom. The walls of the room were hung with scenes of what I imagined was the Scottish Highlands, with the requisite mountains and stags at bay. Holmes and I peered idly at one.

"I hope you gentlemen enjoyed your meal," Lord Rosebery said, coming up to us. He indicated the painting. "It is a McCulloch. He depicts Scotland as a country of bens and glens." He shrugged. "Which is true enough, but not the whole story."

A footman offered cigars from an elaborate case, and another servant lit them.

Lord Rosebery turned to Holmes. "I hear you are investigating Scottish Nationalism, Mr Holmes. You are looking for rebellious sects."

Holmes bowed. "I have found no evidence that any such political organisation exists, at least nothing on the scale of the Irish movement."

Lord Rosebery took a long puff on his cigar. "Political nationalism in Scotland was killed by Jacobitism, then the chance of home rule came to naught because it was coupled with the Irish Question."

"What is your position on the independence of Scotland, Lord Rosebery?" Holmes asked.

"I have made my position clear, Mr Holmes: I am for Union and Empire, but I will not castigate those who are uncomfortable with the present arrangements for governing the United Kingdom." Lord Rosebery smiled. "I hope you will forgive me, gentlemen, if I say the English do not make much effort to alleviate the sensitivities of the other nationalities who share these islands. You will recall the words of the jubilee hymn sung before the Queen at Saint Paul's Cathedral last month by five hundred choirboys. No? It ends,

> *Where England's flag lies wide unfurled,*
> *All tyrant's wrongs repelling.*

*England's* flag; that was vexing to those of the Queen's subjects who are Scots, Welsh and Irish."

Lord Rosebery regarded the end of his cigar. "In many ways, we Scots are closer to the French than the English. The English prefer gentlemen dilettantes to professionals, rule of thumb to precision, and precedents to reasoned argument. Above all an Englishman must never give the impression he is focusing his mental powers on any problem. We remain aloof. Governing the Empire must seem an effortless, gentlemanly amusement; a hobby one shares with members of an elite caste."

A pair of footmen appeared with a tray of glasses and a decanter of whisky.

"Do help yourselves," said Lord Rosebery. "We stand on no ceremony tonight. Burns, as I said in my opening remarks, was a democrat."

I received a glass of whisky and inhaled its peaty aroma with the greatest pleasure.

Lord Rosebery took a sip of whisky. "Enough of politics, gentlemen; let us finish our drinks and join the ladies."

He turned to me. "If I had known the author of the excellent Sherlock Holmes mystery stories was a medical doctor, I might have abnegated my duty as a host this evening and consulted you on my many and various ailments, insomnia being the chief one." He smiled. "But I believe I have already discovered the agent of my malady and effected a partial cure. I have excised a parasitic growth that was draining my energy and bringing my intellect down to that of a mere brute."

"A cancer?" I asked softly.

"Indeed, Doctor; a malignant entity known as the British Imperial Cabinet. I am heartily glad to be retired and rid of it. Campbell-Bannerman, and particularly that fellow Harcourt in full flow would beat down the constitution of a Hercules, and at least that gentleman had a cudgel to defend his interests."

I chuckled, then started as I looked over Lord Rosebery's shoulder and saw the man who had toasted me across the supper table examining a painting. Lord Rosebery followed my gaze. "Have you met Baron von Feldberg?"

He brought the baron to join us, made the introductions and then excused himself as a servant appeared and whispered something in his ear.

"We meet at last, Herr Doctor," Baron von Feldberg said to me in unaccented English.

I blinked at him.

"I suppose I should be angry with you, sir," he continued. "You have inconvenienced me and invaded my privacy."

I stiffened. "I have done nothing of the sort – at least not directly—"

"How would it be if I advised the Kaiser of my ill-treatment here, and he directed the same might be meted out to the English in Prussia? How would you like that, Doctor?"

Holmes appeared beside us. "I believe the only British people living in the state of Prussia, apart from your Kaiser's mother, are governesses. I would advise you not to cross swords with them. You may find that our British governesses are made of sterner stuff than you can manage. Mine was a gorgon."

The baron smiled. "Do you English take nothing seriously?"

Holmes wagged his finger. "British, Herr Baron. My colleague may have Scottish blood in his veins."

I considered. "Interestingly enough, that could well—"

The baron held out his hand to me. "I very much enjoy your stories, Doctor, as does His Imperial Highness. He devours his *Times* every day with his breakfast egg, and he has the *Strand Magazine, Punch* and *Comic Cuts* sent by courier to wherever he is."

We shook hands, and Baron von Feldberg leaned forward and continued in a low tone. "I enjoyed hearing of your little charade from my managers. In compliment to your ingenuity, please accept with my best wishes the case of champagne you borrowed. I hope it is not too sweet for your taste; I know you English like everything a little dryer than we Germans."

He put a finger to his cheek and smiled. "That reminds me. The Kaiser is making a study of English humour, your *badinage*, as he calls it. I have been instructed to gather materials to help him understand what is the true English (I'm sorry, British) wit. Can you think of any books or magazines that might be instructive?"

"He takes *Punch*," I said doubtfully.

"And as His Imperial Majesty also takes *The Times*," said Holmes, "he is well served for humour. Almost everything in that newspaper is in an ironic vein and should be taken with a pinch of salt."

Baron von Feldberg frowned. "I understood the Duke of Edinburgh and his wife were to be the guests of honour this evening. I do hope they are well and nothing is amiss."

"A slight indisposition, I understand," Holmes answered.

The baron bowed, thanked us and withdrew.

I turned to Holmes. "Baron von Feldberg was having a little fun with us. And we are no further forward on the abduction case. We have missed our deadline; tomorrow the affair may be in the Continental papers."

Holmes narrowed his eyes. "There is a saying about the last laugh, my friend. We are not finished with Baron von Feldberg. And we have much to do before midnight."

"Lord Rosebery's opening speech was instructive, Holmes," I said as we joined the stream of gentlemen moving towards the drawing room. "I didn't know Burns was a supporter of democracy."

"He went from Jacobite to Jacobin," Holmes said. "Burns lauded the American and French revolutions and sent cannon, or carronades at least, to the revolutionaries in Paris." He smiled. "It is interesting, is it not, that His Lordship managed to praise Burns as a champion of democracy and as a staunch Imperialist in a single paragraph of his oration. It shows how far Scots must trim their sails if they are to thrive in the management of Great Britain and her colonies."

"That is unfair," I retorted. "Lord Rosebery recognises that the British Empire is the only empire in history within which people may hope for improvement through work and application rather than an accident of birth or race."

Holmes chuckled. "You might have debated that with Mr Parnell and the Irish, or better yet with Caesar Augustus."

My reply was drowned by a skirl of bagpipes as the piper slow marched into the salon. A gorgeously dressed lady festooned with diamonds and pearls and a portly, bearded gentleman processed into the chamber behind him. The guests who were sitting stood, gentlemen bowed, and ladies curtsied.

Lord Rosebery appeared beside Holmes. "Here are our guests of honour, a little late, but the more welcome." He smiled. "I hope you will forgive me for not letting you in on our secret, gentlemen; I have a weakness for dramatic effects. My colleagues in the Cabinet often remarked on that defect of character, among my many other wee faults." He strode across the room to the couple, bowed and shook their hands.

"What the deuce?" I began. "Is that the Prince of Wales?"

Holmes shook his head. "His younger brother, Prince Alfred of Great Britain, Duke of *Saxe-Coburg und Gotha*, Duke of Edinburgh, etc., etc. And the lady on his arm is of course his wife, the Grand Duchess Maria Alexandrovna of Russia."

He sighed. "If someone would be kind enough to fling the Stone of Destiny in through the window, we could go home, wash our hands of the whole affair and have an early night."

LORD ROSEBERY

## 12 DO OR DEE

Lord Rosebery introduced Holmes and me to the Duke of Edinburgh.

"Have you eaten, your Royal Highness?" His Lordship asked.

"We have not," the duke replied. "My wife has taken no sustenance other than dry biscuits since we were captured. Rather prettily, our abductors provided her with *Maries*. We are both ravenous."

"I will have a meal laid out in my private dining room." Lord Rosebery bowed and hurried away.

The duke turned to Holmes. "You must join me at the table, Mr Holmes and Doctor Watson, and I shall tell you all. My brother has informed me you were indefatigable in your search for me, and for my dear wife, of course."

Holmes and I bowed, and the duke continued. "We will make no ceremony or fuss; we are abominably late, and Lord Rosebery must see to his guests. I hope you will have a glass of wine with me while I refresh the inner duke. My wife will make her arrangements with the ladies."

Lord Rosebery returned and ushered us across a magnificent marble hall hung with old masters and into an exquisitely decorated dining room. The Duke of Edinburgh, Holmes and I were seated at one end of a long table under a portrait of Lord Rosebery. The duchess and a clutch of ladies occupied the far end of the table under a crepe-draped portrait of the late Lady Rosebery. A dozen or more servants bustled around us laying plates and cutlery for the duke and duchess and providing Holmes and me with glasses, a fresh decanter of port and bowls of fruit and nuts.

"Say what you will," the duke said when he had settled himself and sampled the red wine offered him. "Grand Duchess Maria Alexandrovna was magnificent. When we were ambushed, my wife so industriously beat the rascals about the head with her parasol that they had either to subdue her or retreat from the field in ignominy. The scoundrels persevered, but at the cost of capturing the duchess as well as me. Ha! They had no idea what a fish they had landed!"

"Why did Her Royal Highness not escape when she could?" I asked.

"I conceive that you are not married to a Russian grand duchess, Doctor, the daughter of a tsar." The duke smiled. "You may not be aware that in such a case a husband is kept under strict control by the head of the household. When we are in London, Maria is prepared to allow me to take luncheon at my club (an all-male establishment, obviously) and permit regular excursions to Ascot and Cowes in season, but unsupervised gallivanting with revolutionaries is not to be sanctioned. My wife has strong views on radicals and their freedom from moral constraints, and she suspected there might be common strumpets in their rebellious lair."

He took another sip of wine and smiled. "She was in her terms proved right, as I shall relate."

The duke indicated for a waiter hovering beside us with a decanter to fill Holmes' glass and mine with red wine. "The window blinds of our coach were closed tight, but I could tell from the noise and clatter that we drove at first along the busy arteries of London. I am sure we crossed a park and then the Thames. The streets became narrower as we moved through meaner locales, then widened as we left the bustle of the city and entered a leafy suburb."

I took a sip of wine and frowned. Even my uneducated palate could tell it was a far superior vintage to that we had taken earlier.

The duke saw my expression and mistook my frown for doubt. "A shaft of light peeped in on one side of the window blind, Doctor, and it was filtered green by the foliage above us. Thus I deduced we were in the suburbs. Much like in your excellent story of the Greek Interpreter."

I bowed.

A waiter laid a plate of soup before the duke, and he crumbled bread into it and began to eat. "My wife and I were held at gunpoint in the carriage by two bearded desperadoes who seemed even more uneasy than we were. They grasped their pistols, old-fashioned rim-fire pieces with unguarded triggers, with little regard for our or their own safety. The road was often bumpy, and I feared an accident might occur and one or more of us injured. I considered disarming the fellows (despite their imposing beards, they were of slight build, and I still had my stick and pistol), but again it was possible someone might be hurt in the fracas. I had to factor into my scheme the scoundrels' accomplices and the response of my dear wife."

He sipped his wine and shrugged. "I suggested a truce; the duchess and I would make no move to escape and our captors would put up their pistols. They readily agreed, and our situation became more comfortable. Incidentally, as they pocketed their revolvers, I noted the chambers were clear: they were not loaded."

The waiter returned with more soup and we waited while the prince ate. "Do I detect prunes in this chicken soup?" he asked.

"You do," I answered.

"An odd combination," the prince replied with a smile, "but a very satisfactory one."

He sat back in his chair, patted his lips with a napkin and continued. "We were required to get down in a grassy lane bordered with high hedges and transfer to another coach. As we were ushered between carriages, I was astonished to see a young girl up on the box of the villains' equipage, holding the reins. She smiled and waved at me with a familiarity that caused my wife to abandon her previously buoyant mood and adopt her more usual restrained character."

"The duchess was not downcast," I exclaimed. "Even under the frightful circumstances you were in."

"Father Sergei, her chaplain, is something of a seer," the duke answered. "When we were in Coburg earlier this year, he prophesied that an outrage would be perpetrated against the duchess while she was in England for the Queen's Diamond Jubilee. He convinced my wife she should not stir from the safety of our palace. I poured scorn on the Sibyl and all his works, and I vowed I would consider it my duty to attend the celebrations alone if the duchess did not care to join me."

He sighed. "My wife has a high sense of duty, and when I reminded her that the Jubilee would be the first occasion when she, as the consort of a reigning duke, would take precedence over her English sisters-in-law, the tide turned, and she agreed to come."

He shook his head. "Naturally, when the prophesied outrage did occur, Maria and the priest were vindicated, and I was in disgrace again. Or 'in the soup' as my carriage driver in Sydney taught me. That was one of his tamer expressions, most were so vulgar that I could not use them even on the lower deck of my armoured cruiser, ha ha!"

The duke caught Holmes' impatient glance at me, and he continued his narrative. "The carriage stopped at a villa with a high-walled garden, and we were shown upstairs to bedrooms which were small, but adequate, with gas lighting, a shared bathroom and the usual offices. We were reminded of our parole and invited to dine at six. The girl brought jugs of hot water and towels."

A waiter presented the duke with a dish of haggis flanked by mashed potato and mashed turnips.

He frowned at the plate. "The girl served our food: plain, but wholesome fare." He looked up and smiled. "I refer only to the food, gentlemen; in fact the girl was very appealing, and I had high hopes of deepening my acquaintance with her if Maria, as I confidently expected, was speedily ransomed by the Tsar. I was sure our British Parliament would agonise for weeks over the expense of redeeming a Royal prince from durance vile, and the officials of my own dukedom are not renowned for their speedy decision making. I imagined I would be in my captors' hands for some time."

He shrugged. "It was not to be, and here we are at this interesting dinner. Have you any idea what meat, if meat it is, this mince is made from?"

"It would not be in your Royal Highness's best interests to enquire," Holmes replied in a confidential tone.

The duke nodded. "The Grand Duchess would have no truck with the girl as an attendant. She ordered her Russian lady's maid be instantly kidnapped from Clarence House and brought to her, as no other person on earth understood her hair. She also required the presence of her personal chaplain so she might make her devotions, but she graciously gave our captors a deadline of Sunday morning to perform that abduction."

He chuckled. "My Dear One refused to join us downstairs for dinner, berating the scoundrels for incompetence in not stealing her jewels. How, she asked, could she appear for dinner in a walking dress and without her evening emeralds? A tray of food was therefore delivered to her room, but it was not to her satisfaction, and she subsisted on dry biscuits and a light Sauterne. She pronounced the biscuits to be mere copies of the true *Maries* purveyed by appointment to the Russian Court by Messrs Peek Frean."

The duke stirred his meal with his fork. "My wife is almost as scathing on English cuisine as she is of our parliamentary system. She believes not only that we overcook our vegetables, but that the Commons is filled with radicals and nihilists. In her opinion, the country is little better than an ill-fed, howling democracy." He frowned, "What exactly is this orange substance?"

"Neeps," I offered.

"A new word for me, Doctor." The duke chuckled again. "I made an effort before my marriage to learn some Russian. '*Niet*' for our 'no' proved to be useful, as My Beloved uses it constantly. I continued my Russian studies after my marriage and 'tantrum' was one of the first words I learned (it is, as you might expect, a feminine noun)."

"Your abduction must have been a terrible experience, Your Royal Highness," I suggested.

He laughed outright. "I am a retired naval officer, gentlemen; after thirty-odd years in the Service it takes more than a few scallywags with empty revolvers to ruffle my feathers." He ate a tentative forkful of neeps and narrowed his eyes. "In the Navy, particularly in my youth, we did not have the cool rooms and bakeries we now have on our ships, and we were not over-nice with regard to victuals." He peered down at his plate. "I thought I was inured to – well." He put down his knife and fork. "What is for pudding?"

"Whisky trifle, then cheese and biscuits," I answered.

"No," the duke said firmly. "I am done. That excellent soup has set me up. One must be careful not to overeat after an emotional experience; it can heat the blood to a dangerous level. Pass the port and nuts."

The duke glanced at the ladies' end of the table and lowered his voice. "Actually, I thought my captors capital fellows, much like the young officers in the wardroom of my cruiser, the *Galatea*. After my wife retired to her room with her evening headache, the company downstairs dined merrily. We lit our cigars (which she abhors) and played *chemin-de-fer*. I won four shillings and this amber cravat-pin. I entertained my captors with nautical airs on the violin: music is my passion."

He bent across the table and lowered his voice even further. "It was the first time I have played a gambling game with a girl, a lady, well, no, a girl in fact. And the first time I have seen a girl of not more than sixteen years smoke a cigar. I have to say Miss Stuart was highly competent at both those activities."

He leaned back in his seat. "Our captors let us loose this afternoon, dropping us off at the cab rank by Westminster Bridge at ten to four. We got home to Clarence House, and I was about to send a telegram of regret for this evening, when my wife stayed me.

She was adamant we must attend Lord Rosebery's dinner. We might even have been on time, but she and her maid needed to be reacquainted in floods of tears before her hair could be attempted upon, and the duchess and I then attended an interminable service of thanksgiving conducted by Father Sergei in her private chapel."

The duke shrugged. "I felt the goodwill of our Russian Orthodox Sibyl was worth a Mass."

He smiled and lowered his voice again. "Thinking of Miss Stuart, I don't know about you, gentlemen, but I have come to the opinion that ladies, well, perhaps not ladies, but girls, need not be as—"

He stopped as his wife called a question down the table in French.

"Neeps," he answered her, and turned back to Holmes. "Gentlemen, to business. I would not have it generally known, but I not only gave my parole as an ex-naval officer, I made a pact with my captors as a condition of our release. Firstly, I agreed not to give information on my abductors' identities to the police or other authorities, other than the generalities I have acquainted you with, and then I made a solemn promise I would do what I could to right a wrong. Do you know anything of a Scottish royal crown in our possession, that is, in the possession of the English?"

"Taken from the baggage of the deposed King John Balliol of Scotland by Edward the First in 1299," said Holmes.

The duke frowned. "That may be so, I do not have details."

"I too have little information," said Holmes. "I only know the crown's existence has been denied by a high official of the government and by representatives of the College of Heralds."

"The government denies it exists?" the duke said with a long, slow smile.

Holmes returned the smile. "Emphatically."

The duke pursed his lips. "After such a statement by a high official of the government we must, of course, be satisfied. Nevertheless, if this missing crown were a coronet belonging to the duchy of *Saxe-Coburg und Gotha*, I would move heaven and earth to recover it. I would be derelict in my duty to my people if I did not. And now I am pledged to my captors to make every effort to find the crown. After all, I am Duke of Edinburgh: I have an equal duty to my

Scottish subjects. May I engage you in the matter, Mr Holmes?"

"To recover the crown to what purpose?" Holmes asked.

"To return it to Scotland. My captors vow their sole aim is to restore the crown to its rightful owners and place it with the Scottish Crown Jewels in Edinburgh Castle, there to be used as the will of the people of Scotland directs."

Holmes bowed. "In that case, I am at your service."

The prince leaned forward and lowered his voice to an almost inaudible whisper. "We might keep this between ourselves. If my mother got to hear, there would be repercussions. Even my nephew, Willy, is afraid of Mama." He raised his eyebrows. "The Queen can be definite in her views. She does not care for Maria: I break no confidences, the rift is well-known in our circles."

He sighed. "It is all very well for my older brother, Bertie; he can get away to Paris now and then. I am stuck in Coburg, a pleasant town but staid in its ways. There are no pretty things like Miss Stuart in Coburg (or in Gotha for that matter). It is an odd fact, but a fact nevertheless, that Bertie, the Prince of Wales and future king, may range abroad through Paris, even in the Montmartre district, without consequences (beyond my mother's censure), but I – ha!" He sighed again. "She really was rather lovely."

"Did your captors mention the Stone of Scone?" I asked. "Or Prussia?"

"The stone of what? We talked mostly of sport. Miss Stuart has decided views on racehorses and their pedigrees. She fancies my brother's horse Persimmon in the Goodwood Cup. I might hazard a guinea or two."

The duke tone hardened. "I have a duty in this matter of the Crown, Mr Holmes. Blood is everything, is it not? And the blood of Stuart monarchs runs in my veins."

We stood as the ladies left the table, gathered by the door of the dining room and were led away by footmen. The duke smiled a wry smile at Holmes and me. "You must meet my wife."

We followed the duke as a footman led him into a cosy sitting room where the ladies sat on overstuffed sofas and armchairs and tea was served. The duke presented us to the Imperial Grand Duchess. "Our indefatigable investigators," he declared.

Holmes bowed and held out the bracelet and locket and the ring he had found in the carriage. "May I return these to you, Your Imperial and Royal Highness?"

The duchess smiled. "Ah, you found them, Doctor. How clever of you. Father Sergei prophesied that you would."

"This is Doctor Watson, *Madame*," Holmes answered, indicating me with a sweep of his arm. "I am Sherlock Holmes, the consulting detective."

The duchess blinked at Holmes and held out her hand. "I am extraordinarily pleased to meet you, Mr Holmes. It is much like meeting Robin Hood or perhaps Mr Pickwick. I had thought you entirely fictional."

The Duke of Edinburgh took me aside as Holmes and the duchess continued their conversation.

"I am a great admirer of your works, Doctor Watson," the duke said. "But, do you tell me in all truth that the gentleman now talking with my wife is Sherlock Holmes, the master detective? Come now, Doctor, I believe you play a greater role in the matter than you will admit. Is not this Mr Sherlock Holmes a shadow figure set up for the amusement of the public? A puppet? He does not seem so very astute; I do not believe he knew the source of the grey mince."

I pursed my lips. "A puppet might be taking things too far, Your Royal Highness, but I will admit I am obliged to diminish my role in these little affairs to some degree. Ah, here is Holmes."

"I am afraid that we must leave you, sir," Holmes said. "We must return—"

He stopped as a page entered the room and looked around. The boy spotted me and held out a salver with a telegram on it. "Mr Sherlock Holmes, sir?"

Holmes took the telegram from the tray and read it. "More wreaths have been discovered, this time adorning statues in Parliament Square. It seems our conspirators have moved from the Scottish play to Julius Caesar."

"Any answer, sir?" the page asked me. I waved him away.

"The first message, found on Disraeli's statue is again in Gaelic," said Holmes. "Yet more maudlin barditry, I expect. The second, on the statue of Richard the Lionheart, is more direct."

*Lay the proud usurpers low,*
*Tyrants fall in every foe,*
*Liberty's in every blow!*
*Let us do or dee.*

I narrowed my eyes. "Let us do or dee? Is that reference to the River Dee? Could they be planning an attack on the Queen at Balmoral?"

"Dee is Scots for die," said Holmes. "Let us do or die; think the Charge of the Light Brigade at Balaclava."

Lord Rosebery appeared once more beside Holmes; he bowed to the Duke of Edinburgh and smiled at me. "Did I hear you quoting Burns, Doctor? You'll have Scots blood in your veins, I fancy."

"Well, as a matter of fact, my middle name—"

"Lord Rosebery," Holmes said over me. "Do you know anything of thistle wreaths with silk bands and verses?"

Lord Rosebery frowned. "I do. A wreath appeared on my front door this evening. I conceive it is from a well-wisher, as the sentiment written on the silk band is a quotation from my address at last year's Robert Burns centenary."

"You know nothing of other wreaths?"

"I do not."

Holmes gestured for me to show Lord Rosebery my notebook and the transcriptions of the first wreath, and Holmes handed him the message he had just received.

"This is Burns," said Lord Rosebery. "The verse is from his poem *Scots Wha Hae*."

"The tyrant is the king of England?" I asked.

"Yes, Edward the Second and all associated with him and with English oppression of Scotland generally. Burns wrote when the Highland Clearances were fresh in people's minds and the proscription on the Gaelic language and Highland dress and music had only recently been lifted."

Holmes glanced at his watch and then at me.

"You'll not leave us so soon, gentlemen?" Lord Rosebery said. "You'll miss the dancing. I borrowed some Highland troops from Lord Wolseley."

Holmes bowed. "We must make our farewells. I thank Your Lordship and Your Royal Highness for a most stimulating evening."

Holmes chatted with the duke and Lord Rosebery for a moment, and I made our farewells with the duchess.

"My husband has told me all," she said with a confiding smile. She looked over her shoulder, gave Holmes an amused glance and turned back to me. "I know who is man and master in your collaboration."

"I say, Your Royal Highness—"

"Imperial and Royal Highness," the duchess said stiffly. She smiled and tapped me playfully on the shoulder with her fan. "The world knows you English are maestros of deception, Doctor, but we of the Blood Imperial are not so easily deluded."

"Come," said Holmes. He instructed a footman at the front door to fetch a cab, and I followed him to the cloak room where we picked up our hats, gloves and sticks, and I my pistol.

I yawned. "Home?"

"Paddington Station. I have engaged a special train."

The footman led us outside to a waiting hansom.

"Holmes, I don't understand," I said as we settled ourselves and the cab set off for Paddington. "How can you act for the Duke of Edinburgh? You aim to recover the crown of Scotland for the villains who abducted him and very probably stole the Stone of Scone, when at the same time you act for the British Crown to recover the Stone!"

Holmes chuckled. "Where have I heard the duke's remark about the primacy of blood before?"

"Smoke and mirrors," I muttered to myself. "Mirrors and smoke."

## 13. SPOILS OF WAR

Holmes and I were greeted by an official of the Great Western Railway Company at the entrance to Paddington Station, and he ushered us across the crowded concourse to a platform where a train huffed and puffed as if in a hurry to be off. A single first-class carriage with private notices pasted on the windows was attached to the engine.

We climbed into the middle compartment. Holmes lay along his seat, tipped his hat forward and folded his arms across his chest. I sat opposite him and took childlike satisfaction in nodding to the railway official for him to signal the driver to depart.

We rattled through the darkened city at a fine pace, and soon we were passing suburban developments and then fields, grey-black in the soft moonlight. I pondered on the strange turn the abduction case had taken. I could not yet fathom a connection between the menacing verses, the return of the duke and duchess, the mythical Golden Crown and, of course, the missing Stone of Destiny. I felt we were moving forward, but towards what goal I could not tell. What might we find at Windsor?

The train slowed, its wheels screeching as we crossed a set of points, and Holmes stirred. "I suggest you load your piece, Watson," he said from under his hat brim. "I do not expect any violence, but there's a possibility I've read the runes wrongly, and we are up against a more desperate crew than I anticipate."

I loaded my gun, checking the chamber under the hammer was empty.

Holmes sat up and straightened his hat. "I believe an attempt will be made tonight on the vaults at Windsor Castle."

"The fiend!" I exclaimed, thumping my fist on my knee. "The charming baron sups with a peer of England, I mean Great Britain, and yet he plans a dastardly attack on one of her fortresses. There's your Prussian for you. And the Kaiser is behind it all, I do not doubt. What sort of grandson would do such a thing to his grandmother?"

Our train shuddered to a halt, and we stepped once more onto the platform of Windsor Station. The building was dark and deserted save for a fat railway policeman who led us to the exit, muttering crossly to himself and yawning copiously. He unlocked a metal grill across the gateway and let us out, and I followed Holmes to a carriage outside the station with its blinds down and the driver hunched on his box, fast asleep.

"I ordered a cab at an hourly rate through the railway company," Holmes said, heaving himself aboard.

I woke the cabby, clambered in after Holmes, and we covered the short distance to the imposing gateway to Windsor Castle in a few minutes. Holmes jumped down from the cab, and I followed him to the gate. He ignored the sentries in front of their boxes on either side, and he banged on the iron bars of the gate with his stick, demanding entrance.

A tall sergeant, made even more imposing by the huge bearskin he wore, stepped out of the guardroom, folded his arms and regarded Holmes through narrowed eyes. Two guardsmen armed with rifles and bayonets peeked out of the doorway behind him.

"We're closed," the sergeant said in a strong Scots accent.

Holmes produced the envelope Mycroft had given him and passed it through the gate. The sergeant accepted the letter with evident reluctance, peered at the seal in the light from a hanging oil lamp and shook his head. "I'll have tae fetch my officer."

Holmes snatched back the envelope, broke the seal with a sweep of his hand, scattering wax over the sergeant and me, and removed the single sheet of paper inside. He held it to the light of the lamp and read aloud.

"To whom it may concern. By this authority, our valued and trusted servant Mr Sherlock Holmes may enter our castle at Windsor and access all rooms, vaults and chambers without let or hindrance. We command our guards and officials to assist Mr Sherlock Holmes in any way he may require.

Signed this day, Victoria. Titles etc., etc."

The sergeant, guards and I stiffened to attention. Holmes folded the paper, put it back in its envelope and returned it to his pocket. "Kindly direct me to the Vaults," he said.

The sergeant opened the gate with a key from a ring on his belt and let us in. He beckoned one of his men. "Murray, go with the gentlemen and show them to the Vaults."

He turned to another guard and murmured instructions. The soldier handed his rifle to the sergeant, tucked his bearskin under his arm and pelted towards the castle.

Murray ushered Holmes and me along a path, through several gates and into an inner courtyard. We followed him to the Armoury, a large, stone-buttressed building with an entrance at the top of a flight of steps and several arched doorways at ground level, all blocked by iron grills.

The sentry box at the bottom of the steps was empty, and a rifle with a fixed bayonet leaned against the inner wall of the box.

"My God, Holmes," I said with a thrill of horror. "We are too late."

He gestured for silence, and we listened. I heard a girlish giggle coming from a little way off, then another. Holmes ordered Murray to take post in front of the sentry box, and he and I followed a tendril of tobacco smoke towards the source of the sounds. We came around a buttress and found a soldier leaning against the castle wall smoking a cigarette. A young, dark-haired girl in a flowery dress hung on his shoulder, whispering in his ear.

"Get back on guard!" Holmes ordered. The soldier gaped at us, dropped his cigarette and raced away.

The girl tripped across the grass and smiled up at me.

"Miss Stuart, I presume," Holmes said.

To my astonishment, the girl threw her arms about my neck and smiled in a most alluring and inappropriate manner.

Holmes turned away. "That's enough tomfoolery Watson, come along."

"This is Miss Stuart?" I asked Holmes as I gently disengaged her hands. "She is one of the abductors?"

"She is, and she is using her wiles in an attempt to delay us. Now grab her by the collar (or whatever the female equivalent of a collar is) and follow me."

I extracted myself from Miss Stewart's embrace and stood her against the Castle wall. "Now, young lady," I said sternly, "you heard what my friend said. Shall you come quietly?"

The girl curtsied. "I'll go with you, sir, and most happily."

"Very well," I said, smoothing my moustache. I motioned her before me, and we followed Holmes back to the entrance. Private Murray had disappeared. The guardsman standing stiffly outside his sentry box brought his rifle to the salute.

Holmes strode past the guard, climbed the steps, swung open the unlocked iron grill of one of the archways, and disappeared into the dark tunnel beyond. Gently ushering Miss Stewart before me, I followed Holmes down several flights of stone stairs dimly lit by lanterns set in alcoves. We came to a junction where our tunnel and another met in a small antechamber with two arched openings, each blocked by iron-barred gates. Holmes tried the first grill, which was locked, then the second, which swung open. We ducked under a low arch and entered a windowless chamber, its walls of dressed stone, lit by a single candle in a wall sconce.

I peered around the room and made out two young men in dark suits, one a youth and the other a little older, who lounged against an ancient ironbound door smoking cigarettes. The girl danced across the chamber to join them.

"What then, Masters Elwood?" Holmes said in a stern voice. "Would you take arms against your queen? I saw you with this young minx at Windsor Station."

The two boys exchanged smiles, and the older boy ruffled Miss Stuart's hair affectionately. "We meant no harm to the Queen, Mr Holmes," he replied in a faint Scots accent. "In fact, we were there to show our loyalty."

Holmes laughed. "No, no, you young deceivers, you wanted to make sure I was on the train to Scotland with Her Majesty, giving you free rein here tonight when you knew the garrison would be preoccupied with the Burns celebrations. But you must admit, I foxed you, for here I am."

"And here we are," said the older boy. I saw as my eyes became more used to the poor light he probably was not yet in his twenties. He nodded to his young companion, and they slid pistols from their belts, aiming at Holmes and me. I instantly drew my revolver, sighting at arm's length on the older of the two boys. "Holmes," I said softly. "The younger boy; I will not shoot a child even if he is a traitor."

"Child, sir?" the boy cried. "Traitor, sir? You'll answer for that remark, Doctor." He swung his revolver and pointed it at my midriff. "Kindly shift your aim to me."

I flicked my eyes to Holmes and raised my eyebrows. Holmes laughed again. "The Duke of Edinburgh told us that when his abductors holstered their pistols, he noticed the chambers were empty; the guns were not loaded."

The older boy grinned, and he hooked his pistol back into his belt. "We'll be happy to admit that fact, Mr Holmes, to every newspaper reporter who might care to interview us." His younger companion twirled his gun around the trigger, Buffalo Bill fashion, and returned it to his belt. I put my weapon back in its holster, feeling slightly foolish.

The older boy stepped forward and held out his hand. "Nathan Elwood, at your service, gentlemen."

We shook hands.

"And may I introduce my brother, Saul?"

I shook the boy's hand and frowned. "I know you."

Saul bowed.

"The young messenger in Regent Street with the diamond ring," Holmes said. "And Nathan was the aristocratic lounger in Baker Street. His trouser seat was polished by the school benches at Eton, and his shoes by his junior form servant, his fag. They watched the progress of our investigation and tweaked our noses."

I blinked at the boys.

Nathan smiled. "And you, Mr Holmes were the American gentleman in the white hat and fancy waistcoat who spent so long eyeing my reflection in the plate-glass window of the wine shop in Baker Street. You were your visitor to a 't', sir, except in one regard."

Holmes narrowed his eyes as he considered. "My walk."

Nathan nodded. "Your visitor had an odd, mincing gait far removed from your manly stride, Mr Holmes. You must think of these things when you take on a character."

"Thank you for the advice, Mr Elwood."

"We will publicly confess to removing the stone, gentlemen," Nathan said, "and kidnapping—"

"Abducting," I suggested.

"Eh? Very well, thank you Doctor, abducting the Duke of Edinburgh and his wife and breaking into the vaults of Windsor Castle. Our arrest will revive the cause of Scottish Nationalism and light a fire of liberty from ben to glen. We might mention the French Revolution and the Albanian League against the Ottomans."

Holmes sniffed. "On the whole, I doubt that the Albanian reference would be well received, and the French Revolution is not looked upon with approbation by most residents of these isles."

"Nevertheless, the penny dreadful newspapers can make a great deal of hay with very little straw," I suggested.

"A muddled metaphor, but a good point, Watson." Holmes turned back to the boys. "Gentlemen, please be so kind as to tell me what you are doing here."

Light from a lantern flooded the room, and I heard the click of a heavy revolver being cocked. "We are here," said a voice in a strong Scots accent, "to restore to the people of Scotland what is rightfully theirs. And we will brook no interference, Mr Holmes."

Holmes narrowed his eyes. "I suggest you turn your light away and lower your pistol, for it will avail you not at all. By this time a company of Guards has occupied the courtyard and all exits from the Castle will be double-stopped: you have no chance of escape."

I felt for the butt of my pistol and held it in the long pause before the beam of light shifted away from Holmes and to the ironbound door set into the wall.

A clergyman came into the chamber wearing a long, black surplice. He bowed to me, and he threw Nathan a packet of candles and Saul a box of matches. The boys lit the candles and set them in the corners of the room, and at last I could see the chamber clearly, and recognise Canon Blood!

He held up a bunch of keys. "What we have come to collect is behind that door, Mr Holmes. We intend to return a symbol, justly the property of Scotland, to the custody of that nation."

"Where did you get the keys?" I asked.

"I am personal chaplain to the warden of the Castle," Canon Blood replied in a stiff tone.

"That's how he got the boys into the Armoury," said Holmes. "The canon stole—"

"Borrowed," interjected the canon.

"Very well, *borrowed* the keys to this chamber from the warden. How is he, by the way?"

"Still sleeping soundly after a heavy meal of haggis, tatties and neeps. It is the anniversary of the demise of Robert Burns this evening."

"We have come from a celebration at Lord Rosebery's," I said.

"Are you a Scot, Doctor?" the canon asked with a smile. "I had an idea you might be."

"Well, I wouldn't go quite so far—"

"Drugged?" Holmes asked.

"The neeps," answered Canon Blood. "The Warden is fond of neeps."

There was a loud clamour and the thunder of heavy boots in the corridor, and an officer in formal mess uniform burst into the room brandishing a revolver. Guardsmen carrying rifles with fixed bayonets crowded behind him.

"What devilry is this?" the officer cried in a Scots accent. "What are unauthorised persons doing here in the Vaults?"

Holmes stepped forward. "I am Sherlock Holmes, consulting detective. Your sergeant no doubt sent a message to you from the gatehouse. I carry a personal authorisation from the Queen."

The officer looked Holmes up and down. "And I am not Captain A. R. Ferguson of the Her Majesty's Scots Guards, I am the Chang the Chinese Giant."

He dismissed Holmes with a wave of his revolver. "Ye'll all consider yourselves my prisoners; any trouble at all and I'll have ye in irons." He turned to his men. "Sergeant Grant stand fast and disarm the villains. Corporal Fraser assemble the detachment outside the door. None shall pass save with my permission."

"Aye, sir." The corporal saluted and led his men out.

I handed the sergeant my pistol, and the canon and Elwood brothers did the same.

"Now," Captain Ferguson said, giving Holmes a cold look. "Let's have no more nonsense. I'm in no mood for any havering tonight of all nights, with my soup going cold—"

"I demand the Balliol Crown in the name of the people of Scotland," said Canon Blood.

"Who are you to demand anything?" the captain replied, poking the canon in the chest with a white gloved finger.

"I am Isaac Blood, descendant of Colonel Thomas Blood who liberated the Crown Jewels from the Tower of London in 1671. I intend to return the Golden Crown of Scotland to its lawful place as the chief Honour of Scotland."

Captain Ferguson frowned. "I do not understand you, sir. What crown of Scotland is this? The Scottish Honours are in Edinburgh Castle. My company had the privilege of guarding them a year ago. I know of no other crown of Scotland." He snapped his finger at the sergeant. "Consult the inventory."

The sergeant took a sheaf of papers from a satchel at his side, held them to a candle sconce and frowned as he read aloud. "You are charged on perrril of your life tae guard the items on this list – etc., and so on." He flicked through several pages and ran his finger down a sheet. "There's no gold crown of Scotland mentioned, Captain, no' a single one."

"There, the Golden Crown of Scotland is not in the inventory of items kept in these chambers," Captain Ferguson said with a smug smile. "You are on a fool's errand, gentlemen, and your presence here is a felony. How the devil did you get past the sentry?"

The girl giggled, and I gave her a cold look.

"There are no records," said Canon Blood. "The English do not want it known they have the Crown, but it is here. You may have my word on it."

Captain Ferguson confronted Canon Blood. "How do you know?"

The canon drew himself to his full height. "A Scots gentleman is not be required to give his reasons, once he has given his word."

Canon Blood and Captain Ferguson regarded each other with cold, inimical stares.

"Captain," Holmes said, breaking the tense silence. "If the Golden Crown is not on your list, I fail to see how you are charged with the task of guarding it. Let us calm ourselves, and merely open the vault and see if the crown exists. If it is not there, what harm?"

A skirl of bagpipe music came from the yard outside, and I recognised the tune from our evening with Lord Roseberry. "They are piping in the haggis."

A soldier appeared at the door with a tray of glasses and a decanter of whisky. At a nod from Captain Ferguson, he poured us each a glass. I started forward when the girl took one, but Holmes held my arm.

"Canon Blood?" Holmes held up his glass of whisky. "A toast to the Golden Crown?"

The canon shook his head. "First to the memory of General Charles Gordon of Khartoum. And success to British arms against his murderers, the followers of the mad Mahdi in the Sudan." He drained his glass and called for another.

"General Gordon," we chorused.

Holmes turned to Captain Ferguson and raised his eyebrows. The captain swirled the whisky in his glass as he considered, then he frowned and shook his head. "No, sir. Whatever authority you may invoke, I must consult my superiors before we go any further in this matter. There may be agreements or conventions I am not party to. I have sent word to my colonel, but he hosts our Burns Night supper, so we must wait for him with what equanimity we can muster."

I offered Holmes my cigar case. "Whatever the outcome," I murmured, "it will not look good that the treasures of Windsor Castle were under the protection of the Scots Guards at the time of a raid by Scottish Nationalists. The newspapers—"

"What was that you said, sir," Canon Blood cried. "You impugn the loyalty of a Scots regiment at your peril, Doctor. The Scots Guards have taken a personal oath to the Queen! I must ask you to withdraw your remarks and apologise to the captain here or face the consequences."

Captain Ferguson stepped forward. "The Scots Guards is my regiment and I'll be the one to defend its honour."

Canon Blood poked the captain in the chest. "And I remind you, Captain," he said fiercely, "that Queen's Regulations do not perrrmit you to duel, and I further inform you that my family has called out more gentlemen than any other in these isles (not counting Ireland, naturally)."

Captain Douglas batted the canon's hand away. "And I remind you, Canon, that you are my prisoner, and I am responsible for your sorry life. I'll no' have Doctor Watson there take it withoot I'll have to face my colonel for derrreliction of duty."

Holmes took my arm. "We might move to the side here and let them come to their conclusions," he said quietly. He drew me across the chamber to where the two boys and the girl stood.

He smiled at the boys. "Your father was the Earl of Elwood."

"Aye, sir, he is sadly deceased, but we keep his name," said Nathan. "Our mother, also sadly deceased, was Scots." He sniffed. "Our stepfather is an Englishman."

"You are at Eton?" I asked.

"We are," Nathan answered with a smile. "Or were."

"What are your plans?" I asked.

"We'll not have Hamish endure Eton, sir," said Saul. "Nor will we return to the school. We have resigned."

I frowned. "Hamish? The boy we met in the Abbey?"

Holmes bent forward, plucked off the girl's dark wig and revealed a fair-haired boy. "James (Hamish in Scots) Elwood of the Westminster Abbey Choir."

The boy bowed and grinned at me.

I gaped at him "You were the flower girl in Regent Street! I bought a daisy from you!"

"He gave you fair warning, my dear fellow," said Holmes. "Remember Ophelia, daisies are for deception."

I wagged my finger at the boy. "You young scoundrel; I should take my hairbrush to you."

"I have no intention of allowing you to do so, Doctor Watson," James Elwood said in a surprisingly firm voice. He put his hands on his hips and glared at me. "I'll not accept English domination from this day onwards. Do your worst, sir, and take the consequences."

His eldest brother ruffled James' hair. "Hamish means no disrespect, Doctor. He was not carving his initials into the Coronation Chair when the dean caught him, he was hiding behind it ready to open the Abbey side door for us to take the stone. He accepted a thrashing from the dean so as not to give our plans away, but it's the last time he'll submit to English tyranny. That's why we can't put him to Eton with us; we'd spend every waking hour fighting his battles."

"So, we resigned," said Saul.

I frowned. "Can you do that?"

Ethan shrugged. "We consider it is a matter of not paying the fees and not turning up for lessons. We'll tutor Hamish at a Scottish school, and Saul and I will apply for Edinburgh University. Our uncle, the Earl of Elwood after our father's death, will take us in."

"What possessed you to kid– to abduct the Duke of Edinburgh," I asked.

"We meant no harm to the duke," Saul said. "We wished to offer him our hospitality until we had completed our arrangements for the Scottish monarchy to be revived. We wrote in general terms to sound out the feelings of Marie of Bavaria, but we did not receive a favourable reply. We therefore hoped to persuade the duke to accept sovereignty of the Scottish nation (he has Stuart blood in him through his ancestors) so that, when the sad time comes and our Queen is no more, he and his brother would be co-equal monarchs and friendly relations between England and Scotland would be assured."

"To be frank with you gentlemen," Nathan said in his soft voice, "we soon fervently wished to return the grand duchess and the duke; particularly, if I may make so bold, the lady."

Saul nodded. "And the royal gentleman is fond of music; he makes his attempts on the violin, and unfortunately we had one in the canon's house. Brawling cats wasn't in it, Mr Holmes."

"What is your relationship with Mr Macdonald, the illusionist and Mr McNair of the News Agency of the North?" Holmes snapped.

The boys frowned. "I don't believe we know the gentlemen," said Nathan.

"What of the wreaths and verses?" I asked.

"That was Saul's idea," said Nathan. "We wished to give the English fair warning of our aims; we have done nothing underhand."

"And the Stone?" I asked.

The boys exchanged amused glances.

Holmes turned to me. "You may remember I suspected more than one man, but less than a whole number of men. I meant the Canon and young Elwood. They took the Stone of Scone."

"Ha!" I said coldly, glaring at James. "The boy lies as readily as our pageboy."

"I resent that, sir!" cried James.

"And I!" cried Nathan

"And I!" cried Saul. "I will require satisfaction for you giving my brother the lie."

"I am the eldest," Nathan said to his brothers in a menacing tone. "It is for me to act in the matter."

"But I am the better shot," Saul said reasonably.

"We might move again to let them thrash out the question," said Holmes. "Come, James."

We moved to a quieter corner of the chamber. The argument between Captain Douglas and the canon had grown fiery, and the two Elwood boys were shaking their fists at each other.

"You really must not call me a liar, gentlemen," James said in a voice close to tears. "It is a most unfair accusation. The Stone of Destiny was never in Westminster Abbey. The Stone is in a safe place known only to the Lord of the – well, I must not say. King Edward was fobbed off with a drain cover. We took the stone to make that fact known. We intended to return it when the government admitted it is fake. You will recall you asked me if I filched the Stone of Destiny, which I hadn't. I did not lie."

"A Scottish sophist," Holmes said, frowning down at the boy. "Very well, but your nonsense in the Abbey did not fool me. I knew the Stone (or drain cover) never left the Abbey. The sandstone particles you sprinkled so carefully along the floor in a trail to the river exit did not dupe me or my brother, though he would have had me believe he was fooled. Ha!" He smiled. "I unreservedly apologise to you, young Elwood for calling you a liar (frankly, Watson and I have a plethora of duels on hand at the moment or we might be tempted to debate the matter more thoroughly with you)."

I added my apology to Holmes' and shook the boy's hand.

"However, young man," Holmes continued. "You should be ashamed of yourself. You took Doctor Watson's peppermints under false pretences."

James hung his head.

"What do you know of the Sons of the Thistle?" Holmes asked.

The boy looked up and smiled. "I know it well, sir." He began to sing in a sweet treble that rang and echoed in the chamber. He was joined in the chorus by his brothers, Captain Ferguson and the sergeant.

*'Success to our soldiers wherever they be,*
*For they are the lads that still keeps us free;*
*The bravest on earth that ever has been,*
*Are the sons of the thistle and shamrock so green.*

*"Old England is proud, but what would it have been,*
*Were it not for the thistle and shamrock so green."*

The chorus of the song was taken up by the soldiers outside, then by a distant piper.

*"Old England is proud, but what would it have been,*
*Were it not for the thistle and shamrock so green."*

The company applauded, and James took a bow.

"Now away with you," Holmes said. "Pacify your brothers, if you will."

Holmes grinned as the boy tripped across the chamber. "I suspect the rock is secreted under Elwood Minimus's bed. It was no symbol of nationalism for our conspirators; they firmly believe it to be a drain cover. Its theft was a warning to the government that at least one section of Scottish opinion was not fooled by the pathetic sops the Scots have been offered instead of a regular assembly. I do not think they were serious with their offers to Marie of Bavaria or to the Duke of – ah, here is the duke. I invited him to join us."

The Duke of Edinburgh appeared at the door of the chamber wearing the uniform of a British admiral. "I am sorry I'm late, Mr Holmes. The sentries outside were officious. And my wife—" He spread his arms. The sergeant handed him a glass of Scotch.

"Well, gentlemen, lady and captain," he said, looking around. "I am the Duke of Edinburgh, admiral in the Royal Navy, honorary colonel of the London Volunteer Artillery, a royal prince and reigning duke of Saxe-Coburg and Gotha." He smiled. "What's going on? Have you found the Golden Crown?"

"We are at an impasse, Your Royal Highness," Holmes said. "May I present Captain Ferguson of the Scots Guards? We are his prisoners. And this is Canon Blood of Westminster Abbey. He is the chief conspirator in the matter of your abduction and the theft of the Stone of Destiny. The now-beardless Elwood brothers you know, of course."

"I am Nathan, sir," said the oldest boy, shaking the duke's hand. "This is Saul and this James."

"I hope Her Imperial Highness is quite well," said James.

The Duke of Edinburgh gave the youngest boy, still in his floral dress, a narrow look. "My wife is as well as can be expected, under the circumstances. She takes the Boat Train for Paris tomorrow, and then to St Petersburg for a recuperative holiday."

Holmes explained Captain Ferguson's reluctance to open the vault without permission from his superior officer.

"That is easily remedied," the duke said. "I am the captain's superior, by blood, by station and by rank, and this is my mother's home." He faced Captain Ferguson. "Captain, I command you to open the vault."

The captain considered for a moment, then nodded. "Very well, sir, we will enter the vault. But you must all kindly remember I have my men outside armed and as peeved as I am about missing our supper."

Canon Blood chose a large key from the keyring and held it up. Captain Ferguson nodded permission, and the canon inserted the key into the lock and turned it. He and the captain pulled the heavy door open.

The canon picked up his lantern, and the company followed him through the doorway into a rough-hewn chamber with a low stone roof. Directly across from the door were three iron-gated cells. The Elwood boys brought candles, and Holmes and I lit the oil lamps that hung from brackets on the walls.

I examined the cells as the room brightened. Each had a yellowed printed notice affixed to the gate. The first read 'HM the Queen', the second, 'Visitors' and the last 'Misc'. Each cell held stacks of leather cases and portmanteaus, and wooden crates stood on shelves. A pair of baited rat traps lay on the floor of each cell.

"The first chamber holds valuables belonging to Her Majesty (those not kept at the Tower) such as her day and evening jewels and the tiaras and necklaces worn at balls," said Captain Ferguson. "Many of the boxes have not been opened since the death of Prince Albert. The second cell houses similar items belonging to members of the Royal Family and distinguished visitors to the Castle; the Queen's daughters leave some of their British orders and decorations here when they are abroad. The last is for household items: odd sets of cutlery, mismatched vases after breakages and so on. An American delegation came to congratulate the Queen on her golden jubilee in '87, and they made off with dozens of items of cutlery embossed with the Queen's cypher; we now use plain cutlery and store the odd cyphered cutlery and plates here. The Crown Jewels and other ceremonial items used only on special occasions are secured in the Tower of London, of course."

I turned to Canon Blood. "Why did you not attack the Tower like your ancestor?"

He laughed. "We have no interest in English gewgaws. Your Crown Jewels are mere replicas of those sold off or destroyed by Oliver Cromwell; why should the Scots covet them? The Golden Crown of Scotland is far more ancient. We Scots don't want English cast-offs; we want our crown." He held up an antique key. "It is in the long chest on the second shelf to the right of the last cell."

"Canon Blood took the key from the Warden," Holmes explained to the duke.

"Borrowed, sir." Canon Blood handed the key to Captain Ferguson, who looked to the duke.

"Open it," the duke ordered.

Captain Ferguson unlocked the grill and swung it open. He and Canon Blood dragged the long, dusty leather case the canon had indicated from its shelf, carried it out of the cell and deposited it on the floor of the chamber.

The Canon selected another key from the ring, bent down and unlocked and removed a padlock. He undid a pair of straps, lifted the lid of the portmanteau and disclosed a pile of brown-paper-wrapped and wax-sealed parcels. He smiled up at the Duke of Edinburgh and gestured for him to take out the first item.

"No, no," said the duke. "Go ahead. Don't mind me."

"More light," said the canon, and the Elwood brothers held candles over the case as Captain Ferguson bent and picked up a long thin package wrapped in brown paper and tied with twine.

"That is no crown," I said. "A sceptre perhaps?"

Nathan held out his pocketknife. Captain Ferguson cut the twine, undid the parcel and disclosed a spear with a leaf-shaped blade and a short handle. "It's a Zulu assegai," he said. "My father has a couple on the wall of the gunroom at home, souvenirs of the Natal War of '79."

I nodded. "The massacre at Isandlwana and the brave defence of Rorke's Drift."

Holmes took the assegai and examined it through his glass. "Not just any assegai, gentlemen. This was the symbol of authority of Cetchawayu, King of the Zulu nation, who we deposed at the end of the war. I believe he was lodged in Kensington."

"What else?" Canon Blood asked impatiently.

Captain Ferguson delved into the chest once more and brought out a gaudy, moth-eaten yellow umbrella.

"A symbol of office of the deposed King Thibaw of Burma," said Holmes. "You will recall the war in Upper Burma in the eighties."

Captain Ferguson continued to remove packages from the case, revealing souvenirs of the Empire's many wars. One hatbox looked most promising. Captain Ferguson prised off the lid and found not the Golden Crown, but a silver chamber pot studded with gilt bees.

"The bee was the symbol of the House of Bonaparte," said Holmes.

"The rest is mouldy rags," Captain Ferguson said, standing and wiping his gloved hands with his handkerchief.

Holmes knelt and plucked something from the debris at the bottom of the case. He held it to the light of the boys' candles and smiled. It was a thin gold circlet set with dusty gems and with a cap of threadbare and faded royal-blue silk.

"The Golden Crown of Scotland," Canon Blood said in an awestruck voice.

"A literal spoil of war," said Holmes, wrinkling his nose. He handed the crown to Canon Blood.

The captain and the Elwood brothers returned the other trophies to the portmanteau and locked it in its cell, and we trooped out of the vault with the canon leading, carrying the crown high. We assembled again in the antechamber.

"What now?" asked the duke.

Holmes faced Captain Ferguson. "My dear sir, my colleague and I unreservedly apologise if any remark of ours could have been misconstrued as a defamation of the Scots Guards, of Scottish regiments in general or in particular, or of the Scottish nation. We have the highest regard for the history of your corps and of the probity and loyalty of your officers and men. I hope you will take this apology and our hands in the spirit in wish we offer both."

The captain nodded and took his hand. "A fine sentiment, sir, and well put. Let us have a dram together to seal our compact of friendship."

A piper in the yard outside began another tune on the bagpipes as a private came into the chamber with a fresh decanter and a tray of whisky glasses.

"How do they do that on cue?" I asked.

"Tae Rabbie Burns, gentlemen, deed this night," the captain said, holding up his glass.

We drained our glasses.

"And now," the captain continued, "Your Royal Highness and gentlemen, we have only a few hours left of this Burns night and I must dismiss my company so they may take their supper. Then we and the Highlanders in the Queen's service have a mind to dance. You are welcome to join us."

"Alas," said Holmes, "we are engaged." He glanced at his watch. "We must bid you farewell."

"What do we do with these fellows?" I asked, indicating the canon and the Elwood boys.

The duke glanced at young James in his dress and reddened. "I do not intend to lay a charge. We must keep the matter out of the public eye."

Canon Blood grinned. "King Charles gave my ancestor Colonel Blood not only a full pardon, but a considerable pension and lands."

"You are lucky to escape the Rope," the duke growled. "You are in one of the most secure fortresses in Europe, guarded by the Queen's Guards; hold your tongue if you do not wish to remain here at her leisure."

"What of the crown?" I asked Captain Ferguson as he escorted us to the door of the antechamber. "Why is it so important?"

He leaned forward and answered in a low tone. "Canon Blood considers the crown a symbol of the triumph of the proud spirit of the Scottish nation over the shallow world of Hanoverian avarice and greed." He smiled and shrugged. "The canon is an assertive gentleman, even for a Scots clergyman."

"Will you give the crown to him?"

"A tricky business, sir, best left for us Scots to decide. We'll all have a wee talk when my colonel gets here." He saluted the duke, Holmes and me at the door, then he shook my hand and bent towards me again. "I'm an avid reader of your works, Doctor," he said softly, "You'll no' convince me yon fellah is the real Sherlock Holmes, ha, ha. I'm no' so soft as to credit that."

Holmes, the duke and I said our goodbyes to Canon Blood and the Elwood brothers. Young James was tapping his feet to the skirl of the pipes. We passed out of the Castle and walked across to a side gate accompanied by a sergeant and a pair of soldiers, and we were challenged by sentries several times before we reached the gatehouse.

"How did the boys plan to remove the crown, Holmes? They had to pass all these guards, then survive the scrutiny of more guards at the gate."

"They planned to secrete the crown in James' petticoats."

I smoothed my moustache. "Good Lord, Holmes."

We stopped before the main gate, and Holmes addressed the duke. "Your Royal Highness, I booked a supper table this evening at the Café Royal, but we are a little late, and our business is not quite concluded. I wonder if you would do me the honour of accepting my invitation to an early breakfast. I may say it is a purely bachelor affair."

The prince bowed. "I accept with pleasure, sir, on condition it is my treat."

Holmes smiled. "There is one more port of call I wish to make tonight, and again I have the temerity to suggest Your Royal Highness might like to join me. A conspiracy against the Crown must be rooted out from a location not far from here. There may be some danger."

The prince's eyes lit up. "I did not bring my revolver. Should I borrow a weapon from the armoury?"

Holmes smiled and bowed. "We should be glad to have Your Royal Highness as our third musketeer."

The duke hurried back to the castle, and Holmes and I passed through the main gate and waited by our carriage. I took a cigar from my case and lit it with a match. "What will they do with the crown, assuming Captain Ferguson lets it go? Will they bring Marie from Bavaria and crown her as the Queen over the water, or will they press the Duke of Edinburgh to be their sovereign?"

"We must wait and see."

The duke crossed the forecourt beaming at us and waving a long sword in a scabbard. Holmes spoke to our driver, and we clambered into the four-wheeler and set off, the duke's carriage following ours.

"What was that nonsense Canon Blood said about the Crown Jewels?" I asked.

"Oh, it's true enough. His ancestor Colonel Blood snatched several of the Jewels from the tower, crushed St Stephen's crown so it would fit under his accomplice's petticoats and sawed the Great Sceptre of England in half. He was caught, but King Charles II forgave him. Some say Colonel Blood had information on Charles that would have shaken the monarchy. Our kings and their consorts of the period did not have the staid home life of our own dear Queen."

"How did the canon persuade the Warden to inform him of the whereabouts of the Golden Crown? And how did you know the conspirators would strike at the Vault?"

"I looked Canon Blood up in Crockford's register of Anglican clergy and found he is chaplain to the Warden of Windsor Castle, his confessor in fact. The canon's obsession with the Scots crown led him to take up positions in the Abbey and the Castle, two likely places for the prize to be secreted. The boys watched us set off for Scotland with the Queen on the Royal Train, or so they thought. With a Scottish regiment guarding the Vaults, Burns Night was the obvious choice for their venture."

"Confession!" I exclaimed. "Now you see why I do not condone the practice."

THE KAISER

# 14 SONS OF THE THISTLE

The moon was high and bright, and details of fields and copses and darkened farmhouses were clearly visible as we clattered along the narrow road, the sole travellers at that early hour. The weather was still sultry, the atmosphere was heavy and the air in our carriage was close, even with the windows open.

We crossed a stone bridge over the Thames and made our way by the same path the horseless carriage had hurtled along the day before. Our carriage passed the gates of our rented villa.

"I assume we are going to Baron von Feldberg's lair, Holmes. How do you propose to gain entry?"

"I have already effected an entry."

I frowned. After one of his Sibyl-like pronouncements, Holmes was apt to be as taciturn as a Red Indian chieftain, but at one in the morning after a busy day and night, I was stung into demanding an explanation. "How?"

Holmes yawned. "Dogs and handler are drugged: the beasts with doped meat and the gatekeeper with a bottle or two of fine Scotch whisky."

"The high walls and spikes?"

"We will enter through the gates."

"The keys?"

"Obtained by an appeal to patriotism, accompanied by a thumping great bribe."

Holmes smiled at my puzzled look. "You know I left Rankin behind at our rented villa. He spent last evening at the Royal Stag public house. As I had surmised, with the baron in London and the household given notice, the discipline of the servants was not as it should be. The butler set the tone by spending Monday to Wednesday evenings on his favourite stool in the public house. His name is Jevons, and he is from Dumfries."

I groaned. "Another Scot."

"Rankin plied him with drink, mourned the loss of his position with him, offered him government gold and soon made him an ally. The baron is no longer loved by his employees (if he ever was). This evening, the keys of the house were given to Rankin, just before Jevons passed out, the richer by fifty gold sovereigns."

"A heavy bribe."

Holmes smiled. "Remember,

*'English gold has been our bane,*
*Such a parcel of rogues in a nation'."*

Holmes shook his head. "The sentiment is clear enough, but it really does not scan."

The gates of Baron von Feldberg's villa were open and our carriage and the duke's following us passed through unmolested. We drove along a sweeping gravel drive and drew up under the portico of a fine Georgian manor house with newer wings on each side in the same style. The strange gantries at the ends of the building loomed over us and cast long menacing shadows across the lawn.

"They are like miniature Eiffel Towers," I said. "And just as hideous."

Rankin appeared with a ring of keys in his hand. As he made his report to Holmes and the duke, I peered through the tall, dark ground-floor windows of the house, but I could make out nothing of the interior. I walked to the front doors and pushed. To my surprise, they swung open to reveal a marble-floored hall with twin staircases leading to the upper floors and the two wings. The hall had a silent, eerie quality in the bright moonlight.

Holmes came up beside me holding a lantern.

"Servants?" I asked.

"Gone, you will recall they were dismissed; there is only the gatekeeper, and he is in a stupor." He looked at his watch. "The baron is due from London in the morning. We have until dawn."

"What are we doing here, Holmes?" I asked. "Are we searching for the Stone of Destiny? I thought you said—"

"The matter is darker than that," Holmes replied in his irritating, enigmatic style. "We act to prevent a pan-European conflagration."

The duke joined us carrying a lantern, and he, Rankin and I followed Holmes across the black-and-white chequered floor of the hall and through a set of double doors into a fine, large room that formed the front of the west wing. The light from our lamps was reflected in tall pier-glasses and a pair of crystal chandeliers that hung from a plasterwork ceiling. The chamber was a reception room, furnished with elegant side tables, delicate chairs and spindle-legged sofas.

We passed through more double doors into the next room, a dining room facing the garden behind the house, then we returned to the hall, mounted the stairs and continued our reconnaissance on the upper two floors of the west wing. Holmes flashed his light over the opulent furnishings of a sitting room, a music room and a billiard room on the first floor, and well-appointed bedrooms on the floor above. He marched backwards and forwards across each room, apparently at random.

"I say, old man," I said at last. "Shouldn't our attention be focused on the mysterious east wing?"

Holmes smiled. "You are quite right. Lead the way, Rankin."

We followed Rankin downstairs to the hall, up the right-hand staircase and along a corridor lined with paintings of racehorses and glass showcases crowded with china figures.

"Dresden," Holmes said, peering into one case. "Rather fine."

A green-baize-covered door blocked the corridor. Holmes motioned Rankin forward, and he tried several keys from the ring he carried.

"I got these from the porter," Rankin said in a surprisingly cultured Scots tone. "He is a *Prooshyan* and a military type. He attacked the whisky with élan, gentlemen, and only succumbed after the last dram had been expended. I tied him up and left him with the drugged dogs in the gatehouse." Rankin opened the door, and we filed into a library.

The duke shone his lamp along the spines of rows of leather-bound volumes. "Military history for the most part, with some volumes of German illustrated magazines – oh, I say." He pulled one tall volume from the shelf and opened it on a reading desk. "Japanese erotica."

I peered at the drawings and sniffed. "The baron has odd tastes."

The duke returned the book to its place, took up his lantern and led us through a series of rooms: another billiard room, much larger than its equivalent in the opposite wing and set with three tables, a room fitted as a gymnasium with the latest rowing machines and electric horses and the final room on the floor, a chapel with pews for a congregation of fifty or more.

Holmes shone his lantern around the chapel.

"I wonder who the baron invites to worship here," I said. "From the accounts I have heard, his Friday and Saturday night guests are not of a saintly character."

The Duke of Edinburgh poked his head around the door. "Come and see what we've found." He led us up a further flight of stairs to a corridor matching the bedroom floor of the opposite wing. He opened the first door and shone his lamp inside. Instead of the elegant four-poster beds and wardrobes that furnished the guest rooms in the west wing, this room was crammed to the ceiling with bunk beds.

"It's a dormitory," I exclaimed.

"The other rooms on this floor are the same," said the duke. "There's bed space for a hundred or more."

I frowned. "Is Baron von Feldberg opening a boarding school? Or perhaps the villa was a school before he took it over."

"Come," Holmes said, leading the way out.

Rankin stood in the corridor. "I can find no access to the top floor, Mr Holmes, or to the cellar, if there is one. The main stairs go from the ground level to this floor only." He held up three keys from the ring. "These don't fit any doors so far."

Holmes nodded. He paced along the wall of the corridor, sounding the panels with a rap of his knuckles and kneeling to examine the skirting board. He reached the end and stopped before a tall mirror set into the wall with a small table and a vase filled with silk flowers in front of it.

He took out his magnifying glass, peered at the edge of the mirror, turned and smiled. "The occupants of those bunks will use the staircase to reach the newly constructed dining hall and facilities for their ablutions in the back garden; very well. But there should be an upper floor and a basement in this wing matching those in the opposite wing; if so, there must be another method of access. By the rough measurement I took pacing the rooms of the west wing, this corridor is nine feet shorter than its companion on the other side. There is a hidden staircase or lift."

Holmes moved the table aside, slipped his hand behind the mirror and released a hidden catch. The mirror swung away from the wall to reveal a door, which the first of the three odd keys opened, disclosing a landing with narrow stairs leading up and down. We filed through the doorway and followed Holmes up to the next floor.

The second key opened a door into a large room furnished as an office. Shelves of books lined the walls, and crates and packing cases lay against the far wall. A desk piled with technical journals and reference books stood between the curtained windows.

The duke and Rankin went through an archway into the adjoining room. I lit the oil lamp on the desk and picked up a magazine, an issue of *The Electrician* from December of 1895. One article was marked with underlinings, exclamation marks and notes in the margin in German. "I say, Holmes, Baron von Feldberg has an interest in electricity, if the annotations are his."

The Duke of Edinburgh peered through the doorway from the next room. "This is a telegraph office."

Holmes and I joined the duke in a chamber lined with waist-high benches crammed with apparatus. In the farthest corner, a brass tube, six inches in diameter, ran from floor to ceiling like a fireman's pole.

"This equipment is similar to that illustrated in the programme of a lecture my brother Bertie attended last month at the Royal Institution," said the duke. "It was on Mr Marconi's work on 'Signalling in Space without Wires'. Bertie said he slept through most of the demonstration (he's not of a technical bend of mind), but he gave me the programme to show my son, Affie, who's interested in anything electrical. Last month I took the boy to see work on wireless telegraphy being done by the Royal Navy Torpedo School at Devonport."

"What sort of range would a wireless telegraph device have?" Holmes asked.

"I believe our chaps have achieved distances of six thousand yards or more. Call it three miles or so."

Holmes sniffed. "It is at least three hundred miles to Edinburgh and double that to Berlin. The baron would need a much more powerful machine to signal messages to his masters. Could this apparatus be capable of reaching so far?"

I looked closely at the machinery, particularly at a large horn attached to brass fittings and wired to a complicated system of connected boxes. It reminded me of my elderly neighbour's ear trumpet at the Burns dinner. "I believe that is some form of mouthpiece, like a telephone," I said. "This may be a machine to magnify the voice by electrical means, a giant megaphone."

Holmes smiled. "Perhaps, in the event of hostilities between the German Empire and Great Britain, the baron aims to yell rude words at the Queen in Windsor Castle."

I ignored his gibe and idly snapped up a lever on the apparatus in front of me. To my consternation, it came crackling and sparking to life. There was a hiss of hydraulics and the brass pole in the corner of the room slid smoothly up to five feet or so from the floor. An eyepiece or monocular was visible at the base, with a handle on either side.

"A periscope," the duke said, darting to the pole. "I saw one on a Bruce-Partington submarine a couple of years ago." He bent, peered through the eyepiece and twisted the handles. "This device extends through the roof and gives a view across the countryside for miles."

The duke stepped back and invited me to look. An image sprang into sharpness in the bright moonlight. "Windsor Castle. My God, I can see every detail of the battlements." I swung the periscope and viewed the countryside surrounding the villa. I saw our rented house through the trees, and beyond it the few lights still burning in Windsor. A series of flashes in the distance caught my eye. "There's a storm brewing; the weather may break at last."

The duke leaned over a desk in a corner of the room. "Here are notes in German for a message; the topics are itemised. First, 'There is a rumour that Prince Alfred and his wife Grand Duchess Maria have been kidnapped by Irish fanatics'." The duke took a propelling pencil from his pocket and scribbled on the paper. "I substituted 'abducted' for 'kidnapped'."

He frowned. "This section on cavalry tactics is not only out of date, it is badly phrased. And here on the second page is a scandalous rumour about – a certain personage – without the slightest basis in fact." He crossed out a long block of text. "The rest of the message is a report on the defences of our naval facilities at Portsmouth. Ha! It is wildly inaccurate."

Holmes gestured for me to follow him. "We might leave His Royal Highness to his editing while we continue our search."

He turned to Rankin. "See if you can find a way onto the roof; I'd like to take a closer look at those towers."

Holmes led me back through the door and down the secret stairs, past the dormitory floor to the ground floor. The last key on the ring opened a door into a room furnished as a study in the clubroom style. An oil lamp and telephone apparatus stood a fine mahogany desk placed between two closely curtained windows. Opposite the windows, three tall pier glasses hung against the wall with bookshelves set between them; a massive green safe occupied the far corner of the room.

I lit the oil lamp, and Holmes knelt in front of the safe and rubbed his palms together. "As we are here, we might take the opportunity to have a peek at the baron's papers."

I stiffened. "I do not believe we have the right to riffle the contents of the Baron's safe. We have found unusual equipment and the sort of military information one would find in the pages of the *Illustrated London News,* but nothing except mere gossip suggests that the baron is a spy."

Holmes laid out his leather wallet of instruments.

"We cannot prove von Feldberg had anything to do with the abduction of the duke and duchess, the theft of the Stone or the Sons of the Thistle," I said. "We must withdraw."

Holmes selected a pick.

"It will not do, Holmes; it would be like stealing his snuff box." I picked up a tiny box enamelled with the Prussian Imperial eagle from a side table.

"What of the periscope?" Holmes asked as he peered at the safe lock. "You saw that the defences of the Castle are laid bare. What of the reports on Portsmouth and on cavalry tactics?"

I considered. "If the periscope were sighted at Dover or Portsmouth, I would be much more concerned. A spy would be able to count the masts of our fleet and make notes on new vessels, stores and musters. But Windsor Castle is an ancient fortress with little value in a modern war. And the duke says the naval report is wildly inaccurate and the cavalry information dated."

"Windsor has great symbolic value," Holmes said as he inserted a pair of picks into the lock. "Particularly when the Queen is in residence."

I blinked at him. "You cannot think the Prussians mean to lay hands on Her Majesty!"

Holmes smiled. "Let us see what we shall see."

I watched in frustration as Holmes twisted the picks in the lock.

"More light."

I held the lamp high and heard a click as Holmes pulled the safe door open. He took out stacks of papers, envelopes and folders, some tied with legal tape, and leafed through them. He frowned. "Private papers: leases, bank accounts; nothing with a Scottish or military connection."

I sniffed an 'I told you so' sniff.

Holmes stood and narrowed his eyes as he quartered the room. "If not in the safe, then where?"

He searched the room most thoroughly, checking the drawers of the desk and closely examining the bookshelves. He sat at the baron's desk and spread his hands on the leather desktop. "The baron is a careful man. He does not keep incriminating papers in his secret study. I say again, then where?"

He took a sheet of paper from a drawer, dipped a pen into the ink reservoir and drew a rectangle, dividing it into three. He marked the leftmost section with an 'X'. "The kitchens are here, in the basement of the west wing. Again, assuming an architectural balance, we might conjecture a basement under this eastern wing. How is it accessed? The secret stairs go no farther down than this floor."

I pointed to the mirrors that stood against the wall opposite the windows. "The baron favours mirrors, Holmes."

"He does."

I scrutinised the panels and the wooden beading surrounding the mirrors as Holmes crawled along the skirting board between the bookcases, examining the floor through his magnifying glass.

He stood. "I have a feeling that we are missing the wood for the trees."

Holmes sat again in the baron's chair and ran his gloved finger across the top of the desk. He showed me his dust-covered glove and scowled. "The baron's servants are not allowed to venture into this wing of the house. The rooms must therefore be cleaned by the valet or the gatekeeper. Their hearts are evidently not in the work."

Holmes dropped to his knees and glared at the parquet floor through his glass. "Something has been moved."

He went to the desk and disappeared under it. There was a loud click, and he stood, smiling an 'I told you so' smile. He pushed the left end of the desk and it slid, pivoting to the side and exposing a hatch cover with a ring handle. Holmes pulled up the hatch and revealed a staircase.

I took the oil lamp and lighted our way down the stairs to the lower floor. In the basement, we entered a wide corridor that led to a set of steel-shuttered doors.

"Outside access," Holmes said. "Very probably leading to a loading bay from which crates of tinned sausages may be brought into the basement and stored."

I followed him to the end of the corridor, held up my lamp and revealed another heavy steel door. Holmes shone his lantern on the lock. "The gatekeeper does not have keys to the basement, and this is a modern Chubb lock, patented as burglar-proof. I think we might disprove that claim, but it would take too much time. The baron is due here in a few hours." He rapped on the door with his knuckle. "To force this door would require a charge of Dynamite."

Holmes leaned against the wall, shook a cigarette from his packet and offered it to me. "Let's have a think."

I frowned as I took the cigarette. "One thing puzzles me. If the baron regards the abduction of the duke and duchess as a rumour, as we have learned from the message pad upstairs, then he can have had no part in the outrage."

"Indeed."

"If you did not suspect Baron von Feldberg in the matter of the abduction, why then the elaborate charade with the firemen and the Irregulars at his offices in Regent Street?"

Holmes smiled as he lit his cigarette and mine.

"I believe the baron was your target all along, Holmes," I said coldly. "He was the little matter of espionage you mentioned at the Abbey. You co-opted the Stone of Destiny and the abduction investigations to further your interest in Baron von Feldberg."

Holmes shrugged. "I admit things are easier now I have access to Treasury funds. The thought of a Scottish uprising opened the government purse strings and showed how much the Treasury values the contribution of Scotland to its coffers and how near panic they were at the possibility of secession."

I shook my head. "Another thing puzzles me. How is it the notes for the message upstairs contained a reference to the abduction? Is that not strange? I mean, if the baron hasn't visited his villa since Monday morning, how—"

A blaze of electric light illuminated the corridor and a figure standing behind Holmes holding a gun aimed at his head. I grabbed for my revolver.

"Good evening, or rather good morning, Baron von Feldberg," Holmes said, turning. "You are early. We were not expecting you until after dawn."

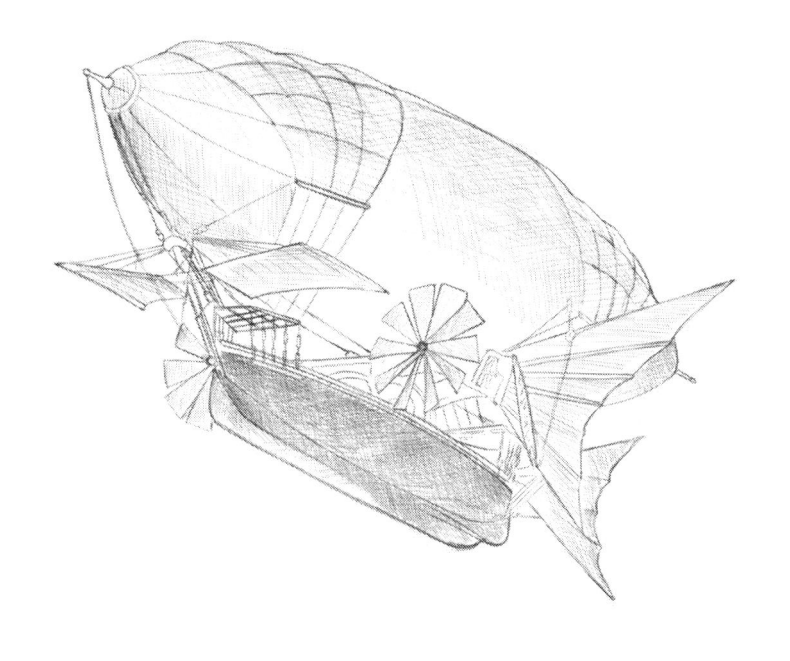

COMES THE DAY

## 15. DER TAG

"Your guns on the floor, if you please," said the baron. He cocked his pistol with a loud click.

Holmes nodded, and I laid my service revolver and lamp down.

"I don't often carry a gun," said Holmes. He took his leaded whip from his pocket. "I am a man of peace."

He flung down the whip, and I saw his back muscles tense for a leap, but the baron's aim did not falter, and another man appeared behind him holding a long-barrelled pistol. The baron reached into his pocket, pulled out a ring of keys and threw it to me.

"The silver Chubb key, Doctor."

I unlocked the heavy steel door and pulled it open. I picked up my lamp, and the baron pushed me through the door in front of him. Holmes followed, guarded by the second man.

The white-painted walls of the basement room we entered were lined with framed maps, and a long table was covered with piles of folders. One wall was fitted with floor-to-ceiling sliding doors.

"Your lamp and lantern on the table, gentlemen."

Holmes and I laid our lights on the table, and we turned to face the baron.

"Heinrich, check upstairs," he ordered. "There may be more of them."

The baron's man snapped to attention, saluted and left the room, stooping to pick up my pistol from the floor of the corridor. He left the heavy door behind him ajar. I glanced at Holmes and saw a twitch of his eyebrow.

The baron wagged his pistol at me. "You thought you were so clever, my friend, but you did not figure into your plans that I contact my gatekeeper by telephone at the same time every night. He did not answer, so I knew something was amiss. I keep at my premises in London, a Daimler horseless carriage capable of travelling over twenty miles in a single hour."

The baron's eyes glittered. "We were here in a trice, in time to foil what our European press calls your perfidious English schemes." He glared at me. "Now really, Mr Meddler, why should I not shoot you and your lackey with you?"

I frowned. "I believe you may be under a misapprehension, Baron von Feldberg. I am Doctor John Watson, an author, and a medical doctor." I indicated Holmes with a careful gesture. "This gentleman is the famous detective, Mr Sherlock Holmes."

"Consulting detective," Holmes corrected me.

The baron laughed. "You do not fool me for a moment with your talk of Sherlock Holmes, the great detective. Come now, Doctor, I am too old a bunny to be tricked in such a fashion. With Mr Mycroft Holmes you are hand-in-glove, and this Sherlock is but a cats-paw."

"This is becoming tiresome," Holmes said, turning to me and poking me in the breast with his finger. "We must have an end to these literary maunderings, Watson."

"But, Holmes, I tried to kill you off at Reichenbach Falls, and I was almost lynched. Our agent was booed in the street. People wore mourning black and the *Strand Magazine* office was mobbed."

"No, no," said Holmes. "I must put my foot down—"

"I demand—" the baron snarled.

Holmes held up his hand. "Just a moment, my dear baron." He turned back to me. "I am considered as real as Robin Hood and Mr Pickwick by a Russian grand duchess!"

I chuckled. "The duke wasn't convinced of your powers. He cited the matter of the haggis—"

"You must listen!" Baron von Feldberg screamed. "You are in my power!" He fired two shots into the ceiling. The enormous reports from the heavy pistol echoed through the chamber.

"I am sorry, Baron," Holmes said in a penitent tone. "You have our complete attention."

The baron nodded. "It must be so, for your very lives are mine."

"Quite," Holmes agreed.

The baron pointed his pistol at me. "You thought with your smoke bombs and your ragamuffin boys you had fooled me, but it was you and Mr Mycroft Holmes who carried out that little charade in Regent Street."

The baron curled his lip. "Your minions dog me in the streets, you invade my business premises in London and you cause me embarrassment – was that the act of an English, I mean British, gentleman? And now you suborn my servants, drug my dogs and into my private house infiltrate yourself. I ask you, Doctor, in all sincerity, why I should not dispose of you?"

The baron's eyes narrowed, and he peered at Holmes. "Why do you smile? I advise you not to make a move; I am the seventh-best shot in England. Your own Prince of Wales says—"

"Hello," said Holmes.

The baron frowned. "To whom do you pretend to speak? This room is completely soundproofed."

Holmes smiled. "Perhaps you should look behind you, Baron."

"Ha! You think me a fool to fall for an old trick. I ask you for the last time, why should I not destroy you out of hand as I would a pair of rabid dogs?"

The Duke of Edinburgh pressed a heavy pistol to the baron's right temple. "*Guten Morgen, Baron von Feldberg.*"

Holmes relieved the baron of his pistol and clapped me on the back. "Our little ruse worked – the duke heard the pistol shots through the open door."

He chuckled. "These people will go on and on before they do anything; it is an interesting psychological weakness, a Hamlet-like urge to procrastinate and soliloquise. Really, Baron, 'Your very lives are mine'! My dear sir, you have been watching far too much melodrama at the Alhambra."

Rankin appeared at the door holding the baron's valet by the collar. He had my pistol in his other hand.

Holmes voice took on an official tone. "Baron von Feldberg, you are not an accredited diplomat and you have no immunity from prosecution. The equipment upstairs, the notes you have made for transmission to Berlin and the papers I expect to find in this room will be more than enough to convict you of espionage. You do not care to be hanged, I suppose? No? Then I require you to remove yourself from our presence and take the morning boat train to the Continent."

We marched the baron and his valet out of the chamber, along the corridor and outside through the metal shutters, now wide open. A horseless carriage stood in a courtyard. I frowned at Holmes, and he caught my look.

Holmes addressed the baron. "Your horseless carriage is sequestered as a spoil of war. You may borrow our cab to the station. Where you go and what you do in Europe is up to you. I understand *Saxe-Coburg und Gotha* is picturesque at this time of year, but you may not find a welcome there."

The Duke of Edinburgh smiled. "On the contrary, Mr Holmes, I shall prepare a suitably warm welcome for the baron should he set foot in my territory."

Baron von Feldberg took a cigar case from his pocket and selected a cigar. I offered him a light. "Thank you, Doctor. What of my Dresden? And my books?"

"I expect your personal effects will be forwarded to you on application to the Foreign Office," I said.

We watched as Rankin ushered the baron and his valet to the cab.

"If you try to return here," Holmes said softly, "we will shoot you down as we would, ah, a pair of rabid dogs. The cab is paid for, but don't forget to tip the driver."

The baron bowed. "*Badinage*, Mr Holmes?" He climbed aboard the carriage followed by his valet, and the driver urged the horse into a trot.

"I heard shots," the duke said as we assembled again in the basement. "I started up just as a fellow with a gun came through the door. Rankin knocked him to the ground, and I relieved him of the doctor's revolver and this."

He held up a pistol with a box-like magazine under the action and a short grip. "It is a Mauser automatic pistol, capable of firing ten rounds in a few seconds."

I shook my head. "Can the Germans apply their genius to nothing but death?"

The duke stiffened. "Bach, Beethoven, Schumann, my dear Doctor. Dürer, Heine, Schiller, Hölderlin—"

"Look at this," Holmes said, to my relief. He indicated a map on the wall, and I held up the lamp to illuminate it.

"A map of the English coast with our forts and batteries laid out," I said. "Our garrisons are marked with details of infantry, cavalry and field guns, with their calibre and range."

The duke peered at a coastal map. "I cannot speak for the Army, but these naval brigades supposedly at Hastings are wholly fictitious."

Holmes picked up a folder from a pile on the table, held it to the lamplight and leafed through it. "These are not: invoices for pistols, rifles and Maxim guns from a firm in Scotland. The destinations are supposedly our garrisons in India and Ireland. Here are others for American-made repeating rifles, artillery pieces and shells."

He picked up another folder. "Lists of members of the Sons of the Thistle organisation and assembly points for cadres of armed insurrectionists with the names and lineage of their captains: an almanac of the Scottish peerage and Scots officers in the Queen's service. And here are records of drafts on the Bank of Scotland in favour of Angus Macdonald."

"The illusionist from the Alhambra," I said.

"Meecham is indeed an illusionist," Holmes replied with a wry smile. He indicated a roll of posters on the table. "Here are bills in English and Gaelic urging civilians to keep calm and obey the orders of the Occupying Power, and a list of punishments for offences against the occupiers. As you may imagine, the penalty for the least infringement of Prussian prerogatives is death." He passed me a folder. "A list of prominent persons in this country who will support the Scottish cause."

I opened it and shook my head. "Holmes, it is headed by Lord Rosebery."

Holmes picked up another fat folder. "Persons who might hinder the revolt and who therefore must be disposed of: the Cabinet and influential Members of Parliament, the staff of the War Office and Admiralty, various earls and other peers, senior clergymen, prominent intellectuals, Socialists of course and members of the Salvation Army. No policemen or detectives, as a note says they are in the pay of the rebels to a man."

Holmes handed the file to me. "You, Mycroft and Doctor Conan-Doyle are listed, and I am not." He sniffed. "I am relegated to a footnote and marked 'refer Kaiser'.

The duke looked over my shoulder. "My family and I are to be imprisoned in Edinburgh Castle."

Holmes turned his attention to the large sliding doors on one side of the room, and Rankin and I helped him slide the first door open. I held the lamp high and gaped in astonishment as the light fell on stack after stack of wooden crates, piled to the ceiling. "A huge warehouse," I exclaimed.

The duke peered at the crates in the light from his lantern. "German rifles of the latest marque. Ah, here is a crate of Hotchkiss machine guns from France; I knew the French would feature in this conspiracy."

I held the lamp higher. "American Dynamite and repeating rifles."

Holmes shone his lantern on one tall stack. "The German sausages the landlady of the Royal Stag spied at Windsor Station."

I shook my head. "Is the whole world aligned against us?"

"The Germans, Russians and Americans are envious of our power, our influence and the global reach the Navy secures for us," said the duke.

"The French are the French, of course," he added. "Theirs is the highest civilisation in the world in terms of art and cuisine, and we cannot trust them an inch."

"What are your intentions, Holmes?" I asked.

"We must remove these arms to a place of safety. The baron was expecting a sizeable contingent of soldiers, presumably Scots insurrectionists, who would be billeted and armed here and awaiting a signal to strike. There are Krupp cannon ready for assembly. A surprise attack by such a well-equipped force would be a devastating blow. We are but twenty miles from Whitehall, an hour's drive in horseless carriages."

"Can we not inform the authorities and let them deal with the matter?" I asked.

"There's no time. Lawyers would have to be engaged, injunctions served and stays of execution accorded the seal of justice. We would be too late; the baron's plans are far advanced. As you said earlier in the evening, Watson, we must act."

"Come now, Doctor," said the duke. "England, I mean Britain expects and so on." He and Holmes smiled at me, and I could think of no counter-argument. "Should we fetch more lamps?"

Rankin peered at a panel on the wall. He flicked a switch, and the room was flooded with electric light.

Holmes smiled. "To put your mind at ease, Watson, with His Royal Highness's permission, I intend to donate these arms (together with the sausages) to Captain Ferguson at Windsor Castle to distribute as he thinks fit."

"Very well," I said. "We must send a galloper to inform him."

The Duke of Edinburgh raised his eyebrows.

"Doctor Watson served with the Berkshires in Afghanistan," Holmes explained. "He is an old campaigner and accustomed to command."

I reddened. "What of the papers?" I asked, nodding at the pile of folders on the table.

"A bonfire," said Holmes. "It is, after all, Burns Night."

Rankin and I carried the folders upstairs. We brought furniture from the servants' rooms and made a pile on the gravel path beside the portico.

"Those names, Holmes!" I shook my head. "The members of the conspiracy. Should we not pass the papers on to the appropriate authority?"

"The names are worthless, my dear fellow. The lists are works of fiction by Mr Angus Macdonald (née Meecham) and his associate Mr Richard McNair of the News Agency of the North. The literary agent of these fictions, though he did not know it, was Baron von Feldberg. His aristocratic patron, though he too may not have been aware of all the facts, was the Kaiser."

Rankin and I dumped the folders onto the pile, and Holmes lit the bonfire with a match. "Mr Macdonald's profession is illusion," Holmes continued as the flames crackled. "He conjured the Sons of the Thistle, a fictional Scottish National Army of twenty-thousand men, in order to cajole gold from Prussia. And he succeeded."

Rankin came from the villa carrying a tray of champagne flutes and two bottles in a cooler.

"A capital notion, Rankin," said the duke. We watched as Rankin opened the first bottle in expert fashion, poured the wine and handed us glasses.

The duke frowned. "We must make it clear to the Kaiser he has been duped, and there are no Sons of the Thistle, but we cannot send that message through diplomatic channels: too many people will know, and Wilhelm will be embarrassed and forced to react. My nephew is a precipitate young man. Only respect for his grandmother keeps him in check."

Holmes raised his glass. "To the Queen."

"The Queen!" cried the company.

"This is very good wine," Holmes said as he held his champagne flute up and watched the liquid glisten in the moonlight, "Say what we may about the baron, we must admit he has excellent taste. His Dresden china is exquisite. Should we not declare it a spoil of war?"

"What is that sound?" I asked. "Is it thunder? I hear a faint regular throbbing, as if from a steam pump in the distance."

Holmes peered towards the Castle, his eyes narrowed. "Rankin, take us to the roof."

We followed Rankin upstairs to the top floor, through a narrow door and out onto the flat roof of the villa. I looked towards Windsor Castle and saw an extraordinary sight. A cigar-shaped object hung in the air with its prow pointed at us and propellers whirling on either side. The airship advanced steadily, and the thrum of its engines grew louder. Suspended from the gas bag was a long boat-like structure in which figures moved.

I recalled the strange events detailed in the American newspapers earlier in the year: the attempted abduction of an officer, his female companion and their horse and buggy by seven-foot creatures, and the woman held captive in a craft exactly like the one I saw above me.

A light appeared on the prow of the vessel, and in its glow I made out a dozen or more occupants and a white and black Imperial ensign flying from a jack staff. I frowned. "Prussians? They crossed the Channel in that contraption?"

"I think not," the duke said. "It's more likely the airship was launched from a cruiser in the Channel. We are just fifty miles from the sea."

He gestured to the tall structures above our heads. "The so-called lightning conductors must be giant couplings designed to hold an airship and let it swing to the wind. There's one at each end of the house, presumably to facilitate faster disembarkation when the time comes."

"The time, Your Royal Highness?" I asked.

"Napoleon planned an air attack across the channel by balloon. The Kaiser has taken a leaf from the French emperor's book. The dormitories on the second floor could accommodate not just Scots secessionists, but Prussian Imperial troops sent over in a fleet of airships. They would reinforce the Sons of the Thistle and operate the heavy arms in the basement."

I frowned. "An invasion from the air? It sounds preposterous."

The light from the airship blinked in an irregular sequence.

"Morse," the duke said, slapping his sword scabbard. "Come, gentlemen, we must prepare to repel boarders."

"Rankin and I have examined the electrical apparatus in some detail," the Duke of Edinburgh said as we assembled in the periscope room.

"In fact, there are two systems. This bank of switches controls a light beam attached to the periscope. The beam is focused on the airship as it hovers overhead, and a message may be transmitted in dots and dashes of light as a heliograph reflects sunlight to transfer information in short and long flashes."

"It is a two-man operation," said Rankin. "One focuses on the airship and the other taps out the message."

"The baron and his valet," I said.

Rankin took the duke's place at the periscope. "Or the duke and I," he said in a cultivated Scots tone far from his previous gruff accent. "His Royal Highness speaks German and knows Morse from the Navy, and I can understand German well enough."

He caught my frown. "I was educated at a Scottish university, Doctor; in Scotland we think it polite to converse with our English brothers and our European cousins in their own languages."

The duke laughed. "Keep a close eye on your Prussian cousins aloft, Mr Rankin," he said. "If they land armed men we will be in trouble. There may be a dozen or so professional soldiers aboard the airship, and she has the weather gauge." He indicated the complicated electrical machinery and the horn. "Here is the second system."

"A giant megaphone?" I asked.

"Something like that," the duke answered. "I believe it's a wireless telephone, similar to the one Mr Marconi demonstrated to my brother. We may be able to talk to the occupants of the airship."

A loud crackle came from the giant horn, then a faint gurgling sound.

"The light is flashing again, sir," said Rankin.

The duke grabbed the periscope, peered into it and dictated to Rankin. "First cordial greetings, then they inform us the initial draft of soldiers is to be delivered tonight, together with a half-dozen senior officers as the core of a planning staff. Their cooks and valets will travel in the entourage of Baron von Feldberg's new wife, arriving on the boat train from Boulogne."

The duke turned to us, his brow furrowed. "We cannot let the airship land; it would mean war."

"And if we shoot them down?" I asked.

"War."

I looked from Holmes, to Rankin to the duke. Anxiety was etched on our countenances.

"Well, gentlemen," the duke said. "Ideas?"

Holmes turned to me. "Watson, you mentioned Dynamite when we were in the basement. Do you recall where the crate was?"

"I do."

"Fetch it," the duke snapped. "And get rifles and ammunition. Go with him, Mr Rankin."

Rankin and I careered down the stairs to the baron's study and through the hatch to the basement. I climbed over a stack of crates and found the one containing American Class A Dynamite. I hefted it and called for Rankin.

"Just a moment, Doctor," he said, leafing through an inventory hung on the wall. "We will need blasting caps or fuzes."

We returned with the case of explosives and rifles and ammunition, but no fuzes or detonators.

Holmes turned to the duke. "What says the Navy?"

"We must blast the top off the towers so the airship cannot dock," the duke said.

"If they land on the lawn?" I asked.

"I believe the contraption will compact itself and be unable to take off again. In that case we will set up a Maxim gun and call on the devils to surrender or we open fire." The duke shrugged. "For the detonator, we must improvise. Who is our best shot?"

I looked at Rankin.

He smiled. "No, Doctor, I studied Philosophy and Mathematics at Edinburgh University. Give me data, and I will calculate a trajectory. And I fished rather than shot pheasants."

"I believe that might be me," I informed the duke.

"Very well. We will pack Dynamite around the tops of the towers. Doctor Watson will take post as near the first tower as he thinks compatible with our awkward situation and his safety; I will take my stand beside him with a second rifle. The doctor will detonate the explosives with gunfire. He will then repeat with the second tower."

I took an unfamiliar Mauser rifle from Rankin, checked the bolt and loaded it with a hand that steadied as I stiffened my upper lip.

The duke led the way to the roof. "Mr Holmes and I will attach explosives to the docking mechanism of the west tower. Mr Rankin and Doctor Watson will take the east. I suggest no more than three sticks, we don't want to blow the roof off. You may use your belts to strap the Dynamite to the struts."

Mr Rankin stuck three sticks of Dynamite into his jacket pocket, I handed him my belt, and he began to climb the east gantry.

"I understand you took your medical degree at London University, Doctor," he said as he climbed.

"I did."

"I considered doctoring, but I am a sensitive soul; I canna stand the sight of blood. Did you know that in the last hundred years or so, Scots universities produced more than ten times as many doctors as the English universities?"

"I did not."

Mr Rankin smiled down at me. "And where are these doctors, Doctor?"

"All over the Empire," I answered with a touch of pride.

"And in England," Mr Rankin said. "The Queen's doctor is a Scot." He strapped the explosives to the tower and climbed down.

We turned to look across the roof to where Holmes clung to the west gantry strapping dynamite to the docking hook.

A double fork of lightning, then another, lit the landscape, catching my companions in shuddering mid-movement as in a tableau, and a long, slow reverberation shook the building.

"The weather has broken at last," I said. I brought the Mauser to my shoulder and aimed, not without a certain trepidation, at the cluster of Dynamite sticks attached to the gantry. The Duke stood beside me with his rifle raised and we exchanged nervous glances as another clap of thunder rolled over us.

Holmes tapped me on the arm and smiled. "I think we might consider a less drastic solution to our problem."

The duke and I lowered our rifles.

"What do you do," Holmes asked, "when you are faced with a mad dog?"

I frowned as I deciphered his meaning. "Throw a stone at it to warn it off," I suggested.

"What if there are no stones?" Holmes asked.

The duke smiled. "You pretend to pick one up. The dog doesn't know whether you have one or not."

The duke barked his words into the wireless telephone horn. His tone in German was far harsher than his calm, patrician English. He saw my look, and he leaned across to me and grinned. "It's the Prussian style." He turned back to the horn and continued his rant.

"They ask him to confirm on his honour as an officer that the gantry towers are mined with explosives," Mr Rankin translated. "He does so, and he suggests the airship had best stand clear as nature may provide our ignition at any moment."

The duke went quiet, and there was nothing from the Prussians.

"They are having a think," said Mr Rankin. "A wee consideration."

The duke stood. "They made certain un-officer-like remarks, and I replied with suitable epithets I hope they convey with my compliments to my nephew. Come, we must secure the lawn against a landing."

We picked up our rifles and followed him downstairs and out onto the lawn. The airship floated perhaps three or four hundred feet above us.

Mr Rankin chuckled. "The duke suggested His Imperial Highness might—"

A flash of lightning was instantly followed by an astoundingly loud double explosion, then a long rumble of thunder. The house shook and debris clattered onto the roof and fell around us as the steel towers folded at the top and crashed through the roof. The west wing seemed to quiver for a few seconds before it slowly collapsed, the floors dropping one by one like a folding concertina. The east wing stood firm, only the top floor demolished by the falling gantry.

"Perhaps two sticks would have sufficed," said the duke after a long silence.

We looked up as the signal light on the airship blinked.

"*Au revoir,*" the duke translated. "Comes the Day! Long live Prussia, long live the Emperor!" The airship turned and headed east, clanking over Windsor Castle.

We stood under the portico of the house, smoking and watching the lightning flashes. Rain pattered on the gravel path, getting heavier by the minute.

"The ship will float back to its cruiser in the Channel with the people of Britain unaware our territory had been violated," the duke said.

"And has it been?" I asked. "Violated, I mean. Is the air above us also British? And if they return to attack us, what can we do? They could drop infernal devices on our magazines and armouries with impunity; the fiends might target our barracks, or even our ships in harbour."

Heavy rain fell on the lawn and gravel path and the bonfire hissed and steamed.

"Did we just hear the opening explosions in a great war?" I continued. "Will not the events of tonight precipitate a catastrophe of European or even global proportions?"

The duke shrugged. "These days every minor incident has that potential. The Prussians spoke of the Day. I believe they mean the death of my mother. Without the restraining and calming influence of the Queen in European affairs, what frightfulness may not be unleashed? I do not doubt the next war will be ignited by the Kaiser losing at billiards to my brother."

I frowned. "The army of Saxe-Coburg and Gotha is part of the Prussian Army."

The duke avoided my eyes.

Holmes checked his watch. "It's nearly dawn. The Café Royal does a capital breakfast. If the telephone apparatus in the study is working, we can call them. Then I must make my report."

We returned to the house. Water streamed down the remaining staircase and puddled in the hall. We made our way along the corridor to the east wing, now strewn with glass and China shepherds and shepherdesses from the showcases, and down to the baron's study. The telephone worked, and I managed to connect with the restaurant and confirm our reservation. I handed the apparatus to Holmes, and he obtained a line to Mycroft's residence in Pall Mall.

"Sherlock," said a tinny voice emanating from the device. "I knew you'd play that old railway coach trick at Windsor. I know how you think: deviously."

"Duplicity runs in the family, Brother."

"What are you bothering me for? Do you know what time it is? I have not yet had my morning apple."

"Baron von Feldberg will be on the early Boat Train to the Continent, the Sons of the Thistle have shut up shop, the Lavender Pond Strangler appears nightly at the Alhambra and you might want to inform the authorities at Boulogne and Dover that the Baron's new wife and entourage should find no welcome on these shores."

"Good news. Well done, Sherlock—"

"And the Golden Crown is now in Scottish hands."

There was a pause, and then Mycroft's voice came from the earpiece in a colder tone. "That is unfortunate. Certain persons will be disappointed you uncovered the wretched thing despite clear indications to keep off the grass."

"My prince and double-duke trumps any pettifogging minister whose powers you might invoke, Mycroft. And he invites you to breakfast."

"Eh? Speak up."

"The Duke of Saxe-Coburg, Gotha *und* Edinburgh commands you to breakfast."

"Get thee behind me, Sherlock!" The tinny voice cried.

"*Lèse-majesté*, Brother? His Royal Highness proposes the Café Royal."

"The Café Royal?" the voice said in a thoughtful tone. Holmes turned to me and the duke. "My brother is smiling. I can hear it."

"A broiled fowl perhaps," said Mycroft. "With bacon, a chop or two, and eggs and sausages on the side. And with black pudding. And crumpets; I pine for crumpets."

"And an entry for your diary," said Holmes, "Watson and I are 'At Home' at five on Tuesday. There will be seedcake."

There was a long silence, and I thought the instrument might have been disconnected.

Holmes turned to me. "I could not accept any financial reward or distinction for doing my duty in regard to the abduction, I therefore chose to request the His Highness and Her Imperial and Royal Highness the Duchess join us for tea."

Holmes bowed to the duke. "The Duke and Duchess of Edinburgh will call at 221b Baker Street on Tuesday at five of the clock. That will put paid to any street gossip about the low quality of Mrs Hudson's household." Holmes turned back to the telephone.

"Distinction?" I murmured, frowning.

"Sir Sherlock," the Duke of Edinburgh said, raising his eyebrows.

I blinked at him in astonishment, and we laughed aloud.

Holmes addressed the telephone mouthpiece. "The Sons of the Thistle may be no more, but the Scottish Question remains unanswered. With or without a Golden Crown, how is the will of the people of Scotland to be expressed by a predominantly English parliament?"

I considered. "Could we not let the Scots people decide? We could frame a—"

"Plebiscite?" the tinny voice cried from the apparatus. "Lord help us, no! We are a parliamentary democracy, Doctor; Parliament debates and decides, expressing the will of the people. Plebiscites are an abnegation of responsibility by government and expressive of the tyranny of the majority: nasty, foreign, populist fripperies. No responsible British government would stoop so low as to allow a *referendum* to dictate its policies. It would mean the dissolution of the Union, the end of civilised rule in these isles and the beginning of the end of the Empire—"

Mycroft was cut off by a long, strangely tinny rumbling noise.

"What was that?" the duke asked. "More thunder?"

"Excuse me, Your Royal Highness," said Mycroft. "A slight touch of bilious catarrh."

The apparatus went dead, and Holmes replaced the earpiece in its cradle. He led the duke, Mr Rankin and me outside. Dawn had come at last, and wan sunlight filtered through a grey, overcast sky. The bonfire was out, and the rain had lessened to a drizzle splattering on the gravel path.

"My brother shows how dependent we are on our bellies," Holmes said as we stood under the portico. "In his full, roast-beef-of-old-England form, these affairs would have been instantly solved and dismissed by Mycroft, and I would not have been involved."

He frowned. "Perhaps if I'd eaten Mrs Hudson's porridge, I'd have had the intellectual energy to solve the cases sooner. There is a monograph on the connection between food and mental facility that cries out to be written – by a Frenchman, of course."

We said our *au revoirs* to the duke and agreed to meet at the Café Royal later in the morning. He hitched his sword, climbed into his carriage and saluted as he was driven through the gates of the villa.

I checked the gatekeeper and dogs in the lodge and found them still sleeping peacefully. I helped Mr Rankin load our belongings onto the baron's Daimler and put up the elephant-hide hood against the rain.

Holmes and I shook Mr Rankin's hand and thanked him. Holmes said he would telegraph the Castle from Windsor Station, and suggested Mr Rankin might wait for Captain Ferguson and his men and arrange the transfer of the arms and supplies.

I tested the Daimler's steering tiller, examined the engine and filled the fuel tank from a tin attached to the rear of the vehicle. "The machine has a hot tube ignition system, Holmes."

"Can nothing be done?" he asked, taking a cigar from his cigar case.

"No, that's a good thing, in fact, but I shouldn't light that cigar until we are moving."

Holmes sniffed and climbed onto the box. I swung the starting handle, the engine clattered into life and I leapt up beside him. I put on a pair of the baron's goggles and handed the other to Holmes. "The legal limit is now fourteen miles per hour. As the baron said, we will be in London in a trice."

I released the brake and we were off. I followed the gravel path, wiggling the tiller to get used to its range of motion, and I steered the carriage through the gates of the villa, turned onto the road and settled at a steady cruising speed.

"Mrs Hudson will be pleased with your notion of tea with the prince," I said over the clatter of the engine. "She longs to upstage Mrs Campbell from number ninety-seven. And it is some time since you have had an aristocrat in your chambers, if you discount the Pearly King."

"Mrs Hudson is already pleased," said Holmes.

"You found her hair tongs!"

Holmes grinned. "The Duchess of Edinburgh offered me a ring from her finger as thanks for our meagre efforts on her behalf; I declined, of course, but she insisted on rewarding us (Her Imperial and Royal Highness is used to command), and I was obliged to admit that I was short one pair of Maxim's electric hair tongs. The duchess said she had a couple of pairs at Clarence House, and if I did not mind the monogram 'MH' entwined in gold leaf and enamel on the handles, she would send one to 221b in the morning."

He smiled. "The letters refer to the duchess, 'M' for Marie, and 'H' for her grandfather, Nicholas II; the letter 'H' is pronounced as 'N' in the Russian alphabet."

"I have an idea Mrs Hudson's Christian name begins with the letter 'M'," I said. "Naturally, I have never enquired. In any event, it will do for 'Mrs'."

I glanced at Holmes. "Our driver studied Philosophy and Mathematics at Edinburgh University."

"Yes, he was assigned to us to make sure we kept off the grass." Holmes smiled. "Ha! Trying to get a Scotsman to go against his conscience is like herding cats."

Holmes took a packet from his pocket. "Peppermint? I retrieved them from a penitent young James Elwood who I confidently expect to see on the boards (he divulged to me his ambition to be an actor)."

"He would make a convincing Iago," I said as I took a peppermint.

"I see him in the Scottish play," Holmes said.

"In the title role," I asked. "As Mac—"

Holmes put his finger to his lips. "Tut, tut, Watson, name not what may not be named. We don't want Scots spirits abroad in Berkshire."

"I'm sorry, I meant, as the Scottish king?"

Holmes sniffed. "Something like that."

We passed the Royal Stag and turned onto the high road. I opened the throttle and the Daimler picked up speed, whipping rain into our faces. I allowed myself a celebratory 'parp, parp' from the vehicle's horn.

Holmes laughed aloud. "I can't wait to see Mycroft's reaction when I show him our expense account.

## Author's Notes

We know from Watson's notebooks that Sherlock Holmes was offered a knighthood by Edward VII soon after his accession. He refused the honour.

King John Balliol of Scotland was relieved of the golden crown of Scotland by customs officials at Dover in 1299. King Edward ordered it should be sent to Canterbury Cathedral, but whether the crown was kept there or returned to Scotland is lost in the misty glens of history.

For many of the arguments made by proponents of Scottish independence in this book, I relied on the excellent work *The Claims of Scotland* (1968) by philosopher H. J. Paton in which he proposed that 'under the Crown and within the framework of the United Kingdom, Scotland should have her own parliament with genuine legislative authority in Scottish affairs' (p. 254).

The opinions expressed by the characters in this novel are not necessarily my own, but any errors or misattributions are mine alone.

ALSO FROM MIKE HOGAN

The Sherlock Holmes and Young Winston Trilogy

\* The Deadwood Stage
\* The Jubilee Plot
\* The Giant Moles

A review of The Jubilee Plot by Davis Ruffle, author of the acclaimed Lyme Regis Trilogy and other Sherlock Holmes books;

'Holmes and Watson team up once more with the schoolboy, Winston Churchill in a dark tale of politics and political uprising and plotting. As with his previous outing, Mike Hogan's own plotting is second to none. The pace is leisurely at times and then grips hard when required. The book opens with a gorgeous scene between Holmes and Watson in which Watson is trying to do the 'household' accounts. He fails to bring home the importance of frugality to Holmes and that becomes a recurring theme of the tale. 'Take the underground', cries the good Doctor. The result: a cab!

The dialogue in this opening scene displays the warmth of the characters to each other and Mr Hogan's unerring way with dialogue which is witty without ever being forced.

This scene is closely followed by one involving Lord Salisbury which matches the opening scene in its splendid dialogue.

The novel goes from strength to strength after that, plots and sub-plots fly by all deftly handled.

Moriarty makes an entrance, still the Napoleon of crime that we know him to be, but with the saving grace of being an Englishman! This is the kind of pastiche that gives pastiches a good name. I am inclined to think it's the one of the best pastiches of the last twenty years.'

## About the Author

Mike is British and currently divides his time between America, Asia and Europe. He writes novels, plays and screenplays. He is an avid Holmesian and a Monty Python and Frasier fan. His obsessions are Shakespeare, Ancient Rome and the Royal Navy. Among his favourite modern writers are Patrick O'Brian, Mary Beard, Robert Harris, Stephen Ambrose, Rick Atkinson, Gore Vidal and Tom Wolfe.

For more information visit
http://kaleidoscopeproductions.co.uk.

Printed in Great Britain
by Amazon